HER
DEADLY
ROSE

BOOKS BY CAROLYN ARNOLD

Ties That Bind

Justified

Sacrifice

Found Innocent

Just Cause

Deadly Impulse

In the Line of Duty

Power Struggle

Shades of Justice

What We Bury

Girl on the Run

Her Dark Grave

Murder at the Lake

Life Sentence

SARA AND SEAN COZY MYSTERY SERIES

Bowled Over Americano

Wedding Bells Brew Murder

MATTHEW CONNOR ADVENTURE SERIES

City of Gold

The Secret of the Lost Pharaoh

The Legend of Gasparilla and His Treasure

STANDALONE

Assassination of a Dignitary

Pearls of Deception

Midlife Psychic

CAROLYN ARNOLD

HER DEADLY ROSE

bookouture

Published by Bookouture in 2024

An imprint of Storyfire Ltd.
Carmelite House
50 Victoria Embankment
London EC4Y 0DZ

www.bookouture.com

Storyfire Ltd's authorised representative in the EEA is Hachette Ireland
8 Castlecourt Centre
Castleknock Road
Castleknock
Dublin 15, D15 YF6A
Ireland

To Carol Bennett,
a great friend and powerful cheerleader to have in my corner.

PROLOGUE

The watcher stood on the sidelines, the place to which they were always relegated. Sometimes from a greater distance than today, but it didn't matter because whatever the view, the girl's movements and timing were flawless. Everything came effortlessly to her. She could do no wrong. A natural, America's rising star. Or so the papers across the country said. That only made the watcher hate her more.

If the girl was in a gilded cage, the door was open, but she stayed of her own choosing. She loved it there, but who wouldn't? Being tended to by hands eager to offer their assistance and support. She had people to respond to her every beck and call, who were more than willing to elevate her to the height of her grand aspirations.

The watcher was pushed out, no longer needed or desired. It mattered none that they had been there from the beginning. The girl had practically spat in the watcher's face. The rejection seared an indelible mark, rendering its damage and setting things into motion.

Even so, the watcher was willing to give her one more chance to change her mind, to concede. They weren't without mercy. But if the girl remained obstinate, the watcher was prepared to follow through. Only moments left until she'd choose her fate. If she failed to comply with the watcher's desire, they would get redemption and the final say. The girl would find out too late what her pride had cost her. By then, her cries and pleas would fall upon unhearing and uncaring ears. The watcher would observe the girl's eyes widen in terror and fill with tears as her throat began to close and her body convulsed as it fought for life. She would reach out to the watcher, but they would stand there resolute. No turning away. Not until the last breath left her body.

ONE

The skaters glided around on the ice like prima ballerinas dancing on air, the rink beneath them an extension of themselves. Their movements were fluid and expertly coordinated as they swept in and out of each other's arms to "(I've Had) The Time of My Life" pumping through the arena's speakers.

Amanda could hardly keep her eyes off them, but one thing competing for her attention was the reaction of her daughter, Zoe, sitting beside her. The nine-year-old's mouth was frozen in a huge grin, and her beautiful blue eyes were wide and glistening with delight. Amanda hardly blamed her. This all-stars event had attracted some of the best talent in the world to take to the ice. It had sold out within a couple of days of its announcement and was being televised live.

There wasn't a more perfect way to spend a Saturday afternoon leading up to Christmas than with her friends Patty Glover and Katherine Graves and her daughter. It gave her and Patty a reprieve from their day job that centered around darkness. Patty was a detective in Sex Crimes with the Prince William County Police Department, and Amanda a detective with their Homicide Unit. Even better, the tickets were a gift from Patty. The generosity was prompted by the fact that the show's lead attraction was Michaela Glover, Patty's niece and Olympic hopeful, born and raised right here in Woodbridge, Virginia.

As the song built to its crescendo, the female figure skater sped toward her partner and, at the last possible moment, executed a perfectly timed leap into the air. Her partner caught her with grace and continued to suspend her body above his as the two of them spun in a circle that slowly died to a stop. The woman slid down her companion's body, landing gracefully, and they pressed their foreheads together as the music faded out.

The crowd roared, rising to their feet to give the couple a standing ovation.

"Mandy, I want to be a skater!" Zoe exclaimed as she popped to her feet, pointing at the ice. "She's *soooo* beautiful. Like a princess."

The female skater was in a sequined costume with a V-shaped neckline. Her blond hair was swept into a bun and framed by a braid. "That she is," Amanda said as she stood. Seeing life through the eyes of a child was magical. Nothing else quite measured up to this level of bliss and satisfaction. At least for Amanda.

"Bravo!" Patty said, standing and clapping.

Katherine rose last and was grinning too. Though it would be hard not to. The entire show was spectacular. The only sad thing was that it was nearing its end.

The skaters who had just finished glided to one end of the rink, and the announcer came over the loudspeakers. "And now we welcome all the amazing talent who have entertained us today. Give a big round of applause as our all-stars take to the ice for one final encore."

The skaters filtered onto the rink as "Rise Up" with its powerful lyrics vibrated in the background. Watching the ensemble share the ice in a choreographed routine was moving and breathtaking. Amanda couldn't stop smiling, and it had been a while since she truly felt this happy.

Amanda searched for Patty's niece but couldn't spot her. She had yet to meet her, but Patty had pointed her out the second she took to the ice in the first half. The young woman may be about to make a dramatic solo entrance.

At the crescendo, the group of skaters bloomed out from center ice, their costumes creating the illusion of an exploding starburst before closing back in. The song ended with the group tucked together.

The announcer's voice rang out again. This time he called each skater or duo, in turn, to take a bow. Single roses were tossed onto the ice, along with some small bunches banded together with ribbon. Zoe had a rose for Michaela and was doing a good job of patiently waiting.

Patty nudged Amanda's shoulder and leaned in. "I don't see Michaela. Do you?"

"No. Maybe she's coming in last? She was a huge draw for the event."

"Could be." Patty bobbed her head, her gaze on the rink where the last of the skaters were making their way off the ice.

"And to the local star of today's event..."

Amanda smiled at Patty as if to say, *see?*

"Michaela Glover!"

Zoe widened her eyes and looked at Amanda. "Now?"

She was wondering if this was when she should throw the rose. "One minute."

The crowd's cheering became thunderous but dampened after a few moments when Michaela didn't show. The crowd started chanting her name. Some booed. Eventually, the announcer called a close to the show.

Zoe dropped her arm holding the rose. "Mandy?"

"Something must be wrong," Patty said to Amanda, panic

flooding her voice, as she bent over and rummaged under the bench for her purse.

Amanda put a hand on her shoulder. "Let's not rush to assume that."

Patty, who was now dangling her purse by its strap, looked into Amanda's eyes. At first, Amanda thought her friend was going to crumble apart, her mind straight to the worst-case scenario. There was certainly a storm in her eyes, but it started to recede, her gaze softening. She took a deep breath. "You're right. It could be anything."

"An injury in her earlier set? She wouldn't want to aggravate it further," Katherine piped in.

An injury might sound like a horrible thing, but given her and Patty's line of work, it was nothing.

"Let's go find out," Patty said. "You guys need to meet her anyway."

"Yeah!" Zoe squealed and bounced up and down. "Yes, yes, yes! I still have a rose for her."

"It sounds like someone is just a little excited by that prospect," Amanda said, grinning at both of her friends.

"Mickey! Mickey!" Zoe chanted. Patty had told her one of Michaela's nicknames, and Zoe clearly wanted to show off her inside knowledge. She raised her arm and nearly hit Amanda in the eye with the rose.

People in the row behind them were laughing at Zoe's enthusiasm. Leave it to a child to put smiles on people's faces. But when the rose almost hit her a second time, Amanda put out an instinctive hand. "Just put that down, okay? Please."

"Fine." Zoe stuck out her lower lip.

They eventually made it out of the stands into the ring of the arena but came to a temporary standstill. It didn't seem like anyone was in a hurry to leave and enjoy the rest of their Saturday afternoon.

"Where can we find this beautiful niece of yours?"

Katherine asked Patty. "The show was absolutely amazing, and the bit with your niece... above." She smiled, letting the expression linger as her eyes danced over the crowd.

"I expected her to have a set in the second half, but I guess the others needed a chance." Patty laughed. "But they put her up in a dressing room. The other skaters are sharing two locker rooms."

"That's impressive." Amanda was happy that her friend seemed to be feeling better.

Patty claimed to know where the dressing room was and led the way through the mass of people. Amanda kept a tight hold of her daughter's hand, possibly too tight, as Zoe squirmed and complained. Amanda released slightly. Her job gave her a front-row seat to the evil of the world, making her well aware of what miscreants would do with a sweet girl like Zoe. Not to mention Amanda already had the scare of her life when Zoe was taken by a sex-trafficking ring. Thankfully, before the unthinkable took place, with Patty's help and the rest of the PWCPD, they rescued the girl.

"You're hurting me." Zoe tugged and wriggled free. Her arm with the rose swung out, and a passerby knocked it out of her hand.

The rose fell to the floor, and Amanda failed to reach it before a man walked on it, crushing the petals beneath his boots.

"No! It's ruined." Zoe's eyes beaded with tears. "It was for Mickey."

"I'll get you a new one." Amanda sounded more confident than she was feeling. At this point, the vendors might have shut up shop. She confirmed the location of the dressing room and told Patty and Katherine they'd meet them there in a few minutes. Then she took Zoe's hand and walked with determination to the first cart they came to. They were out of single roses, but Amanda bought Zoe a bunch of three roses tied with a red ribbon.

They caught up with Patty and Katherine just as they reached Michaela's dressing room.

"I never imagined we'd get here at the same time," Amanda said to them.

"You must have elbowed your way through that crowd better than us," said Katherine with a smile.

"We got extra roses for Mickey!" Most of what Zoe had said since the first skater took to the ice flew from her with the exuberance of an exclamation mark. She lifted the bunch and nearly hit both Patty and Katherine in the face.

Amanda gently swept the roses aside. "Watch what you're doing before you poke someone's eye out." She enlarged hers while making a silly face, and Zoe laughed before lowering the flowers.

"I'm so excited to introduce you guys." Patty knocked on the door.

A few seconds passed. No answer.

Patty rapped again and leaned toward the door. "Mickey, it's me. Open up."

No response.

Patty drew back. "That's strange. She wouldn't just leave." She turned the handle and pushed the door open.

Then she let out a blood-curdling scream.

TWO

The next moments were pure adrenaline and chaos. Amanda had Katherine take Zoe outside while she called dispatch. Zoe had protested some, wanting to meet Michaela and give her the roses. Amanda told her to take them with her for now. She'd explain why later.

Amanda had closed the door on Michaela's dressing room, but not before seeing enough to know the Olympic hopeful was gone. No longer the vibrant, young woman who had taken to the ice as an apparition floating over the surface. Her skin no longer held a glow. Her eyes were widened like she'd been terrified in her last moments and were marked by petechiae. A clear tell that she had been starved of oxygen and suffocated. Never an easy way to go. And while there was no visible ligature or bruising around her neck to indicate manual strangulation, there was a pool of vomit. Not exactly a smoking gun, but it supported asphyxiation as well.

There were signs of a possible altercation, or at least a struggle for survival. The floor was a mess. Several roses were scattered about, including trios tied with ribbon. A purse was tipped over on its side. Cream-colored liquid had seeped from

the lid of a sports bottle next to it. A card lay just outside the
reach of Michaela's left hand.

Amanda would look at everything in the room in more
detail soon enough. But the gist was a young woman, in prime
health, doesn't usually keel over on her own. That alone made
her death suspicious, making the dressing room and everything
inside it a potential murder scene. And that meant taking the
necessary precautions to avoid contamination. The clock
couldn't be reset and evidence restored if the determination of
homicide was made later.

Officer Brandt was posted outside the dressing room, while
other officers collected names and statements from as many
people as possible before allowing them to leave the arena.
Amanda was most interested in knowing if anyone suspicious
was seen hanging around Michaela's dressing room.

The arena staff and those traveling with the show were
sequestered to the two locker rooms. Officers would take their
information, but they'd be on hand for more detailed questioning if it became necessary.

The television network that had covered the event was fast
to catch the news that one of the skaters was dead and was
making the lives of some uniformed officers hell. The threat of
arrest barely had any effect on getting them to vacate the arena.

Amanda hung up after finishing her slew of calls. In addi-
tion to dispatch, who would request a medical examiner and
crime scene investigators, she had called her detective partner,
Trent Stenson, and her boyfriend, Logan. She let Logan know
the situation and that Zoe would be coming home. He'd offered
to come get her, and she'd taken him up on it. That would free
Katherine to take Patty home and possibly stay with her.
Amanda had one more call to make, that being to her boss,
Sergeant Scott Malone, but Patty's loud sniffling had her
pausing.

Patty was seated on a chair in the arena manager's office,

eyes blank and distant. She'd open her mouth wide in agony and slowly close it. Rarely did a sound utter from her lips.

Amanda dropped into the chair next to her and put her arm around her friend. She was trembling beneath her touch.

"This can't be happening. It's... it's like a bad nightmare, and I want to wake up."

Amanda's heart broke for Patty. After all, she knew the cutting pain of deep loss, having buried her husband, Kevin, and six-year-old daughter, Lindsey. The fact it was nearly ten years ago did little to remove the ache that lived in her chest, ready to be poked and revived with little provocation. "I know, sweetheart." She rubbed her friend's arm.

"What happened in there, Amanda? I saw Michaela and then I couldn't take much more in. It's like my brain shut it all out." For Patty to use her full given name was rare. Family and friends typically dropped the formality and called her Mandy. Amanda surmised Patty was bracing herself, trying to erect a shield around her heart, going into cop mode.

She wouldn't be doing Patty any favors by sugarcoating her response. Her friend would see through it anyway. But there wasn't a reason to mention the petechiae. "There may have been a struggle..."

"Are you telling me that someone killed her?" Patty's voice cracked with the question. Her chin quivered.

"All I can say is I promise to get to the truth of what happened to her. You have my word." It niggled that she hadn't seen Michaela's phone, though it could still be at the bottom of her purse.

Patty's eyes were pooled with tears as she nodded. "I saw that she'd been sick... There was vomit on the floor."

Amanda was impressed Patty had absorbed that much. "There was. It was alongside a sports bottle. Maybe her drink didn't agree with her." Though the puke could have come from another person who had been in the room.

Patty straightened and twisted her body to face Amanda. "She loves her protein shakes, has them every time after coming off the ice. But..." Her chin quivered, and her eyes pooled with tears. "Mick is deathly allergic to peanuts. If she ingested any... Oh my God. But wait, that makes no sense. She should have had her EpiPen. Unless..." Patty sobbed, sniffled, and eventually shook her head. "Did someone take it so she couldn't use it?"

Amanda hadn't seen an EpiPen either, though it too could still be inside Michaela's purse. It was also entirely possible Michaela lost consciousness before she was able to reach it. But there was a darker possibility, as Patty suggested. That someone had deliberately taken her EpiPen and phone so Michaela would die. Amanda rubbed her friend's back. "As I said, I promise I'll find out what happened." She'd vow justice in the event of murder, but it was a fallible system. "Do you know of anyone who had an issue with Michaela?"

Patty pulled some tissues from her purse and dabbed her cheeks, sniffled. "I thought everyone loved her."

If this was murder, sadly, the truth was on the flip side of that statement. Unless they were looking at someone who had been obsessed with Michaela and harbored a warped view of love. "Does Michaela have any other family that I could reach out to? You don't need to carry all this on your shoulders." All Amanda knew about the family was Michaela's mother was long out of the picture.

"Both her parents were never part of her life, but Mickey has a brother. They're not close, though."

"What's his name and where can I reach him? I can let him know."

"If the news doesn't beat you to it. They're probably swarming all over this."

"Don't you worry about that, okay?" She'd make banishing the media her personal problem if she had to.

"Her brother's name is Tyson Bolton." Patty pulled her phone from her purse, tapped away on it, and said she'd forwarded the contact card to Amanda. Her phone pinged in confirmation. Patty added, "Oh, there's one other person you should talk to. I'm surprised I haven't seen her since all this... My mind. I just can't think clearly."

Her resilient friend didn't need placating, but empathy would always be welcome. "That makes sense, Patty. Who is it?"

"Tara Coolidge, Mickey's agent. She was supposed to be here today. She might be able to direct your attention to someone, but she lives here in Woodbridge. Mick's coach would likely know more about what's going on in her day-to-day life, though. She's based in Colorado Springs. That's why Mick lived out there." Patty fussed on her phone again, and a second later, Amanda's device was beeping with the notification of two more text messages.

Amanda looked at them this time, noting the coach's name was Jolene Flynn. "You said Tara was here. What about Jolene?"

Patty shook her head. "Not here today, far as I know. She's more focused on the competition side of things, rather than shows like this one."

"All right, well, I'll track them down and have a talk with them."

Patty palmed her phone. "What am I going to do? What's going to happen now?" As a seasoned detective with Sex Crimes, Patty would be trained to keep calm in a crisis and remain objective. She'd know exactly what needed to be done, but all her training understandably dissolved when the victim was her niece.

"I've made the phone calls. I'm just waiting for everyone to show up, but Katherine's going to take you home. She'll stay with you too if you'd like."

Patty stiffened. "No way I'm leaving Mick. Please don't make me."

Amanda squeezed her friend's hands. "She's gone, Patty. There's nothing more you can do here. Trust me, okay?"

Heaving sobs rocked Patty's body, and Amanda pinched her eyes shut, trying to tune out the pain emanating from her friend in massive waves. She just sat there holding the space until Patty calmed a little.

Thoughts of the agent provided some distraction. If she was supposed to be here today, where was she now? And was her seeming disappearance connected with Michaela's untimely death?

THREE

By five o'clock, the investigation into the death of Michaela Glover was in full swing. A medical examiner hadn't arrived last Amanda knew, but Crime Scene Investigators Emma Blair and Isabelle Donnelly were already at work on the scene. Officers had taken information from the remaining audience members and sent them on their way. Logan came and picked up Zoe, and Katherine took Amanda's Honda Civic they had carpooled in and left with Patty. Sergeant Malone was on his way, but he'd be delayed. Since it was Saturday and nearing the holidays, he and his wife were visiting their sons in Washington, which was a forty-five-minute drive away.

The media presence had grown outside. Before long, it was likely Michaela's name would be tossed around. That's if it already wasn't. The threat of arrest seemed to be having no effect, tempting Amanda to elevate things from talk to action. Trent had convinced her to let it go by assuring her she was of better use inside the arena. She just hoped Michaela's brother didn't hear about his sister's death through some news report. But she'd done all she could, for now, in that regard. She'd sent a uniformed officer to his house, but no one came to the door. And this wasn't the sort of news one delivered over the phone.

She and Trent were walking to Michaela's dressing room, counting on the CSIs to give them some answers.

Officer Leo Brandt dipped his head at them as they approached.

"A medical examiner arrive yet?" She had her fingers crossed in her head that Hans Rideout would be the one dispatched from the Office of the Chief Medical Examiner in Manassas. He had a wicked sense of morgue humor and a robotic attention to detail.

"Not yet. I gotta tell you, this one is rough. It's always such a shame when someone so young and bright goes. Just an unfair world."

"Amen to that," Trent said. Her partner retained his faith in a greater being, unlike her. She and God hadn't reconciled since she lost her family in the car crash.

"How's Patty holding up?" Leo asked.

When Amanda had handed the post to him, she'd filled him in some. "About as well as could be expected."

"And how about you?"

"I just plan on doing my job." Pure, unadulterated focus was the only way she'd get through this.

"I hear ya. Just bootie up first if you're going in." Leo's grim expression fractured at his turn of phrase, giving way to the briefest of smiles. But finding pockets of levity was crucial to remaining grounded when dealing with death and murder. He waved a hand. "You know what I mean. Do you need some?"

"We come prepared." Trent pulled two pairs of booties out of a pocket and extended one set to Amanda.

"Or at least one of us does." She reached for them, and their fingers grazed. Her cheeks heated, and she hated herself for the unwelcome reaction, but he must have felt something too. He was peering into her eyes. Time slowed. She pressed her lips into a smile. "Thanks." *And just when I thought I had buried my feelings for him!*

"Don't mention it. Besides, it's not like you thought you'd be involved in this today."

"Say that again." The day's turn inflicted whiplash. From relaxation to a death investigation. Just like that.

They put on the booties, then softly rapped their knuckles on the door and stepped inside the dressing room when CSI Blair called out the okay. She and Trent stayed near the door when they saw the tight space. They were already carrying out a careful and choreographed dance around Michaela's body.

Everything looked much the same as Amanda remembered it except for the evidence markers now laid out on the floor. Also the card that had been near Michaela's left hand was no longer there, nor her purse. But she noticed a bouquet of assorted flowers in a glass vase on a table to her right that she hadn't seen last time. An empty card stick was in the center of the pink and purple blooms. It was most likely the one that had been on the floor.

CSI Emma Blair stopped taking photographs and looked at them. "I heard this beautiful young woman is the niece of one of our own."

That news would have spread fast among the many officers on scene. "Detective Patty Glover from Sex Crimes." Amanda had steadied herself before replying, but speaking the words still rocked her to the core. Her friend's life would be forever changed. Such intense grief was like battling a moody seductress who was determined to isolate and claim her victims. It had succeeded with Amanda, causing her to cut out her parents, siblings, nieces, and nephews from her life for a time. Back then, she couldn't stand to see other people happy. Blood relatives or otherwise. Her existence became work, home, and one-night stands with strangers. The latter was a form of punishment for living when her husband, daughter, and unborn child had died.

"That poor woman." Blair pursed her lips, and her eyes beaded with unshed tears.

"Makes a person speechless, honestly. I was here for the show and with Patty when Michaela was found."

"Oh, Amanda. I'm sorry to hear that." Isabelle Donnelly, the other CSI, who had just been absorbing the conversation joined in.

"I appreciate the kind words, but let's just find out what happened here. Hopefully, provide Patty with some closure." Amanda's breath hitched on the last word. Closure was deceitful. An explanation could be accepted one minute and found wanting the next.

"How is she holding up?" Donnelly asked, seemingly not in any rush. But she housed a calm spirit and harnessed the canny ability to slow and stretch out time. It had to be her efficient yet relaxed and low-key approach to life. Her personal concern for other people's welfare was one of her most redeeming qualities.

"About as well as you can imagine. Katherine is with her."

"Katherine? Oh, Graves?" Blair asked, and after Amanda nodded, she raised her eyebrows in surprise. "I didn't know you were friends. I thought you were oil and water."

"That changed." Amanda smiled. Her first introduction to Katherine came when she stepped in as interim sergeant for Homicide. Their discord wasn't a well-guarded secret. Thankfully, they landed in a place of mutual respect and understanding. But a couple of years ago, Katherine had retired her badge to work with her aunt at her diner in Dumfries, just ten minutes from Woodbridge. "So, what can you tell us?" She nudged her head to the scene, wanting desperately to get some answers. To start, whether they were definitively looking at murder.

"Hard to say exactly," Blair said. "There appears to have

been an altercation, but there could be another explanation for the mess."

"*Hard to say?* Are you forgetting about what we found?" Donnelly shot back.

"It's not conclusive, Isabelle." Blair's tone disclosed zero amusement.

"What isn't?" Amanda cut in before their debate gained traction. They usually got along well, but they could both be opinionated.

Donnelly retrieved a plastic evidence bag from her collection case and handed it to Amanda.

A small card was inside. "Is this the one from near her body?"

Donnelly nodded.

The first thing Amanda noted was the size and paper stock. Typical dimensions of a business card, but with the grade and thickness of regular copy paper. The side facing up was blank, which she found odd. Typically, a florist's card had the shop's name stamped on the back. She flipped it over and found a handwritten message.

Trent leaned over and snapped a picture with his tablet before she had a chance to read it.

Her focus was first on penmanship. "The writing is cramped and compact and angles to the left... This was written by a southpaw." But as she read the words out loud, tremors ran through her. "'You'll be sorry you turned your back on me after all I did for you.'"

With that, all her doubts vanished. Michaela Glover was murdered.

FOUR

It took a few beats for Amanda's focus to return. Such an ominous message had to be related to Michaela's death. Upon closer inspection, the card looked like it had been cut to size. Home-made. Had it come with the bouquet though? It was possible that the plastic card holder was recycled from a previous time.

The seed of an idea was slowly moving in, but it was rough at the edges, needing more to round it out. She expanded her view, and her eyes landed on the scattering of roses on the floor. Some were single stems. Others were in batches of two or three tied with red ribbon. All except for one.

"Amanda?" Trent prompted. He must have sensed her mind busily processing away.

Clarity clicked in. She recalled the display of roses when she bought more with Zoe. "Make sure you process that trio of roses right there. The one with the black ribbon," she said, pointing it out to Blair.

The investigator angled her head. "What is special about them?"

"The arena was only selling roses tied with *red* ribbon."

"Huh, interesting. Okay, so someone brought them in from outside? But why?" Blair asked.

She shrugged. "That I don't know yet. I don't even know if it means anything. The card was definitely brought in, though. But did it accompany the roses or the bouquet? Either?" *And so the questions begin...* It was the curse of any new investigation. But as her father, the former police chief for the PWCPD, had drilled into her, every stone, no matter how seemingly inconsequential, needed to be turned over.

"Even if we find that out, where does it get us? On another score, there's no name on the card. We could assume Michaela would know the sender based on the message. Again, not like that helps us," Trent pointed out.

Amanda heard his words, but her focus was on proving murderous intent. She pointed at the vomit on the floor and the spilled drink. "Patty told me that her niece loved protein shakes. It's probably what you'll find in the sports bottle and what's been spilled on the floor. But she also said that she had a fatal allergy to peanuts. Is there a fast way to tell if the drink had peanuts in it?"

"Peanuts, you say?" Blair took the bottle into her gloved hands, lifted the lid, and brought it to her nose.

"Do you really think you should—" Amanda was cringing, not sure how wise that move was when they didn't know how Michaela had died yet.

Blair sniffed deeply and drew back. "Oh, yeah. It's mild, but it's there."

"If you can smell it, Michaela would have. Why would she drink it?" Trent asked.

Amanda shared a possible scenario. "She returned to her dressing room looking forward to her shake, flips the cap, drinks some, thinking nothing more of it. By then it's too late? Either way, there's no alternative in my mind. Michaela was murdered." Of all she had said, Amanda was most confident in that conclusion.

Trent bobbed his head. "Well, she certainly didn't put peanuts in her drink, which means that someone else did. But who?"

"You tell me, and we can all go home." Amanda smiled, but it faded quickly as her gaze landed on Michaela. She opened her mouth, about to ask if they'd found Michaela's phone or EpiPen when the door to the dressing room opened.

"I was just being rhetorical," Trent muttered.

Hans Rideout shuffled inside with his assistant, Liam Baker, at his shoulder. Both were decked in overalls and booties. "Wowie. Tight quarters. Everyone's in here."

"Just looking for some answers," Amanda said.

"Of course you are." The light in Rideout's eyes shadowed as they landed on Michaela's prone body. "Another young woman. Sadly, death doesn't discriminate. And this one was especially talented. I've been following this girl's career. She would have claimed that Olympic gold and been the first Black woman to do so. What an impact. She'd have been a role model to young girls everywhere, just like Debi Thomas, who took a bronze in figure skating and made history."

Amanda hadn't known the ME liked figure skating, but she didn't really know much about his personal life. She also excused herself for never hearing of Debi Thomas before either. "I'm sure she would have." She based this solely on knowing if the girl was anything like Patty, she was ambitious, focused, and somewhat of a perfectionist.

"You guys about finished with the area around the vic?" Rideout asked the CSIs.

"That we are." Blair stepped aside, and Donnelly took the bag with the card back from Amanda and returned it to her collection kit.

Rideout and Liam came further into the room. The space

was rather compact to start with, but packing in six people and one prone body was testing its limits. She and Trent should probably step outside to allow them room to work, but they were so close to having some solid answers.

Rideout had barely hunched beside Michaela's body when Amanda said, "Trent and I found out she had a severe allergy to peanuts. CSI Blair detected the smell of peanuts in the drink inside the vic's sports bottle. It would appear that she drank some. We were thinking death came as a result." She wasn't normally like this, rushing everything along.

Rideout's mouth settled in a scowl, clearly not a fan of being force-fed cause of death. The tension in the room became tangible. She knew instantly that she'd overstepped.

"Obviously you're the expert," she backpedaled.

"That you're right about," Rideout said with a dry wit, but the warning was there to let him make the determinations in future. In that regard, he took it about as well as a general practitioner did when a patient self-diagnosed from researching their symptoms online. "There is petechiae in her eyes..." He pried her jaw open and looked in her mouth. "Some on the inside of her lips. Her throat also appears to be swollen shut." He lifted one of Michaela's hands and flipped it over, then the other. "Hmm. She also has a minor rash on her left palm. I'd say she came into contact with something that irritated her skin."

"There was a card that looked like it fell from her left hand. Maybe from that," Amanda said, wishing for duct tape to cover her mouth.

"Anything's possible," Rideout said. "You could smell it in the drink?" He directed the question to Blair, who nodded. "Likely a crude peanut oil."

"Not exactly hard to come by. You can pick it up from most grocery stores," Amanda said.

"Making it far too common to trace to a buyer." Trent sighed.

Rideout sank onto his heels. "There is vomit. It is *possible* that cause of death was anaphylaxis, *but* that isn't my final answer. I'll need to run some tests on her back at the morgue. Obviously, I'll analyze her stomach contents and what she threw up before I'd conclude definitively."

Anaphylaxis meant death from an allergic reaction. She thought she'd feel better hearing that from Rideout's lips, but it had the opposite effect. At least it was more than they had a moment ago. "I appreciate your preliminary assessment."

"Though even if she was having a severe allergic reaction, she would have had time to get out of the room and flag down help. Why didn't she?" Rideout met Amanda's gaze. Apparently, if she saw fit to play ME, he was going to play detective.

"Huh. I can think of one explanation, but it's not pretty," Trent piped up.

Rideout held out his hand to encourage him to continue.

"Someone could have blocked the door from the inside, preventing her from leaving."

"Which would mean the person stayed and watched her die," Liam added and shrugged when everyone looked at him. "Murder is murder. There's no way to put lipstick on that particular pig."

Amanda shook the cartoonish imagery. "Assuming she ingested peanut oil, how long would it have taken to kill her?" Not that Amanda doubted that she had ingested it. The math worked. A tainted drink and a dead body. One plus one in that equation equaled murder.

"A severe allergy to peanuts can be fatal within thirty minutes."

Michaela would have known she was going to die. She'd suffered. Just as the story of the room told them. The dropped bottle, the rummaged purse, the scattered roses. She'd obviously tried to stay upright and breathe but had been disoriented and uncoordinated. Was the horrific scenario that Trent and Liam had just fabricated more truth than fiction? Amanda's heart squeezed, thinking of the sheer terror the poor girl would have experienced in her final moments. It also hurt to think about sharing this much with Patty. "That's a long time for someone to hang around watching her die."

"That's just an approximate," Rideout said.

"And did the killer just get fortunate that no one stopped by to see Michaela?" Amanda added and went on to answer her own question. "Though, I suppose they did."

"Actually, if you'll pardon me. These reactions can also come on fast and strong," Liam said in conflict to his boss. "That's the case for my brother and his allergy to nuts." He added this when all eyes in the room fell on him again. "It's why he always keeps an EpiPen handy. Was there one?"

Both investigators shook their heads.

"No, I processed her bag and the contents," Donnelly said. "Most of which were on the floor. Lip gloss, a pack of tissues, a key ring and fob for a Subaru, but no EpiPen."

Amanda felt chilled. "Patty said she always had one."

"Don't know what else to say. No EpiPen," Donnelly affirmed.

"Any phone?" Amanda asked.

"None that we found," Blair put in.

Trent looked at Amanda, and she read his thoughts. This supported murder. Whoever had added peanut oil to her drink wanted to ensure she wasn't going to get help. Removing the EpiPen would ensure she couldn't get the necessary medication. But why take her phone? They'd just hypothesized the killer would have been present until her final breath. That alone would have prevented Michaela from calling someone. And where was the phone now? Could there be more to this? Something on the phone the killer didn't want discovered? Her stomach knotted with tension. The pressure to close this case was immense. This beautiful girl with ambition and talent *just gone.* What a waste. "Someone wanted to ensure Michaela suffered before she died. They were so committed to that end result, they stuck around and watched it happen." She'd recapped it out loud to help it sink in. Even after all the evil she'd seen, it was hard to comprehend.

"To make it even worse, she probably knew her killer," Trent said.

That was *worse...* "Valid point. They had to know about her allergy and gain access to her dressing room without raising alarm. Possibly more than once. The first time to take her EpiPen and phone, unless they did that while waiting for her." Either way, the entire picture was a bleak one.

Trent nodded.

"Though, I suppose they could have just as easily followed her back here to watch her die." Amanda shuddered in the aftermath of her statement. Working in homicide had calloused her somewhat, but it was either let that happen or risk complete burnout. She turned to Rideout. "Would you be able to estimate time of death? If it helps, her last set was just before intermission at two o'clock, and we found her about three thirty. She's still wearing her costume from that number."

"What I'm seeing supports death within that timeframe. It's rather hard to narrow it down more than that."

"I had a feeling you'd say that." She was aware the body underwent several changes upon death, but most became notable over a greater length of time. To Trent, she said, "We need to confirm when she got back here and who else might have been around."

"I'm with you," Trent said. "Let's go talk to some people."

She hesitated to leave Michaela, but she had a job to do. Sadly, the girl wouldn't know she had left anyhow. "One more thing," she said to the investigators, "please make sure to collect the garbage and recycling from all the bins in the arena. We're not likely to find her phone, but the killer might have tossed her EpiPen."

"Consider it done," Blair said.

Amanda thanked her and left with Trent. He had his phone out and was looking at something on the screen.

"That girl was murdered no matter how you slice it," she said, and he looked up at her.

"Agreed."

"And there's that black ribbon. I can't seem to shake its presence. Does it bother you at all?"

"Huh, great minds, they say..." He twisted his phone and flashed his screen just long enough for her to see a Google results page. "You know how I get into the meaning of things sometimes. Well, black roses signify death, but they would have really stood out among all the red ones. Did the killer give Michaela the next best thing? Three red roses tied with a *black* ribbon. A harbinger of death?"

It seemed so. Had the killer selected the black ribbon with intent? Either way, Amanda had a strong suspicion it factored in somehow. Just like that card.

FIVE

Amanda and Trent left Rideout, Liam, and the CSIs to their work and called in for a trace on Michaela's phone. It came back quickly and didn't advance the investigation. The last known location was the arena, and it wasn't currently giving off a signal.

"I'd like to know where the heck that agent is. She can't even be bothered to call me back." The fact she was AWOL and unreachable didn't sit well for her. Sending a uniformed officer by her house might not be a bad idea. As it was, she notified the officer at the arena door to send the agent to them if she turned up.

"We're probably best not to read too much into it. Besides, didn't you leave a message for the coach too?"

Her partner, the voice of reason. He had the ability to ground her when she needed it and to remind her to give people the benefit of the doubt sometimes. She told him that she had called the coach before he arrived. "I did, but the agent bothers me more. She was apparently supposed to be here today, but now, conveniently, she's not. Something's hinky with that alone if you ask me."

"I get it. Maybe just give it a bit longer. We'll talk to the arena manager, and if we're done with that and we still haven't heard from the agent, we'll get a car to her house."

"Okay."

The arena's manager was easy enough to track down. He was sequestered with his staff in one of the locker rooms. They collected him there and spoke with him back in his office.

Ron Hampton was in his fifties with a full head of hair and fine lines around his eyes. "This is just a damn shame. For all that talent just to be gone. Do you know what happened yet? What caused her... death?"

Amanda surmised by the manager's awkwardness with saying *death* that he hadn't encountered much loss in his life. Then again, the unexpected passing of a young person was hard to accept. "The investigation has just started."

"Investigation? Then she didn't die of natural causes?"

"We don't believe so." She would have thought two detectives sitting across from him would have told him that much. Trent even had his tablet in hand ready to peck whatever Ron told them in for the record.

"Oh." His eyes widened. "Then someone, someone..."

"We don't have all the answers yet," Amanda started. "We are hoping you can help us."

"I'm not sure how, but I'll do whatever I can." Ron leaned forward, clasping his hands on his desk.

"Michaela Glover was found in her dressing room," she said. "Can anyone access it?"

"I don't see why not. I mean there's no locks on the door or security placed to watch over it. At least none provided by the arena."

Amanda perked at that distinction, but she supposed this was a skating arena, not some stadium. Even the dressing room was makeshift and located near the main locker rooms. Still, she asked, "Did she come with her own?"

"There's one security guy with the show, but he was rather busy watching the secured area just to the side of the rink. It's where the skaters go on and come off the ice. I never saw him watching over her room, but you'd best talk to her agent."

Amanda didn't want to let him know they hadn't been able to reach her and start a rumor flying around. "The agent being Tara Coolidge?" She just wanted to ensure they were talking about the same person.

"That's right. She was around, but I haven't seen her in some time. She might have left."

So she was *here…* "When did you last see her?"

"Around intermission. She was coming out of Michaela's dressing room. You haven't spoken to her yet?"

Tingles traveled down Amanda's arms, raising the hairs in their wake. The timing was damning by itself, but even more now Tara had seemingly vanished. Amanda resisted the urge to look at Trent. But if Coolidge hadn't called back by the time they finished with Ron, she'd be hopping in a car and going to her house herself. "Not yet. You mentioned that she might have left. Do you know why she would have?" It was curious what innocent explanation there could be for leaving during her client's homecoming performance.

Ron winced. "It looked like they had a bit of a tiff. Michaela didn't look too happy with her anyway."

Amanda's shoulders stiffened. Could it be that simple? The girl's agent had killed her? "What gave you that impression?"

"Michaela held up a hand before turning and walking to her dressing room. Not a wave goodbye, more like a gesture to indicate 'talk to the hand.'"

"Any idea what they were discussing?" Trent asked.

"Nah. I couldn't hear anything from where I was."

Trent shifted in his chair. "What was the agent's reaction when Michaela dismissed her and walked off?"

"She looked ticked off. Her face was all bunched up in a

nasty scowl." Ron wriggled with shivers. "That one has a temper."

Amanda made a mental note of his opinion. Whenever they tracked this agent down, she'd need to answer a lot of questions. In the meantime, Amanda wanted to understand the dynamics at the arena. "We understand Michaela was the only skater assigned a dressing room. Why was that?"

A tight smile. "She was a local, born and raised right here in Woodbridge." Ron squared his shoulders and raised his chin. "We wanted to treat her like the star she was."

Amanda saw a flip side to that. How the special treatment could give rise to jealousy among Michaela's fellow skaters. Before she could speak, Ron did.

"Do you think that was a bad idea? I just wanted to show her that her town was behind her. I sure hope that the Prince William County PD are taking the matter of her death seriously."

"I assure you that we are." Amanda's mind started building up a list of faceless suspects. Aside from the agent and fellow skaters, it was possible a deranged fan had taken her life. It could even work within the scope of the threatening note. It wasn't uncommon for stalkers to build up a fantasy life with the object of their desire in their minds. And as the manager clearly pointed out, Michaela was a star. She'd have a following. "Was Michaela the reason the show sold out so quickly?"

"I would bet on that."

"Did you see any fans approach her or show her unwanted attention?" she fired back.

Ron's brow tightened, and his gaze intensified. "Heavens no. Nothing inappropriate. Some were tailing her to the dressing room, but they dispersed when Michaela ran into her agent, and they started to talk."

"This was once intermission was underway then?" she asked.

"Not quite. Her set had finished, but things were still wrapping up in the auditorium. These fans were early comers."

That confirmed activity in the corridor, but it wouldn't have reached full stride yet. "What do you consider appropriate attention?" She just wanted a clear idea of his definition.

"They were looking for autographs. Some handed her roses."

She perked up at that. "Tied in ribbon?"

"Some yes."

"Did you see any tied with black ribbon?" Trent asked, looking up from his tablet, beating her to it.

"Black? No, the arena only sells red."

That was just as Amanda had thought. So where had that bunch come from? If she was a gambler, she'd wager it came with the card from the killer's home. "What about a card?"

"Nope, never saw anyone hand her one."

Amanda nodded. "So besides the fans looking for her autograph around intermission, did you see anyone hanging around outside of her room?"

"It's not like I was just standing around. I'm a pretty busy guy. Lots of moving parts to oversee. I wanted to make sure the show went off without a hitch and... Yeah, well, I'll stop talking. Obviously, I failed. Not that I could have prevented whatever happened to that girl." He squinted, a silent petition for more information again. Amanda had to give him credit for persistence.

"If we wanted to track down everyone who was here today, how could we go about that?" Amanda knew that officers had gathered names and numbers of those they could, but some would have left before they locked the arena down.

"Well, it wouldn't be an easy feat."

"But it is possible?" Trent put in.

"It is. For the most part anyhow."

Amanda angled her head. "What do you mean?"

"Ninety percent of the tickets were sold online. Those buyers needed to enter their information obviously, but we also sold some at the door when the event was announced. Our priority was collecting money, not names. And if one buyer bought multiple tickets, there would only be one name on file, not one for each seat. We obviously scan all the tickets as people arrive, but I'm not sure how that helps you."

Amanda failed to see how too. And giving it further thought, it was unlikely Michaela's killer would put their name out there to find. It was a haystack and, at this point, wasn't worth their efforts to dig in but at least they were forearmed. "Can you tell us more about this conversation with the agent?"

"Not really. As I said, I didn't overhear anything."

"But the agent came out of her dressing room?" It was one tidbit he'd dropped earlier that was a potential diamond.

"That's right. And after they parted ways, Michaela went in. I assumed she was going to rest before her next set after the break. It turned out, she never had another one, but she was expected for the encore at the end, which she never... Well, you know."

She assumed his point was she'd never showed, though for good reason. "Did you see anyone else turn up at her dressing room door?"

"Like I said, I had to keep moving. There was a situation I had to take care of with the sound system."

"A man of many talents," Trent said.

"Or wearer of many hats. A necessity around here."

The door to the office burst open, and a petite brunette stood in the doorway, cheeks flushed, breathing rushed. "Ron, what the hell is going on? Are you the detectives I'm supposed to talk to?" She settled her emerald eyes on them.

Ron's mouth gaped open, just as Officer Wyatt came up behind the woman. "Sorry, Detectives, this one got away from me. I told her to wait," he hissed.

"Did something happen to Michaela?" the woman rushed out. "I told a police officer outside who I was, and they said I had to talk to you."

Amanda nodded at Wyatt, and he backed out of the room and closed the door behind him.

"What is going on?" The woman was practically screeching.

"Ma'am, we're Detectives Steele, and Stenson," Amanda said. "Who are you?"

The woman leveled a fiery gaze at Amanda then let it travel to Trent. "Tara Coolidge, Mick's agent."

SIX

"I can't believe this is happening. She's really dead?" The agent's voice reached a higher octave with every word that left her mouth. Tara Coolidge was wearing a coat, but she was rubbing her arms as if she were chilled. Amanda wasn't going to correct the tense she'd used. This *had* happened.

Amanda and Trent remained with the agent in Ron's office, while he reluctantly returned to the locker room. Tara took his chair.

Amanda tried to get a read on the woman, but she was guarded. That combined with her disappearing act and what they learned from Ron didn't help her case. "We appreciate Michaela's death may come as a shock to you, but—"

"A shock?" Tara burst out. "That's putting it a touch mildly. I thought I'd find out the news had it wrong when they said a star skater was found dead. I certainly never expected it to be Mick."

At least, for now, it seemed Michaela's name had been held back. But none of this changed the fact the agent had been who-knows-where for the past several hours. And had been the last person seen with Michaela. Amanda could play this interview one of two ways. One, go at the agent directly, confront her with what they knew. Or two, build up to it. The latter would be more conducive to getting Tara to talk. At best, she'd trip herself up. In the least, she'd likely offer some valuable insights for the investigation. "Were you and Michaela close?"

Tara sniffled and nodded. "I've worked with her since she was six years old. I started as her coach. Eventually I also assumed the role of agent for her, especially once she began winning national junior titles. I remained just a coach for my other girls. I set up sessions for Mick with top coaches across the country starting from when she was around eight, but she only caught the eyes of a world-renowned Olympic coach in recent years. Michaela started working with her a few months before her nineteenth birthday."

"Jolene Flynn?" Amanda countered.

Tara blinked slowly. "That's her."

"And that's when Michaela moved to Colorado Springs?" Trent interjected.

"That's right."

Michaela was twenty-one now so... "Two years ago?"

"Closer to two and a half given when her birthday falls."

"I tried reaching Jolene but wasn't able to get through. She never came for this event?" Amanda already knew the answer, but wanted to get Tara's take.

Tara shook her head. "No. She coaches the Olympic disciplines rather than ice shows like this. She's in Washington this weekend, but for reasons unrelated to the show. Some family gathering from what I understand."

Close enough to pop by and kill her client, but why? "If you could help me understand something. I'm rather in the dark when it comes to the world of figure skating. You got other coaches lined up when she was eight?"

Tara nodded. "Michaela's exceptional talent was clear even then. I knew I couldn't coach her to her full potential, so I needed to get her on the big guns' radars. That's how elite coaching works, Detective. Jolene is the best of the best. She doesn't coach just anybody."

"What does an agent do versus a coach?" Amanda had an inkling but wanted all uncertainties squashed.

"Acting as an agent, my main responsibility is procuring sponsorships for Mick, but I also worked with Jolene to get Michaela here today. Publicity goes far with corporate sponsors. Whereas Jolene's job as coach was to train her so she was ready for competitions, and ultimately the Olympics."

"For your job then, it's easy enough to do remotely," Amanda said.

"That's right. There was no need to uproot myself."

"You said that you started with Michaela at the age of six. You knew her for most of her life, watched her grow up. You must have been close." Amanda approached this conversationally. Tara could offer valuable insight into Michaela's life, but Amanda wanted to see if she could spot any fractures in their relationship. Being aggressive wouldn't get them anywhere.

Tara blew out a deep breath. "She was like a daughter to me. We did a lot of growing up together too. As for her training, getting started early was imperative. If a kid can walk, put them in skates. Figure skating isn't an easy world to be a part of. It takes dedication and commitment. Mick trained six days a week for several hours a day. She also adhered to a rather strict diet. That's when her sweet tooth didn't get the best of her."

"Wow." The hard work wasn't a shock, but it must have come with a hefty price tag. She didn't know much about Michaela's upbringing other than the fact her parents weren't in her life. "Who paid for all of this?" She couldn't imagine Patty covering the bill on a cop's salary.

"Her grandmother in the beginning, but it wasn't long before Mick started winning competitions. That made her attractive to sponsors, and they started to cover all the expenses."

Michaela's grandmother must have taken her in after the mother took off. She hadn't really gotten into the minutiae of Michaela's upbringing with Patty, or thought to inquire who assumed guardianship of the girl. When discussing who to notify Patty hadn't mentioned the grandma either. "You feel that way about all your clients? Like they are your children?"

"Absolutely. I put my heart and soul into them and their futures."

Amanda detected a conflict between the agent's words and behavior. "If you were so close with Michaela, where were you in the last several hours? Why leave the arena?"

Tara's jaw stiffened. "I don't see how that's relevant."

Silence.

One second. Two. Three.

"Oh my God, are you telling me that she was... that someone *killed* her?" Fat tears beaded on Tara's eyelashes.

"Sorry to say that it looks that way," Amanda told her, trying to soften the delivery by prefacing it with the apology.

Tara slumped in her chair. "I'm at a loss for words."

"Well, I need you to answer my question about your whereabouts," Amanda said firmly. "The show ended at three o'clock. You're just showing up now, three hours later. You said the news brought you back, but I tried calling you and even left a voicemail."

"That was you..." Tara paled, and she laid a hand over her stomach. "I haven't listened to your message. I just saw the unidentified number and figured the voicemail would be some mechanical robot talking in Chinese."

Amanda stiffened. "Your whereabouts, Ms. Coolidge? If you're not comfortable talking here, we can take this conversation to Central Station." That was where the PWCPD Homicide Unit was housed.

"No, I'll talk. Just..." Tara unfolded her arms and toyed with the metal pull that dangled from her coat zipper.

"Ms. Coolidge," Amanda prompted.

Seconds of silence.

"All right, suit yourself." Amanda braced her hands on the table as if ready to stand. "Let's go."

"No, no, please. I'm sorry. I don't mean to be evasive. It's just that I'm a nervous wreck. You guys are looking at me like I'm a killer."

"Are you?" Amanda volleyed back.

"Absolutely not. But I clearly had poor timing for stepping out."

Amanda and Trent let the silence stretch.

Eventually, she offered, "I left during intermission and had a couple of drinks at the Tipsy Moose Alehouse."

Amanda was a regular customer of the restaurant. "What would make you do that? Why leave when your client was performing? Someone you just told us you thought of as a daughter." The agent's demeanor and responses weren't sitting well. She could have been telling them the truth but leaving out other parts. What was to say she hadn't slipped back into the dressing room before leaving?

"I needed to give myself some space, and it wasn't like Michaela was due out for another set after intermission."

Being generous, that response was only half an answer. "Space from what?"

"In the grand scheme, it was nothing. I should have stayed." Tara blew out a breath and pressed her lips in a straight line.

Amanda's patience was wearing thin, though Tara was saying more than she might have realized. Between her responses and body language, she was clearly hiding something. Had it been Michaela's murder? It could explain her shifty and unsettled energy. She had been a part of Michaela's life since she was a child and would have known about her peanut allergy. Killing her, even if she felt justified, would have extracted an emotional toll. "Did your leaving have anything to do with your heated conversation with Michaela?" It was apparent by now that Tara wasn't going to volunteer this information.

She locked eyes with Amanda's. "You know about that? How? You know what? Never mind. I suppose it might have looked like an argument to someone on the outside."

"Was it?" Amanda flung back. Sometimes short, direct inquiries were the most effective.

"Not really."

"It was bad enough the conversation pushed you to leave the arena to day drink," Trent pointed out.

"You don't get it, all right. Mick was twenty-one going on thirteen. She could be rather immature."

Amanda found that hard to reconcile with a star athlete already at the top of her field, bound for the Olympics. "Is this your way of telling us she overreacted to something?"

"She excelled at that."

Amanda summoned her patience. It would seem she'd need to pull every word out of this woman. "What was it over this time?"

"Just business. It's nothing that should concern the police."

"A young woman is dead. We decide what concerns us," Trent pushed out. A closed statement not suggesting it was open for debate. Moving this conversation to Central would be imminent if she didn't start talking.

Tara licked her lips but said nothing as she unzipped her coat and shucked out of it. She let the jacket sit bunched up at the base of her back. "I'm telling you it's not consequential, but Mick didn't always understand or appreciate the business side of things. Her head was in the clouds. Winning gold at the Olympics. Having the largest, most prestigious sponsors. She dreamed of being the next Yuna Kim." She paused there, and must have read Amanda's and Trent's expressions that they weren't familiar with the name. "She's one of the most successful skaters of all time and won gold in ladies' single skating at the 2010 Winter Olympics in Vancouver. She was an incredible free skater, and Mick modelled her axel technique. In simple terms, that's a type of spinning jump," she added when they must have looked blank again.

Tara's response was superfluous and off track. "Nothing wrong with having lofty goals and working toward their fulfillment. But it hasn't been missed that you still haven't told us specifically what upset Michaela from your conversation." If Tara's convoluted detour was intentional, Amanda wasn't going to let her off so easily.

"I'm working on getting her a sponsorship deal with Active Spirit." The statement came out on a sigh.

"They specialize in top-of-the-line athletic wear," Trent said. "I take it from your sigh that negotiations aren't going well?"

"I wouldn't leap there. Brokering these types of deals just takes time. There are a lot of hands involved, lawyers, board members."

"So Michaela didn't think you were moving things along fast enough?" Trent asked.

Tara nodded.

Amanda was never a fan of the nonverbal response, especially from someone who hadn't gained her trust. "Run us through this conversation with Michaela. How did it go exactly?"

"Even calling it a conversation is giving it too much credit. It was a few seconds' exchange. She asked me how it was going with Active Spirit, and I told her I was on top of it. She dismissed me with a wave, turned her back on me, and walked off. Like a teenager having a snit."

It was tough to reconcile this simple *exchange* as being what prompted the agent to tuck tail and leave the arena. "That's all? Are you sure there wasn't more to this?"

"Not on my end."

Trent stretched his legs out under the table and sat back. "How long have you been working on this deal with Active Spirit?"

"A few months, which is nothing for a sponsorship of this magnitude. As I said, many hands are involved."

"And that was when you last saw her? Just at intermission?" Amanda asked.

"That's right."

"And this was where?" Amanda asked, knowing the answer according to the arena manager.

"Outside her dressing room."

"Did you go inside with her to extend your chat?" Amanda asked.

"No."

"So you weren't in her dressing room?" Amanda was curious if she'd admit to being there moments before her conversation with Michaela.

"I never said that. Someone had dropped off a bouquet for her at the front ticket booth. That employee flagged me down when I was walking by and asked that I take them to her dressing room. I was coming out when I crossed paths with Michaela. What am I missing?" Tara stiffened, and her cheeks flushed.

Top marks went to Tara if she was acting here. She'd have to know they'd just need to have a brief chat with the arena employee to confirm her story. "We'll get to that. Is it a normal occurrence during events such as this? People dropping off flowers at the venue for a beloved skater?"

"It happens sometimes." Tara was responding to the point, her gaze blanked over.

"Do you know who delivered them? Was there a card?"

She'd like to confirm where the one with Michaela's body had originated.

"I wasn't paying much attention. The girl from the ticket booth might be able to tell you."

"It seems like something easy enough to notice," Amanda put out.

"I was a little preoccupied."

"With what?" Their argument hadn't happened yet.

"Oh, just the sponsorship deal."

"Surely, their headquarters are closed on the weekend," Trent pointed out.

"That doesn't stop me from considering ways to strengthen my proposal."

Amanda could relate. Here she was working on a Saturday. At this rate, Sunday too. It likely wasn't easy to get corporations to part with their money, but if Tara was obsessed about them on the weekend, talks likely weren't going well. But how would that support Tara murdering Michaela? In fact, seeing motive was proving difficult. "So, just to be clear, the last time you saw her was...?"

"That chat around the start of intermission, after which we went our separate ways."

"Did you tell her you were leaving the arena?" Amanda asked.

"No way. Nothing good would have come from that, and I seriously didn't have the bandwidth to handle it if she lost her temper with me. Her earlier attitude was enough. Listen, I've been cooperative, and you haven't even told me what happened to her. I feel I deserve to know."

Amanda recoiled at the agent's attitude. Patty didn't know the cause of death yet, and it was her niece. "To start, Michaela was found in her dressing room."

"Oh. That's why you're so... interested." Tara paled and

held a hand over her heart. "I swear I never would have hurt that girl."

Amanda disregarded her claim. "We were told there was a security guy who came with the show."

"Henry. What about him?"

"Was he ever tasked with watching over Michaela's dressing room?" she asked.

"No. He was to keep fans from going into the cordoned-off section where the skaters prepare to go on the ice and where they come off."

Fans... As she thought before, one of them could be the killer.

"Please, just tell me what killed her," Tara said, her voice cracking.

"It looks like a fatal allergic reaction." Amanda provided that much as bait to confirm the woman's knowledge.

"Michaela has a severe peanut allergy, but there's no way. That can't be right. Mick always has an EpiPen with her, and I have one." She dug into her purse.

Tara wasn't likely to come out brandishing a gun, but better safe than sorry. "Ma'am, I'm going to need you to—"

Tara had already set her cell phone on the table and was now holding up an EpiPen. "She could have just called me."

"Except that she couldn't," Amanda said. "Her phone is gone. So is her EpiPen."

"What? That's impossible. Or did this person... this *monster* take them? They wanted her to die." She shrunk into herself. "This is a nightmare."

"Which, sadly, is also reality." Amanda couldn't let the fact this was the death of a friend's loved one consume her. Instead, she'd choose to let it *fuel* her. "Who knew about her allergy to peanuts? Was it something that venues were alerted to ahead of events or competitions?" Zoe's school sent home a letter at the start of every school year reminding parents it was a nut-free environment. Surely, something similar was enforced for public events involving performers with allergies. As Amanda asked, she realized just how deep that would make the suspect pool.

"We did notify arena management," Tara said. "But there's only so much I can do. I can't make them post signs or change everything to nut-free."

"Do any of them take those measures?" Trent asked.

"Some, but it's not like Mick's allergy is a well-guarded secret. The opposite, in fact."

This confirmation was overwhelming. It made it more possible one of Michaela's fans or a crazed stalker did this. "Then anyone who followed her career was likely to know?"

"No doubt. I just can't believe someone did this on purpose." A wrinkle creased her brow, her eyes hooded and dark, begging for a reason.

"Did you see anyone heading toward her room as you were leaving?" Amanda asked.

"No."

"Any obsessive fans or possible stalkers?" Trent put in.

"She had a few that toed the line. She was a rising star in a popular, glamorous sport, a future Olympic champion. You don't reach her level without collecting some whack jobs along the way. But why would they kill her?"

"She might not have lived up to the fantasies they created in their minds," Amanda volleyed back, and the agent sagged in her chair. "Do you have any names you can give us?"

"No. It was just people who always commented on her social channels, or came to her competitions. Big fans, but not to an unsettling degree."

"Did she ever receive any threatening fan mail?" She and Trent had worked on another case involving a high-profile celebrity and considered the same possibility. They learned there was a fine line between admiration and obsession. The card given to Michaela wasn't far from mind either.

"Not that I'm aware of." Tara narrowed her eyes.

"Did Michaela have any boyfriends?" Trent asked.

"She didn't have time for that."

"Then no recent breakups? Someone who didn't take the news well?" Amanda asked.

"If there was someone, I don't know about them."

There was another group of people who came to Amanda's mind. Not a new thought but one that needed to be explored further. The world of figure skating would, no doubt, be fiercely competitive. What if jealousy had pushed one of Michaela's rivals to murder her? "Michaela was the only skater to score a dressing room for this show. Did that upset anyone?" It was a stretch but if this person felt lost in Michaela's shadow, they could have felt she owed them somehow too.

"There was a lot of complaining about that, but to think of someone going to the extreme of... of... I can't imagine it." Tara wasn't making eye contact, and that niggled.

"But someone is coming to mind, aren't they?" Amanda asked.

Tara met Amanda's gaze now. "Wendy Nicholson. But for her to go to this extreme? I just don't see it."

Amanda remembered Wendy from her performance today, placing her in the arena. "What was the relationship like between her and Michaela?"

"Fraught with tension and competitive spirit."

Was that all it took to commit cold-blooded murder? It was hard to reconcile the graceful skater she'd seen on the ice with a homicidal lunatic. Wendy was also talented, so why would she throw her future away by killing Michaela? But she had to explore the possibility further. "Did it ever get physical between them?"

"I've seen videos where they were yelling at each other. Michaela never mentioned things ever coming to fists."

"What were they yelling about?" Trent asked.

"Frustration over when Michaela had access to the rink. Wendy's coach also works out of Colorado Springs and trains at the Olympic Training Center there. There's usually a friendly rivalry between the two camps, but Jolene's clients get top pick on practice times."

Tara's words opened another avenue that hadn't occurred to Amanda before. They were focused on who had it out for Michaela, but what if she was a casualty of Jolene's success? After all, she seemed to have her pick of the best young skaters. An agent might have schemed to get Michaela out of the way so their client could advance in her place. Or maybe a fellow skater or their family saw it as a way to vacate a slot for themselves.

"Surely, you aren't seriously considering everyone with the show a suspect," Tara said, breaking the few seconds of silence.

"At this point, everyone is a suspect," Amanda said. "I know Wendy was in the show today. Do you know if Wendy's agent or coach is here?"

"Her coach, Lilian Berry, is."

Trent tapped on his tablet.

Considering that all of Michaela's competitors, their agents, coaches, and even the security guy, Henry, would know about her allergy, any one of them could have slipped into her dressing room and killed her without suspicion. "There was a handwritten note in Michaela's room that read, 'You'll be sorry you turned your back on me after all I did for you.'" Amanda paused to gauge Tara's reaction. Her cheeks flushed. "Do you know anyone who might have reason to say all that?"

Tara swallowed roughly. "No. But toes get stepped on in the climb to the top. Intentionally or not."

It felt like a token offering and had come quickly. "Sounds like you've given this some thought."

"I've been thinking about it since you asked about jealous competitors."

"Anyone else coming to mind besides Wendy?" Trent asked.

"No."

Though Amanda wondered how much faith they could place in that answer. Tara was based here, while Michaela lived hundreds of miles away. "What kind of person was Michaela?" Amanda wanted to explore if fame had gone to the young skater's head.

"She was down to earth and humble. It didn't seem to matter how many competitions she won. She'd take them with pride, but with a humble spirit. She was ambitious, like I said, but I never saw her rub any of her success in someone's face."

Niece like aunt. Despite Patty's record of taking many dangerous predators off the street, she viewed it as her civic duty and purpose. Like any good cop the badge was about service not recognition.

Tara let out a staggered breath. "I'm still trying to accept that she's dead, that someone murdered her. Do you know how she ingested peanuts?"

"It seems that someone tampered with her protein shake. Did she ever leave it unattended? Possibly while she was performing or had stepped out to use the restroom?" Amanda was confident of what the answer would be, and it chilled her.

Tara slowly met Amanda's eyes. "Actually, I saw it when I dropped off the flowers. Mick would have been finishing up her act then."

But I never expected that... Amanda wished she could read the woman's mind to gauge her innocence. But it wasn't looking good.

SEVEN

As Amanda studied the agent across from her, she was trying to speculate motive. It was possible Tara Coolidge stood to profit from her death through a will or life insurance. But what would push her to that point? She would be making good money with Michaela alive. Amanda could think of one possibility. It fit the spirit of the note, and if she was on the right track, it also explained why Tara wasn't forthcoming about her conversation with Michaela. "Ms. Coolidge, you tell us you thought of Michaela as a daughter, but I get the sense there was more tension between you than you're letting on. Maybe she wasn't happy with your work anymore. Did Michaela ever threaten to fire you?"

Tara's body stiffened. "No way. She never would. Nope."

"You told us she didn't think things were moving fast enough with Active Spirit. So, she never threatened to let you go? You're predominantly a coach, correct? Maybe she felt she needed an agent with more experience?" Amanda reiterated.

Tara's cheeks were a bright red, but she shook her head.

"Did you stand to inherit anything from her if she died?" Amanda circled back to her thinking from a moment ago.

"Unbelievable. You really think I killed her?"

"Please just answer Detective Steele's question," Trent said.

"Well, Mick set up a will at my nudging. Before you read anything into that, I had her best interests at heart. She was making good money, and as tough as it is for a twenty-one-year-old to think of their mortality, I encouraged her to. Far as I know her estate was set to go to her aunt, Patty Glover. Am I going to need a lawyer?"

"It's your right, but we're just talking with you," Amanda said.

"Really? I feel like I'm being interrogated."

"You tell us that you would never hurt Michaela," Amanda began. "Would you give us a sample of your handwriting?"

Tara looked Amanda straight in the eye. "Fine. Just so that you can move on and find her real killer."

Amanda turned to Trent knowing he'd have a notepad with him. He'd arrived ready to work, unlike her planned day of leisure.

Trent must have read her mind. He tore out a piece of paper and gave it to Tara along with his pen.

"What do you want me to write?" Tara held the pen in her right hand.

The writer of that ominous note was likely left-handed, but Amanda wasn't going to let that fact derail her. Anyone could write with either hand if they put their mind to it. And if Tara wrote the card she'd want to change up her penmanship. "'You'll be sorry you turned your back on me after all I did for you.'"

"Wow, you're being serious right now?"

Amanda didn't say anything and let the silence speak for her. Tara began to write. Her strokes were fluid, not like she was thinking it through as she went along. If she had been trying to make the writing look different, she would have been slower to finish. A few seconds later, she pushed the page and pen across the table.

Trent had brought up a photo of the card on his tablet, and they compared with their layman eyes. Tara's handwriting was bubble-like with a slight right angle. Typically, the tighter and more compact the writing, the more stressed or angry the person. The cursive was even the opposite of the writing on the card. The letters in the words were joined in the note, whereas the tail end to Tara's *r* was incomplete, and when preceding another letter, it didn't flow into the next.

"So?" Tara eventually said. "Am I good to go?"

The writing was nothing like the card, and Amanda said, "We'll need you to stick around the arena for a bit—"

"Why? Obviously, my writing isn't a match." Tara stiffened and darted her gaze at Trent. "I don't understand why it's necessary I stay."

"This is a murder investigation, and we might have more questions for you," Trent told her matter-of-factly.

"What else could I possibly have to tell you?"

"Let's start with where we can reach you once you're cleared to leave the arena," Trent put in.

Tara gave them her home address in Woodbridge, and Trent recorded it to his tablet while Amanda walked to the door and signaled for Officer Wyatt to enter the room.

"Thank you for your cooperation, Ms. Coolidge," she told her. "Officer Wyatt will see you to the locker room now."

"Why?"

"We'll know where to find you. Also, the rest of the show entourage is there," Amanda told her.

"Come on, I'll take you now," Officer Wyatt said kindly.

Tara got up in a huff, grabbed her coat from the chair, and left with Wyatt.

Amanda sat back. "She's a piece of work."

"No argument here, but if we're going by her handwriting, she's likely not the killer."

"Maybe not. But she is holding something back."

"Not going to argue that, but does it matter to the investigation?"

"Can't say. What I *can* say, based on that talk, is that pursuing who knew about Michaela's peanut allergy is a nonstarter. It wasn't exactly kept under wraps."

"True enough. Everyone with the show likely knew she drank a protein shake when she got off the ice too. I expect most of them do something similar."

"Uh-huh. We're best to stick to who had motive."

"When it comes to Tara, I don't see one, at this point," Trent said.

"Me either. Working this from another angle might help. I say we start by finding out where the card came from. Was it with the roses tied with the black ribbon or did it accompany the floral arrangement in the vase? It's time to talk with that person from the ticket booth to see what they can tell us."

"Detectives." A familiar voice had her and Trent looking at the doorway. Sergeant Malone was striding toward them, red-faced and slightly winded. "I was told I'd find you two here. I got here as fast as I could. Where are we with things? I bumped into Rideout and Liam heading out. Preliminary cause of death was anaphylaxis, but it looks like murder?"

"The evidence is pointing us that way." She informed him about the missing EpiPen, phone, and the words in the card.

"'You'll be sorry'? Sounds like a threat to me. Anyone jumping out to you?"

"We've been exploring a few possibilities," Amanda said. "Obsessed fans or stalkers, jealous competitors."

"Her peanut allergy seems to be widespread knowledge," Trent wedged in.

Malone's eyes hardened as he ran a hand over his neatly

groomed beard. "Suggesting the means isn't much of a mystery, though I'd speculate the killer was someone who was close to her. Specifically a person who invested their time, energy, money, or *something* in Michaela and it didn't pay off."

Amanda nodded. "We think the same. I left a voicemail for Michaela's coach, who is supposedly in Washington. She wasn't expected today, but she hasn't returned my call."

"Might be nothing to it. But Washington's not far. It would be easy enough for her to pop by and kill Michaela," Malone said.

The picture of such premeditation was tough to swallow, though possible. "Which we'll take into account, but we had a long talk with Michaela's agent, Tara Coolidge. We ended up releasing her because we don't see a motive for her, and her handwriting isn't a match for the card either."

"Huh. Too bad. There goes a quick close. But there is also a slim chance the card wasn't from the killer."

"Suppose that's true. Though it was almost like it was their opportunity to get the last word." As Amanda said this, how did that reconcile with their earlier theory that the killer stuck around? Being there until Michaela's final breath would have meant ample opportunity to do just that. So why risk writing the card and leaving it behind?

"There's smoke coming from your ears, Steele," Malone said, pulling out her surname, which he rarely did. He had been a friend of her father's and her family's since before she was born.

"I'm just thinking why there was a card in the first place. There wasn't a name on it, but it just seems so spot on for providing motive. It could wind up leading us right to this person," she said.

"Pride, stupidity. Killers are often narcissistic too and feel they are beyond making mistakes. Their need to have the last word, as you just said, could have compelled them to put their grievance into writing. The killer wanted Michaela to know why she was being killed," Trent responded.

Amanda shook her head. "Except we speculated they would have hung around until her final breath. They could have just told her. Why leave a written trail?"

"I'm not sure how much I'd read into it, but you've got good instincts," Malone told her. "You could be on to something. Whatever that is."

At this point she didn't know. "Regardless of why the card exists, I still think accepting it as being written by the killer or being placed by them is the strongest angle to continue working from. We also need to figure out who had motive to kill her. Getting our hands on Michaela's phone records could go a long way to helping us find possible suspects. It might be a while before we get to that. We still have more people to talk to here and..." She let the sentence trail off to nothing, counting on Malone to catch her implication.

Malone smiled. "Is that your way of asking for my help?"

She knew he'd get where she'd been leading him. "I am."

"You have it." There were a few seconds of silence while Malone studied her, barely passing a glance at Trent. "You okay to handle this case?"

She stiffened her posture, not sure why he doubted her ability. She'd proved repeatedly that she could manage investigations that touched close to home. If she wasn't capable, she might as well hand in her badge right now. Living in a small county, it was likely she or someone she knew would be linked to the next victim. "I am."

"I'll need you to back that up. This case demands that you be on top of your game."

"And when am I not?" she countered with a smile.

"I'm just stating it for the record. The PWCPD has a lot of eyes on it at the moment. Outside is a downright zoo. Every media network from the state, maybe some from neighboring ones, are here to cover the story. It's leaked that it's Michaela Glover. I've already fielded a call from Buchanan."

Jeff Buchanan was the PWCPD police chief. He was a good man who wore his authority well and fairly and earned respect from his underlings. Michaela was a celebrity of a sort, and the public would want answers. Now she felt pressure coming from all sides. "Tell me what's being said. Have they mentioned murder?"

"Not that I heard."

She let out a deep breath. "One small mercy."

A few beats of silence passed before Trent broke it.

"We've speculated the card made its way to her one of two ways." Trent told Malone about the roses tied with black ribbon and the floral delivery with a card stick and no card. "We were just going to talk with an arena employee about the origin of the bouquet and if they noticed the card."

"Go. I don't want to hold you up anymore. I'll get on the phone records, and you keep me posted."

She didn't get a chance to respond before Malone turned to leave. To Trent, she said, "So it's not bad enough that a young woman lost her life today, people are trying to make a name for themselves off it." It was a sickening thought, making her more determined to do what she could to bring some fairness and justice to the world.

EIGHT

Amanda and Trent stepped into the locker room holding the arena employees. They were met with a lot of grumpy-looking faces. She could empathize. It was close to eight o'clock at night and hanging around here was no one's idea of a good time. But at least they were alive and breathing. The officer posted at the door told Amanda that he had everyone's information, but she told him to keep everyone a bit longer.

Amanda flagged down the manager, who was sitting on the end of a bench. "We need to know who was working the ticket booth during the show."

Ron's gaze flicked to a brunette in her twenties standing with her arms crossed. "That would be Cindy Morris. Why are you interested in her?"

"Thank you." Amanda brushed him off with a pleasant smile, and she and Trent headed over.

"Cindy Morris?" Trent said.

"That's me."

"I'm Detective Stenson, and this is Detective Steele. We understand that you received some flowers at the ticket booth for Michaela Glover. Is that right?"

"Uh-huh." She slid her bottom lip between her teeth, giving the impression being here was boring the hell out of her. Any other time, Amanda imagined the woman was glued to the screen of her phone. Officers would have asked everyone to stay off them.

"Can you tell us which florist delivered them?" Amanda asked.

"I couldn't tell you. Wasn't there a card?"

Amanda perked at that. "You saw one?"

"I was just assuming so. Usually flowers come with cards."

Usually... That wasn't exactly concrete. "We never found one stamped from a florist. Did the bouquet come from one?"

"A florist? I'd assume so."

"What did the delivery person look like? Or did you see the car they were driving?" Trent had his tablet out and a finger poised over the screen to note her answer.

"Just Plain Jane. Nothing really stood out about her." Cindy shrugged her shoulder. Some people got incredibly nervous and uncomfortable talking to police. This young woman didn't seem at all affected.

"Anything else?" Trent asked. "Age?"

"Twenty-something. She was wearing a gray winter jacket and jeans."

"Any business name on her coat?" Sometimes flower shops had their delivery people wear branded clothing.

"Not that I saw."

"Did she get you to sign for the delivery?" Some florists did, but not all.

"Nope. I just told her I'd get them to Michaela. Then I flagged down Tara, that's her agent, and asked her to deliver them. She just happened to be walking by around that time."

"And this was when?" They had the agent's answer, but in a murder investigation, it was wise to double, triple, even quadruple check responses to see if they continued to line up.

"Not long before intermission."

"Okay, thank you for your help." Amanda gave her a card. "Call if you think of something later."

"Does that mean I can go? I had a date tonight, and I'd like to rescue some of it." Cindy's eyes were wide and full of hope.

"I'm sure it won't be long, and everyone can leave," Amanda told her and watched the young woman's shoulders sag. She left with Trent and turned to him. "We should find out if there are cameras on the front of the arena."

"Short of taking a walk, I know who could answer that question." Trent nudged his head toward the manager.

They crossed back to Ron Hampton, who was now sitting with his hands braced on the rear of the bench, likely to help lend himself some back support.

"Are you sure the employees can't go home? I'll stick around if I must. Though preferably in my office."

"Likely soon," Trent told him, taking the hit of delivering the bad news this time around. "Does the arena have video surveillance?"

"Uh-huh. Cameras are on the front and rear of the building."

"We'd like to have a look at the footage," she told him.

Ron winced. "If it was up to me, I'd just hand it over. But I know the higher ups would insist on a warrant."

Of course they would... "All right, we'll get it sorted." She led the way out of the locker room with Trent at her heels and looked over her shoulder. "We'll bench the origin of the card for now and talk with everyone here."

"Nothing about that sounds overwhelming."

"One person at a time, starting with Wendy Nicholson. But I wouldn't say no to coffee."

"Me either. We have a long night ahead of us."

NINE

Ron soon wrangled up coffee for Amanda and Trent. It was bitter, but it was caffeine and better than nothing if it was going to keep them awake. Amanda released the arena staff, but the people with the show would stay put until they spoke with them. Most came from other parts of the country and probably had flights home booked for the next day. Stepping into the locker room with the skaters and production crew, they were met with a lot of tired and angry-looking faces.

Amanda recognized Wendy Nicholson from the show. She was standing next to a woman who was decades older. She was likely the skater's coach. The two of them were talking but stopped when she and Trent approached.

"Wendy Nicholson?" Amanda asked, though she was confident.

"Yes."

"Detectives Steele, and Stenson. And you are, ma'am?" Amanda leveled her gaze at the older woman.

"Lilian Berry, Wendy's coach. Is there any way we can leave? We have an afternoon flight to catch tomorrow, and Wendy needs her rest."

"I appreciate it's been a rough night, but you've probably heard that Michaela Glover is dead." Amanda tempered her words but had little sympathy for their schedule considering the bigger picture.

"It would be impossible not to. Such a horrible tragedy. What happened to her?" Lilian's voice wasn't charged with emotion, but that could represent her character. She struck Amanda as a confident A-type personality. If one let her, she'd dominate and steer the conversation.

"We believe she was murdered." Amanda set the cold, hard truth out there, curious of the reactions she'd get.

"Oh my God." Wendy laid a hand on her chest and started to cry. Her coach comforted her by putting an arm around her.

From what she saw and felt, the girl was genuinely saddened by this news, and it had Amanda questioning their supposed rivalry. "What was your relationship like with her?

Lilian squared her shoulders. "Should we have a lawyer present?"

"That's up to you, but we'd be curious why you'd feel the need for one." Amanda solidified eye contact with the coach. Her words were likely intended as a threat, a power play on her part, but it was hard to say. She or her client might have something to hide, making having a lawyer in their best interest.

Wendy slipped out from under her coach's arm. "She's just trying to protect me."

The skin on Amanda's neck tightened. "From what?"

"It's nothing to concern yourself with, Detective." Lilian shot her client a reprimanding look.

"It's too late for that," Trent chimed in.

"Fine." Lilian huffed out. "Wendy has taken the hit in the media before, for her hysterics, as one reporter put it. But it was taken out of context."

The coach's wording suggested a specific incident. "What was?"

"The animosity between Wendy and Michaela," Lilian clarified. "It was nothing but a PR stunt instigated by Wendy's agent. A-list celebrities do it all the time. They stage fake fights on social media. It gets fans engaged and talking about them."

"There's nothing between me and Michaela, I swear," Wendy inserted. "It was just for publicity, but it backfired."

When they spoke to Michaela's agent, she hadn't mentioned anything like this. "We heard you screamed at her before."

"A performance. Nothing more," Lilian said on Wendy's behalf. "It was staged and then videotaped."

"Was that something that Michaela's agent was aware of?" Trent asked.

"Who knows? Coolidge is off her game these days," Lilian said.

"You know her?" Amanda was curious how that worked with Tara Coolidge in Woodbridge, and Lilian presumably in Colorado Springs.

Lilian shrugged. "The skating world is small, and word gets around. Apparently, Tara hasn't signed any sponsorships for Michaela in some time and the latest rumor going around was she botched a deal with Active Spirit. Coolidge really should have stuck to her lane and stayed a coach only. She isn't cut out for closing deals with sponsors. At least she did Michaela right by getting Jolene Flynn to train her. That woman is the best, even if by saying so I'm shooting myself in the foot."

If the athletic wear company had rejected Tara, it could explain why she had been acting so strangely when they kept pressing about her negotiations with them. She also could have been lying when she said Michaela hadn't fired her or discussed doing so. But her handwriting didn't match the card. Was that enough to absolve her from suspicion?

"I swear, Detectives, I liked Michaela, respected her." Wendy's voice was small and timid.

She didn't project the image of a cold-blooded killer, but those types rarely screamed their presence in the world. And Wendy had just admitted to putting on one show, so why not another?

"I'd like to know why you went along with this pretend fight, Ms. Berry," Trent said. "You said A-list celebrities do it, but surely Wendy's talent stands on its own."

The skater shot a cold look at her coach. Amanda got the sense the young woman had made that argument several times and came out on the losing end.

Lilian didn't give the impression she'd even noticed Wendy looking at her. "First off, it was Wendy's agent, but, yes, I supported the decision. Figure skating is a fierce sport with even fiercer competition. It takes dedication from a young age, and that effort would be wasted if it didn't pay off. One way to ensure it does is to make our skaters stand out." Lilian squared her shoulders. She was clearly on the defensive.

"But we also become family," Wendy added, glancing over at her coach again.

"Family doesn't always get along," Trent said, and Amanda knew he spoke from experience. Only recently had his aunt been reunited with his family after ten years of estrangement.

"If you're looking at one of us"—Lilian gestured around the room—"then you're wasting your time. No one here would kill Michaela."

"You sound confident in that belief." Amanda was unsure what to make of the coach. It was hard to say if she erected a wall to keep them out or to protect herself or her client. But why did they need protection? And how far would she go to promote Wendy?

"I am."

"As family then, you knew about Michaela's allergy to peanuts?" Trent asked, and Amanda appreciated he was laying the groundwork for further questioning.

"Of course. We all did."

So far motive for Wendy and her coach was unclear, so Amanda would go at it from another angle. Opportunity. "Could you give us a full breakdown of your time since you arrived at the arena and all yours and Wendy's movements from that point?"

"Hold on. Are you being serious?" Lilian asked.

"I assure you I am," Amanda said.

"We were together from the time we arrived at noon," Lilian said, taking the reins. "Wendy had a set at the beginning and second to the end. Then she was due back out during the encore."

Wendy would have been leaving the ice when Michaela was going on. That feasibly gave the skater time to slip into Michaela's dressing room to taint her drink and take her phone and EpiPen before intermission. Lilian had all the time her client was performing to do as she wished. "From the sounds of it you weren't together the *entire* time."

Lilian rolled her eyes. "When Wendy was on the ice, I was rink side with Henry. He's the security guy who came with the show. You can ask him to corroborate what I'm telling you."

"We'll be talking with him." That had been Amanda's intention since first learning of him. "What can you tell us about Henry?"

Lilian's gaze slid across the room and landed on a broad-shouldered man in his fifties. "There's nothing much to tell. He's a big guy but gentle as a teddy bear. He certainly wouldn't have hurt Michaela."

It never failed to irritate Amanda how people tried to do her job. Determining what Henry was capable of was her responsibility. She supposed she should appreciate why Rideout didn't care for her leap to cause of death. "When you left the rink, did you see Michaela preparing to go on?" Amanda asked Wendy.

"Yeah. I guess it will be the last time I'll ever see her." Wendy hiccuped a sob.

Amanda let a few seconds pass before asking, "Once you finished, what did you do?"

"I went to the locker room and got changed into street clothes. I stuck around there until it was time to get ready for my other performance."

Amanda looked at Lilian. "And where were you?"

"I slipped out back for a smoke."

"Anyone see you?" Amanda volleyed back.

"A few people. Actually, Henry popped out for a minute too. You could ask him about that."

"We will." They also had the video camera on the rear of the arena to consult. For now, Amanda was satisfied to move the conversation along another route. "Do you know of anyone who had an issue with Michaela? Any stalkers or admirers?"

"I don't," Wendy said.

"Me either," Lilian put in.

This interview was pretty much tapped out less a few things. "Michaela received a flower delivery to the ticket booth. Is that a common occurrence?" Amanda wanted to verify what Tara Coolidge had told them.

Wendy glanced at her agent. "I never have."

"I can't imagine most of the skaters do, Detective." Lilian's forehead was bunched like she had a headache. "Typically, the venues sell roses and the audience throws them on the ice."

Ones with red ribbons anyway... And why had Michaela's agent led them to believe flower delivery was a normal occurrence? She tucked that question away to readdress later.

"Some people hand them to us after we get off the ice," Wendy put in, and it had Amanda taking notice. "Before, if they're diehard fans."

Amanda straightened. Wendy and Michaela would have

crossed paths in the first half of the show. "Did you notice if anyone handed any to Michaela?"

Wendy shook her head.

"And what about you?" Amanda asked the coach.

"I saw that she was holding some roses when I was leaving the cordoned-off section and she was heading in. That's all. Henry might have seen who gave them to her," Lilian said.

"What about a card or note?" Trent asked.

"I couldn't say."

The arena manager had mentioned fans tailing Michaela after her performance. He hadn't noticed a card. "Thank you for your time and help." Amanda gave the two her business card, and she and Trent set out across the room to talk to Henry.

Could it be that Lilian Berry killed Michaela for some reason they didn't see yet? If her alibi fell through, she had opportunity. And even if it wasn't Lilian, they could be standing in the room with Michaela's killer.

TEN

Amanda and Trent decided to speak with Henry, the security guy, next. They found him leaning against a bank of lockers. At about six foot tall with a bit of a paunch, he wasn't particularly muscled or intimidating, but he was accurately labeled as big. She introduced herself and Trent to him.

"Detectives? Huh, what is going on here?" Henry's brow furrowed into rows of wrinkles.

Amanda found it hard to believe he'd be that in the dark. "You might have heard that Michaela Glover is deceased?"

"Found in her dressing room, or so I heard. That doesn't explain why we needed to hang around though unless... Did someone do this to her?"

His nonchalant manner was somewhat unsettling. "You don't seem too shaken about the idea."

"I don't tend to get worked up unless I know there's reason. But based on your response, I assume I was right?"

"There is evidence that suggests homicide," she confirmed and watched Henry's face fall. "When did you last see her?"

"After her set in the first half. My God, that poor girl." Henry was shaking his head, clearly affected now.

"When she came off the ice?" Trent asked.

"More accurately when she was leaving the cordoned-off area. That's where I stand to make sure only people with the show and other authorized individuals get past."

"Did you notice if Michaela showed up holding any roses?" She was rooting for Lilian Berry, but Henry's responses would be what would save her.

"She was holding a few, yes. She got more after her performance from some eager fans."

"Did any of them pose a threat to her?" Trent asked.

Henry shook his head. "Nothing like that."

"Was she holding any roses tied with black ribbon?" She'd start there and move on to the card.

"You expect I'd notice some small detail like that?"

She shrugged. "Details matter in security."

He smirked and wriggled a pointed finger at her. "Not of that nature. So, no, I really can't say."

"What about a card? Was Michaela handed one from someone?" she volleyed back.

"I don't remember."

That wasn't a no... "Okay, well if you think on it again later, then call me." Amanda gave him her business card but wasn't ready to move on quite yet. "Was anyone in the cordoned-off area when Michaela was leaving?"

"Just me and Lilian. Her client, Wendy, was on the ice."

That eliminated one question she had planned to ask. "But she left with Wendy after her performance?"

"That's right."

His answers lined up to what Lilian told them, but it still didn't alibi her out during Michaela's time-of-death window. "And where did you go during intermission?"

"Mostly here, except for a few minutes when I had a smoke out back."

"Anyone out there at the same time?" Trent asked.

Henry narrowed his eyes. "Ah, Lilian, and a few others with the show. Some arena employees."

Amanda glanced at Trent. Lilian Berry was in the clear. "Is there any surveillance video in the cordoned-off section that you are aware of?" Her hope was they could watch this footage and it would catch the person handing Michaela the roses tied with black ribbon. Possibly the card too. Though she wasn't yet sure it would be worth their time and effort. It was entirely possible both were left in her dressing room or handed straight to her.

"The TV network wasn't back there and there are no cameras in the area that cover that section. That, I can tell you for a fact. Part of the job involves me scoping out the venues for any weak spots. So I notice these things."

"There must be a threat to these skaters then." Trent put it out there in a conversational manner.

"Everyone wants a piece of people who are doing well."

For some reason just the way Henry said that his words landed with impact. *Everyone wants a piece...* They had assumed Michaela's murder wasn't about money, but they couldn't afford to disregard the possibility that it had been. "Were any of the skaters being extorted?"

"I haven't heard of that going on. And I wasn't told to keep a closer eye on one over another."

Amanda nodded. "How long have you worked with the circuit?"

"Seven years."

"Then you know all the girls quite well," Amanda concluded.

"Yeah, but don't go getting any perv ideas. I'm a happily married man with girls of my own."

"I assure you that my mind never went there." *But now that you brought it up...* "I was just voicing my viewpoint that you'd know them. They'd become like family to you too, I'm sure."

"Absolutely. It's why I could tell something was going on with Michaela."

The skin tightened on the back of her neck. "Such as?"

"I asked her, and she told me it was nothing I needed to worry about, but her focus seemed off lately. Today, before she took to the ice, she was really off-kilter. Flustered or preoccupied..."

It was possible that Michaela had received the card with the roses before the show started. The words alone could have upset her. They would Amanda. But why would the killer tip their hand that much in advance? By toying with her, they risked her raising the alarm. And if the card had peanut oil on it, she would have been scratching and even more on alert. It might not have stopped her from performing, but she certainly wouldn't go back to her room and swig back her drink as they had speculated. In fact, all of this made it more likely the killer stepped into the dressing room and handed her the card as she was drinking her tainted shake. But if that's how it had happened, it didn't explain why Michaela was flustered at the beginning of the show. Or was the answer there, and Amanda couldn't see it yet?

ELEVEN

Before Amanda and Trent left Henry, he told them that he thought Michaela had been *off* for at least a couple of months. He had added, though, that it was hard to gauge how long given the fact Michaela wasn't with the show full-time. She and Trent were walking away from him when Tara Coolidge came over to them.

"Is it really necessary I continue to stick around?" She was flushed and fussing with her coat that she had draped over her arm.

Her abrupt response and rush to leave rubbed Amanda wrong. Her client, who she'd described as being like a daughter to her, was murdered and *she* was inconvenienced. "Do you have somewhere you need to be?"

"As a matter of fact I do."

"Where is that?" Trent asked.

The agent slowly fixed her gaze on him. "I don't see how that's a police matter, but if I don't eat something soon, I could pass out. I'm hypoglycemic, and I can tell my sugars are all out of whack." She held out a shaking hand.

"There's a vending machine in the corridor." Amanda remembered passing it and considering a bag of chips.

"I don't like to intake empty calories."

"I'm sorry, but I don't know what else to say. I'm sure you and everyone else will be leaving soon." Amanda may have stretched the truth. Depending on Tara's answers, she might be in for a longer night.

"You can't just keep me here. I have rights."

"Yes, and so do we. You told us that flower deliveries to a venue aren't unusual." Amanda wasn't letting herself be affected by the agent's attitude. It could very easily be chalked up to her medical condition and being *hangry*.

"It's not."

"We were told that it is." Amanda wasn't going to bring Lilian Berry's name up.

"I don't know what else to tell you, but my clients, including Michaela, have received them before."

"All right. Fair enough," Amanda said. "You told us that Michaela had a tense relationship with Wendy, that they were competitive."

"They were."

"But it was all a show," Trent said.

Tara's face bunched up. "Not that I'm aware of."

Amanda resisted looking at Trent so that Tara wouldn't pick up on it. Could it be that Lilian was right and Tara had lost her edge? And if so, was she messing up sponsorship deals? "Okay, we heard differently, but what about the deal with Active Spirit? We heard that was tanked." She intentionally chose a strong word to net a reaction.

Tara clenched her jaw. "I'm guessing Lilian Berry told you that?"

"It doesn't matter where we heard it. Is it true?" Amanda asked.

"Well, if it was her, she has a big mouth. She doesn't even know me. I'm here, and she's in Colorado Springs."

"The world of figure skating is small," Trent put in. "You both seem to have formed opinions of each other."

"Well, some people just rub you the wrong way. And for the record, the deal with Active Spirit isn't dead yet. Or it wasn't anyway. I was still in communication with them."

Amanda was conflicted about whether she should haul Tara Coolidge down to Central. Not liking her wasn't enough to support that action though. Neither were her guarded answers. Other stressors could explain those. Even shock over Michaela's murder on its own. "One more thing, and you can go. We heard that Michaela has been flustered and unfocused in recent months. Do you know anything about that?"

"Not really. Though I'm here, and she's there. But she never mentioned anything over the phone. I suppose she might have felt pressure about performing in her hometown."

It was hard to say if the agent was being forthcoming, but that judgment might be prejudiced by Amanda's lingering first impression of the woman. "Thanks for your time again, Ms. Coolidge. You can go."

"Finally." Tara swept out of the room, her hair blowing up in her haste to leave.

Amanda and Trent weren't far behind, but the officer who had been posted outside stepped into the doorway.

"I said she can go," she told him.

"All I needed to know." The officer smiled and resumed his post.

Once in the corridor, Trent turned to her. "I know we took her off the suspect list, but she's cagey."

"There's something going on with her. Sadly, there's nothing concrete to justify bringing her in. On another note, I don't think video footage is going to help us much either."

"Henry said there wasn't any rink side where the skaters took to the ice anyway."

"Right, but I guess the point I'm wanting to make is, Michaela was likely handed the card within seconds of her drinking the shake. Much before that, she would have been on alert and not have gulped it back."

"Which she must have done. So this all took place in the dressing room."

"I think so. But if she didn't receive the card until later, then it wasn't what had Michaela flustered and unfocused when taking to the ice."

"Right. So what did? We can include that question when we ask around. Ready to go back in?" Trent jacked a thumb over his shoulder, and she nodded.

They spoke with everyone in that locker room. It proved to be a time-consuming and frustrating process that didn't get them far. No one demonstrated a motive for wanting Michaela out of the way. In fact, everyone spoke highly of her and specifically voiced what a shame it was that she was gone before her time. Everyone knew about her allergy and her habit of drinking a protein shake from her sports bottle, but it would take more than that to lay charges, let alone convict. No one could offer insight into her flustered state, though a couple had mentioned they'd noticed. And a few confirmed that Wendy had been in the locker room during, and for a while after, intermission.

It was ten o'clock by the time they'd finished and stepped outside of the locker room.

"Do you think one of them did this?" Trent's tone disclosed he didn't think so.

"I don't. But what's driving me insane is that no one saw anyone aside from her agent leave Michaela's dressing room."

"It's amazing the arena manager saw that much. The corridor would have been crowded during intermission. Easy to slip in and out unnoticed. If they waited for the show to start up again, everyone would have returned to their seats. Again, making it easy to come and go."

"I suppose you're right."

"I am sometimes. So is that it for here? We let everyone go home and head out to Patty's?"

He made it sound so simple when it was the opposite. She'd have to break it to her friend that a cold-blooded killer had, in fact, seen fit to murder her talented niece. But she couldn't let herself sink into that hole. Rather, she had to keep her focus on the job. "She'll be able to tell us more about Michaela's personal life."

"And I assume Michaela was staying with Patty. We could also look through her things and see if that gets us anywhere."

"The cop side of me understands all that. The personal? I'm not looking forward to any of it." She felt if she didn't admit this to Trent, she'd explode.

Trent put a hand on her shoulder, and her heart fluttered. He had to be aware of what his touch did to her, just as she could feel his body tense whenever she grazed his hand or an elbow. She tried to refrain from making contact with him for this very reason. Strong feelings sparked between them that transcended a base attraction, but none of that mattered. She had Logan, and Trent had a girlfriend named Kelsey. Amanda hadn't even pushed herself to find out her last name. Any time she thought of asking, her gut became so coiled with jealousy she cramped up. She knew what it was like to kiss him. It had happened three times. Brief, unforgettable moments in time. She'd even initiated it a year ago and she was with Logan. She'd come clean about the slip, and she and Logan had mostly recovered. Now if only she could purge the residual pull toward her partner.

He cleared his throat but never removed his hand. "I'll be right by your side."

Amanda blew out a puff of breath. "Thank you."

"Always." He removed his hand now, but it left her skin searing.

Her phone rang, and she flinched. She pulled it out, flashing a pressed smile at Trent. "Just startled me."

"I saw that."

Amanda looked at the caller ID and was expecting it would be Jolene Flynn finally getting back to her, but it was Patty. She answered, "Patty—"

"Tell me you have more for me. I'm going crazy here."

Relating to her pain wasn't what Patty needed right now. Something Amanda learned from experience. "We're doing all we can, Patty. Trent and I will be heading to see you very soon."

"Then you do know more. Tell me now. I beg of you."

"It's always best to have these conversations in person. Please, just hold on a bit longer. Is Katherine still there with you?"

"No, I insisted she go home. Let me tell you, she's one stubborn woman, but she eventually left. She took your car with her, so you'll need to pick it up at her place."

Amanda smiled at the *stubborn woman* bit. She'd witnessed that side of Katherine. But for Patty to prevail it would have taken a similar hardheadedness. "All right. We'll see you soon."

A drawn-out pause, followed by, "All right." Patty ended the call without a goodbye.

"We need to get over to Patty's pronto," Amanda said.

Before she and Trent got on their way, they cleared everyone to leave. As they passed the dressing room, crime scene tape crossed it off and a tape seal was on the door. A uniform was posted next to it. The CSIs must have finished up and left. All without saying a word. She'd heard nothing about an EpiPen turning up. Maybe it wouldn't.

She and Trent stepped near the doors to leave but were called back.

"Amanda? You guys are still kicking around?"

Amanda turned to see Blair next to a garbage receptacle. "We are. Thought you were gone though."

"Not so lucky. We're still collecting the waste and recycling bags. We'll take them all back to process later. As in tomorrow."

The fact Blair planned to clock in on Sunday for a case like this one wasn't a surprise, but Amanda said, "Don't blame you there."

"Though tomorrow is only a couple hours out," Trent put in.

"Funny guy," Blair said. "Listen, you should know a few things. One, Liam wanted me to let you guys know that Rideout will be doing the autopsy on Michaela at eight tomorrow morning, but he is confident that cause of death was anaphylaxis."

"He said *confident*?" That surprised Amanda as the ME often didn't resort to making bold statements until he had the bodies back to the morgue.

"Well, as clearly as he'll admit." Blair smiled, but the expression was fleeting. Bags were forming under her eyes, marking the long afternoon and evening. "Before we get to the garbage, though, we'll test the drink, just for due diligence. You also specifically asked about the black ribbon and card, so we'll do that too. What you don't know yet is we found two other items after you left. A blank envelope the right size for the card under the table and a dark wood toggle button. It's not a match for anything in Michaela's dressing room. We'll test it and the rest for trace of peanut oil, prints, DNA..."

A florist card could have come in an envelope, but the quality of the card itself wasn't typical. Its origin remained a mystery. Now, there was a random button. Had it been left by the killer? They could only hope it would turn into a solid lead. They'd check Michaela's things at Patty's just to see if she owned any garment with that type of button. If one had come off, Michaela could have put it in her purse. Then when she was presumably rummaging through it in search of her EpiPen, it fell to the floor and under the table.

"Now that black ribbon that stood out to you... Looking closer at the red ones, it's a different width and design. The red ones are glossy, half an inch wide. The black one has tiny eyelets at the top and bottom edges, giving it a frilly appearance, and is matte with glossy horizontal lines running the length of it. It's also a bit wider at three quarters of an inch."

"We find more of that ribbon, we get our killer." Amanda made it sound as if it were the easiest thing in the world.

"Yeah, that's all." Trent smirked at her.

Before Amanda could respond, Donnelly approached dragging a few bags behind her.

"Anything else before we go see Patty?" Amanda looked at Donnelly hoping for any reason to delay the inevitable, even though Patty's house could also hold some clues among Michaela's things.

"All I have," Blair said. "You, Isabelle?"

"I assume you filled them in on the envelope and the button?" Donnelly asked, and when Blair nodded, she added, "That's it."

Amanda and Trent turned to leave, and Donnelly told them, "Please pass on our sympathies and that our thoughts and prayers are with her."

"Yes, please do," Blair put in.

"We will." Amanda cleared her throat and commanded her legs to move. Eventually they did. No matter how much Amanda wanted to avoid what was coming, there would be no more putting it off. It was time to tell her friend that someone had killed her niece.

TWELVE

The night air was cold and damp and seeped through to the bones. Everyone with the show and the arena employees hadn't wasted any time in leaving. The parking lot was mostly empty aside from a few cars.

"I'm just parked over here." Trent led the way around the side of the building. He unlocked the doors of the department car with the key fob. The lights flashed at the same time headlights in the far corner of the lot fired up. Two shadowed figures cut across the beams and were coming toward them.

"Trent," Amanda said, quietly as a precaution and wishing she had her gun. But all trepidation left when the people stepped under a light post, and she saw who they were. "Unbelievable," she muttered, throwing her arms in the air. "Go home, Wesson."

"Just one comment for the people of Prince William County." Diana Wesson plastered on a smile, showcasing her bleached teeth. The reporter's makeup and complexion were far too flawless for the hour, and she was immaculately dressed. Some people make themselves easy to dislike.

"You know the drill," Trent said. "Take your questions and requests for comment to the Public Information Office."

"The department's PIO isn't saying much of anything at this time. Please, this won't take long."

"I'll take my cue from them." Trent turned to get into the car, but Diana and her cameraman stepped even closer. He pivoted and held up his hand. "I suggest you leave before I'm forced to arrest you."

Diana laughed. "What for? Freedom of speech is my constitutional right."

"Don't you have any self-respect?" Amanda asked her.

"Detective Steele, as charming as always. Tell me, are the rumors true? Were you the one to find Michaela Glover?" She held her microphone in Amanda's face, and she batted it away while glaring at the reporter.

Amanda's composure faltered at being made aware that rumor was flying around. Someone within the PWCPD must have been chin-wagging. Knowing Diana's innate talent for eavesdropping, she could have overheard it. "Go, before I bring you in for assault charges. The way you wave that thing around" —implying the microphone—"someone's going to get hurt."

"Oh, please. Just tell me. Did you find her?"

"Good night, Wesson." Amanda signaled to Trent that she'd reached her limit with the reporter.

Her cameraman took the hint first and lowered his camera. He started to retreat to the *PWC News* van.

Diana looked over her shoulder, then back to Amanda and Trent. "Fine, but this isn't over. I will be getting a statement from you."

"Bye, bye." Amanda waved her off, proud that she hadn't gone a step further and used a one-finger salute to do the job.

Diana finally relented and joined her colleague.

Amanda and Trent got into the car, and she slammed her

door behind her, rocking the body of the vehicle. "What is wrong with these people? With *that* woman? A young girl just died, and she's using it to make a name for herself. Despicable."

"Not going to disagree."

"And setting themselves up in the dark, then pouncing on us? I think I might have pissed my pants." Her vent gave way to laughter. More due to stress from the day than that her words were funny.

"In that case, out of the car," Trent said with a fading smile.

They sat there waiting for the car to warm up and the news van to leave. When it pulled away, it revealed a sedan.

"Is that a Subaru Legacy GT?" Amanda squinted. She just had the profile but was pretty good at picking out makes and models from that alone. Attribute that to her older brother, Kyle, and his love for vehicles. He talked, and she listened.

"I'll take your word on it. It could go with the key fob in Michaela's purse."

"I'd assumed it was for a vehicle she had back in Colorado Springs, but maybe it's a rental."

"One way to find out if Cinderella's a fit." Trent turned the car off, and she followed close behind as he returned inside the arena.

They got past Officer Traci Cochran at the front door without showing their badges, as the cop knew them well. They found the investigators grabbing the bags from the last of the garbage and recycle bins, and they shook their heads at the sight of them.

"Nothing new to report," Blair said preemptively. "Though we're almost done here."

Donnelly yawned and covered her mouth with the back of her arm.

"What's up?" Blair asked them.

"Michaela had a key fob for a Subaru, and there's one

parked at the end of the lot," Amanda said. "Just following a hunch. Could we get it?"

"Ah, sure, but Isabelle and I could look in a minute. As I said we're almost done here."

"We'll just take a quick peek first," Amanda said.

"Suit yourselves." Blair walked over to her collection kit and returned holding a plastic evidence bag with Michaela's purse and its contents. She unzipped the bag and retracted the key fob. Amanda signed for it to maintain a chain of custody.

She and Trent made their way back outside and headed straight to the Subaru. The light post it was parked under did little good. Shadows crawled out around it. It felt like the temperature had dipped a few degrees during their brief detour inside. She shivered as a cold breeze flittered past.

They both put gloves on and activated the flashlight function on their phones. Amanda unlocked the car and opened the driver's door. The car smelled like new, and an air freshener hung from the rearview mirror. It was likely kicking out the faux scent to give the impression of newness. The vehicle wasn't old, but it wasn't straight off the showroom floor either.

Trent opened the back door, the action shaking the vehicle. He did a thorough search under the seats, in the seat pockets, and in the storage areas in the doors. "Nada back here."

"Still looking up here." She lifted a compartment in the console to find a bunched-up used tissue. She shone the flashlight over it, and there was something inside. Amanda's guess was gum. It might tie back to Michaela, but they couldn't afford to make assumptions. She'd make sure that the CSIs processed this. If they were lucky, there was DNA belonging to someone other than Michaela, and they'd net a lead. She shared her find with Trent and walked around and opened the glove box. Inside was the vehicle manual, registration and insurance paperwork, and a booklet with the Royal Auto Rentals logo on the cover. She held it for Trent to see, and he nodded. "We can request the GPS history for the vehicle from them. It could help us track Michaela's movements since she's been in town."

"That could pay off."

"I agree. We could be looking for someone she met with since she arrived. I don't think we've discussed it in so many words, but Michaela's murder was surely premeditated. The killer brought the peanut oil but would also need to know where to find her things."

"They had to know about the dressing room."

"Yeah. All right, well, I think we're done here, no matter. Let's get the key back to Blair and Donnelly and hit the road." She locked up the Subaru, and they returned the key fob to the CSIs, bringing them up to date on the tissue and chewed gum.

"We'll take care of it," Blair said.

Amanda hesitated to leave. There was unlikely anything else that would delay a visit to Patty. But her steps were lighter because finding the Subaru could have provided the strong lead they were waiting for.

THIRTEEN

Amanda's chest ratcheted tighter with every turn that took them closer to Patty's house. When her house came into view, she took a deep, steadying breath.

Trent parked in Patty's driveway and looked over at Amanda. "You ready?"

"Not really, but this isn't about me." In truth, she'd never be *ready*. There was no good time to serve notification. It was a nasty part of the job, as much as it was necessary. In this case, it was already half done. Patty knew her niece was dead and that murder was possible. The confirmation, though, would be rough. It would evaporate all rational ways of excusing her passing. Someone had intentionally caused it. Given how Amanda was brought to her knees with the accidental deaths of Kevin and Lindsey, she couldn't imagine how she would feel if it had been murder. There was no way to soften the blow that would ease Patty's grief.

Patty was waiting at the front door for them, wearing a belted sweater and hugging herself. Her eyes were bloodshot, and it was clear she'd spent the last few hours crying. She would have been going through hell. Not just from trying to process that she'd never speak with her niece again, but speculation was a mind game.

"Hey, honey." Amanda hugged Patty, who fell into the embrace only briefly.

"Come in, come in." Patty backed up, waving her arms wildly to prompt them to move faster.

The house smelled like coffee, and there was a half-empty cup on the table next to the couch. The three of them sat in the living room. No more than a few seconds passed when Patty spoke.

"Just tell me what happened. I need to know the truth. The media's been hounding me for a comment. I've been blocking numbers left and right."

Damn journalists. They were like vultures that fed off the carcasses of misfortune.

"I just have this really bad feeling..." Patty bunched up the fabric of her sweater and twisted it into a ball over her heart.

Amanda distinctly remembered the intense ache that made it hard to catch a breath. Like with every exhale, her chest tightened further. It had taken years after losing Kevin and Lindsey before the pressure eased enough for her to breathe unhindered. The loss was still a scar that was indelibly seared on her heart. "There's no easy way to say this, so I'm just going to come out with it. The evidence points us to murder."

"Murder." The word seemed to scrape from Patty's throat. Her voice was low, and her eyes flooded with fresh tears. "I don't understand how that's possible. Everyone loved her. Mick was... she was..." Patty's chin quivered, quickly predicting the crying jag that arrived with fury.

Amanda wanted to hold her friend, but she refrained. Patty might find it an intrusion to her personal space and grief. Besides, with such a raw wound, there was nothing Amanda could say or do to ease her suffering. "The autopsy is set for the morning, but the medical examiner was confident in saying that she died of anaphylaxis. Her protein shake smelled of peanuts." She'd added that latter part as an afterthought.

Patty licked her lips, and she stared silently into space for a few seconds. "But her EpiPen...?"

"It hasn't been found," Amanda confirmed.

Patty's eyelids lowered, and her shoulders sagged. "That's why you think someone did this to her."

"One of the reasons. Her phone is also missing," Amanda told her. She'd get around to the note in a bit.

"I just don't understand. Who would do this? Why?" The single-word question was thrown out to the universe.

Amanda would do her best to discover the answer, but even if successful, it was unlikely to offer complete solace to her friend. "I'm so sorry, Patty. I wish I had better news." A shiver tore through Amanda, and her own residual grief rolled over her. Quick and devastating, making her breath hitch.

Patty locked eyes with her, as if her grief somehow sensed Amanda's inner turmoil. "Just find who did this to her. But they took her medication and her phone...?"

Amanda nodded and finished Patty's thought. "Whoever did this wanted to ensure that she couldn't get help."

Patty cried out and sniffled, working to compose herself again. "I just can't imagine who could have hated her this much." A few more tears hit her cheeks, and she swiped them away. "She had such a bright future. She would have gone to the Olympics and won. I just know it."

"I have no doubt." Amanda offered her friend a smile, using the expression to suppress her urge to cry in empathy.

"To think that Michaela hasn't been home in a couple of years, and she comes back only to be—" Patty sobbed and blew her nose.

A couple of years... It was just a kernel of an idea, but hearing Patty mention Michaela's travel home had Amanda wondering if they were looking for someone local who had an issue with Michaela. If her recent lack of focus was linked to returning to Woodbridge, was something that had happened two years ago the root cause? If so, this person might not have the financial means or freedom to travel after her. Had the killer taken advantage of her being back home? There was no doubt the words of the note struck a personal chord. "A note was found with Michaela. It read, 'You'll be sorry you turned your back on me after all I did for you.' Do you have any idea who might have written that? Maybe someone from the area?"

Patty blew out a breath. "It's been a couple of years, but she had a boyfriend before she moved to Colorado Springs for training. I don't think he took the news of the breakup well."

"His name?" Trent asked.

"Wendell Smith. Far as I know, he's still around town. He was serious about Michaela, but she turned him down flat. She told him she was far too young to think about marriage."

"Michaela's agent told us she didn't have time for a relationship," Amanda said.

"That's for sure. She pushed herself hard, but becoming the best skater and winning Olympic gold was her sole focus."

"How long were she and Wendell together?" Trent asked.

"Since the start of high school."

He might have thought he'd marry his sweetheart upon graduation, but he must have failed to appreciate just how important it was to Michaela to improve her craft. He could have felt tossed aside when Michaela left for Colorado Springs. They'd speak with Wendell to find out his feelings for her now. "What about anyone else who Michaela might have hurt in pursuit of her Olympic dreams?"

"Her best friend growing up was Deana Jones. She was a skater too, but not as naturally gifted as Michaela. She worked incredibly hard to be half as good. And I don't say this just because I'm a proud aunt. When Michaela set off for Colorado Springs, she cut out everyone from her life before. Everyone but me anyway. She said she had to if she wanted her dream to come true."

They would speak with Deana too, but Amanda was trying to reconcile what could motivate her or Wendell to write that note. What had they done for Michaela that made them feel she'd turned on them? Was it just the time they'd invested in their relationship with Michaela for it to come to nothing? It seemed a reach. After all, it was common for friendships to transform and sometimes evaporate. A reason, a season, or a lifetime. "When did Michaela get to town?"

"Thursday."

Just two days ago... "Did she reach out to Wendell or Deana?"

"Not that I know of, and I wouldn't see why she would. But you realize the whole town would have gotten wind she was coming back with that show. That's if it is someone from the area who did this..."

Just because Patty wasn't aware of any meetups between her niece and former friend or ex, didn't mean they hadn't happened. She could have seen other people while she was in town too. "We found out that Michaela rented a car. She probably had others she wanted to catch up with."

"Pfft, the rental. That girl had such an independent spirit. She insisted on it even though I offered her my car."

"Did she say why it was so important?" Trent asked.

"She liked her freedom and flexibility, but she tried to pitch it as doing me a favor in not wanting to inconvenience me."

There could be more to it than Michaela had let on. The key to solving this case might even hinge on discovering why Michaela required her own car and freedom while in town. Amanda's thoughts were still on who Michaela might have reconnected with. "Do you think Michaela was in touch with her brother since she got here?"

"I doubt it. Tyson can be a piece of work. He's like his

mother. He's selfish to a fault and lacks all maturity to hold a job or build a future for himself. Last I knew he worked at a gas station here in town. I don't know if he still does."

"It doesn't sound like you keep in touch," Trent put in.

Patty shook her head. "I haven't spoken with him in some time. I suppose it's possible he's grown up, but last I knew he was no good with a bad attitude and alcohol habit to boot. He started drinking as a teenager. I blame the media for making booze seem so attractive and sophisticated."

"Is that why they weren't close?" Trent asked.

"It probably didn't help. There are four years between them, with Tyson being older. But once Michaela started doing well for herself financially, he'd often turn up for a handout. I finally told her he wasn't her responsibility, and if she kept bailing him out, he'd never stand on his own two feet."

"So she turned him away?" The words from the card ricocheted in her head. *You'll be sorry you turned your back on me...*

"She started to do that. Yep. The last time was some time ago now, as far as I know."

Amanda glanced over at Trent and found he was looking at her. He must have been thinking it too. They'd notify the brother and have a little chat with him. With Tyson being older, he could have found his younger sister's success hard to accept. Then once she stopped helping him, it could have made him bitter. A feeling that would only intensify if he measured her success against his failures. Had Michaela's refusal to give him money made him desperate enough to kill his own sister? It was horrendous to consider, but it was possible. In Homicide she'd seen a lot, and people lied and hurt each other in unthinkable ways. But if Tyson was an alcoholic, could he have planned and carried out Michaela's murder in such an organized way? It was more feasible that he'd react in the moment when she rejected him rather than premeditate her death. Then again, he could be a high-functioning alcoholic. Regardless, she and Trent would certainly talk to him. "What about the rest of Michaela's family?"

"It's just me, Amanda. Her grandmother, my mother, who raised her died two years ago from cancer."

"That's why Michaela last returned home?" Amanda asked, now understanding why Patty hadn't mentioned the grandmother before.

"Uh-huh. Her grandmother's death hit her hard. Michaela had only left six months prior."

Amanda had known Patty then, but she'd never said a word about losing her mother before now. It was almost hard to believe she hadn't heard some murmuring through the PD's gossip mill either. But she wasn't about to point that out and make Patty feel bad for not mentioning it. The death did explain why she hadn't reached out to Amanda much in the last couple of years though. She'd been grieving and keeping herself busy, likely with work. Amanda could relate to that. Her job was the only thing that had kept her tethered to any resemblance of sanity during the dark years after her family's deaths. And Patty hadn't even been quick to mention her mother's death during this conversation. She had ample opportunity to do so moments ago when first discussing Michaela's return home. "I'm sorry to hear that."

"I never really told anyone. You know I'm a rather private person. I needed the time and space to process my grief and remember my mother the way I needed to."

"I understand," Amanda said.

Patty pressed her lips and nodded.

"Is Michaela's mother dead?" Trent asked.

Patty shook her head. "At least not that I know of. Really that's just a guess. I tried finding her a long time ago. The address on file proved to be a dead end."

"Do you remember where that was?" Trent asked, ready to make note of it.

"Trent, we can look her up," Amanda said kindly.

"Right. Sorry, Patty."

"Don't apologize for being eager to do everything you can. But only God knows where Cheryl is now."

"Does Cheryl share your surname?" Amanda asked.

"Her last name is Glover like mine still, far as I know. Neither of us ever married. Again, far as I know."

"Did Michaela ever know her mother?" Amanda asked.

"Whenever Cheryl came up in conversation, Michaela didn't seem to remember much about her. She was gone from her life by the time she was four. At that point, my mother was assigned full custody of her and Tyson. My dad was gone by then too. She was a brave woman taking on two young children in her fifties."

"Being so young at the time, it makes sense why Michaela wouldn't remember her mother," Amanda said.

"What about Michaela's father?" Trent began. "I'm assuming he wasn't in the picture either for your mother to gain custody."

"Whoever he is. Cheryl, that's my sister, wasn't exactly a nun in those days. Though she tended to run back to one man. Darren Bolton. I know for sure that he's Tyson's father, but he wasn't involved in the kid's life. Darren was too busy being a free spirit." Patty flittered her fingers and rolled her eyes. "But he and Cheryl were rather tight for some time. Why only God would know. It was many years ago, mind you, but you couldn't trust a word out of his mouth."

"Do you know where he is now?" Trent said.

"In town, far as I know. Do you think any of this is relevant to finding who killed Mick?" Patty leveled her gaze at Trent, but Amanda responded.

It was clear that the deep digging into the past wasn't a comfortable experience. "You know what it's like, Patty,"

Amanda said softly. "We just need to find out what we can about Michaela's life, including her past."

"I suppose I know that. It's just tough talking about all this."

"I can appreciate that." Amanda's mind was busy assimilating what they'd found out. The brother might have financial motive. Same too for Darren Bolton or another man who had been with Cheryl Glover. Michaela's success wasn't a secret, and any of them might have seen the opportunity for a payday. "Did Michaela ever mention Darren Bolton, or anyone else reaching out to claim he was her father?"

"If they had, she kept that to herself."

"And could she be that way, Patty? Private like you?" Amanda pieced this together from what Patty just said and her earlier comments about Michaela liking her freedom and independence.

"She had her moments, yes." Patty sounded drained from fielding all the questions and understandably so. They forced her to be objective about a girl she dearly loved who just passed.

"We won't be much longer," Amanda began. "But just a few more things. I get the impression you and Michaela were very close."

"She was the daughter I never had." Patty hiccupped a sob but signaled with a pointed index finger that she had more to say. "We spoke most weeks, messages flipped back and forth. Usually it wasn't much more than trivial everyday life."

"Upon which solid relationships are built," Amanda put in.

The glimmer of a smile. "That's right."

Amanda was awakened to this aspect in the last six months when she was reexamining her relationship with Logan. It was the fact that they could speak easily about the everyday things that brought them together. Before she appreciated how that alone was a gift, she begrudged that he didn't fully get her job. Now she valued that his coming from a background other than law enforcement added a different dimension to their relationship. "I assume she was staying with you while she was in town?"

Patty shook her head. "I wanted her to, but she insisted on renting a hotel room. Goes back to her being a private person."

Again, Amanda was curious if Michaela had intentionally set up space between them. Whether it led to her murder would remain to be seen. "Where was she staying?"

"Lux Suites. She also has... *had*... her superstitious rituals like any other professional athlete. For her that meant solitude and meditation every evening. But she did give me a key to her room. Are you wanting to look through her things?"

"It might help us," Amanda admitted.

"I'll get you the key before you leave. I assume you never found the keycard in her things?"

Amanda shook her head, but its absence may be easy to explain. Whenever Amanda had one, she'd slip it into a slot in her phone case. "Did Michaela keep her phone in a case?"

"Yeah. It had a bedazzled 'M' on the front."

"Did it have slots for cards?" Amanda asked.

"I suspect so."

Amanda wagered once they found Michaela's phone, they'd have the hotel keycard. "What was her room number?"

"Six-oh-seven."

"I'm sure you spent a lot of time catching up while she was here," Amanda started. "Did she mention being nervous about the show and performing for her hometown?"

Patty shook her head. "Never. She came alive on the ice. That girl was born under a bright star."

"We heard that Michaela was flustered and preoccupied before taking to the ice this afternoon. Even that this lack of focus might go back a couple of months. Do you have any idea why?" Amanda asked.

"Not that she shared with me. I thought we were close, but now it feels like she held a lot back from me."

"You can be close to someone and not tell them everything," Amanda told her.

"Bless you for saying that."

Amanda gave her a pressed-lip smile. She also considered that people often held things back to protect another person's feelings. Was that the scenario here? Were Michaela's secrets something that would hurt Patty? Had any of them gotten Michaela killed?

"Would you run us through her day, as you understood it?" Trent asked.

"I know she mentioned she wanted to get to the arena well before the show, so she wasn't rushed. She hated being late for anything. I couldn't tell you what time she got there."

If she had arrived early, someone could have tainted her drink before the event. Though if the killer did this too much in advance, they'd risk her drinking it earlier and getting help. Regardless, they'd find out when Michaela had turned up at the arena and who else was kicking around. "When she wasn't with you, do you have any idea what she would have been doing?" The further they could walk in Michaela's steps, the better chance they'd have of finding the young woman's killer.

"I'm sure she would have visited her grandmother's grave. It's something she likes to do by herself. She was close with her, and her death hit her hard, as I said." She rubbed her temples. "I'm losing my mind."

"You're doing just fine." It was amazing how shock and denial could be a protective shield. "Where was your mother buried?" She stuck with Patty's relationship to the woman, hoping that it would help her friend see that she was here if she ever wanted to talk about her death.

"Eagle Cemetery."

Her family's final resting place. "Just one more thing. Who inherits Michaela's estate?"

Patty's eyes filled with tears again. "I have a copy of her will here. It's all to come to me."

"Do you have any idea how much that is...?" Amanda swallowed roughly, feeling incredibly uncomfortable at needing to ask, but it might end up mattering. That's if the killer's motive was entangled with money.

Patty nodded. "It would be close to two million."

"Wow," Trent said. "She did extremely well for herself."

"Prize money and sponsorships added up fast. But she worked hard for it," Patty quickly added.

Trent put his hand up. "No argument there."

Amanda stood. "All right, Patty, we're going to leave you now. Call if you think of or need anything. But we'll need that hotel room key before we go."

"Oh, yes, let me get it." Patty walked farther into the house and returned with it a few moments later. By that point, Amanda and Trent were at the front door, ready to leave.

Patty handed it over to her, and Amanda gave Patty another hug before she left with Trent.

He got behind the wheel and fastened his seatbelt. "Michaela's keycard is likely with her phone, which we think is with the killer. Do you think they'd have a reason to go into her hotel room?"

"Since we don't know why she was killed, we can't begin to presume." She made a quick call to the on-duty uniform sergeant to have an officer sent over to watch the room. When she finished, Trent spoke.

"Do you think it's necessary to speak with the rest of Michaela's family?"

She shook her head. "To start, we don't know if Bolton is her father, and her mother hasn't been seen or heard from in years. We're far too busy to track down a ghost without reason. But the brother? Yeah, we need to have a talk with him. We're already going to notify him about Michaela, but I'd like to find out how he took Michaela turning him down for a handout."

"Patty thought he last asked some time ago. I suppose even if it was, he could have resented Michaela, even seen her rejection as her turning her back on him. That would fit the tone of the note."

"Uh-huh."

"Though was he capable of carrying out the murder? Patty said he was unstable and an alcoholic."

She was surprised by how often they thought alike. It was just one reason why they made great partners. "There is the possibility he's a high-functioning alcoholic."

"Hmm. Possible, I suppose. He did start drinking as a teenager, so lots of practice under his belt."

"It's also possible that the brother approached Michaela when she was in town. Patty wasn't always around. Michaela turns him away again, he can't take it, and snaps. He could be deluded and think his sibling owed him. Even that he made sacrifices for her advancement. That could fit the 'all I did for you' part of the note."

"Despite the fact she'd earned everything she got. Now, there's no doubt he'd know about her peanut allergy, but did he know about her protein shake and private dressing room?"

"I say we go ask him." Amanda let her thoughts run wild with this theory. Motive was potentially there. He was short on money and unable to follow his sister across the US. Her being home would have presented an opportunity. Had Tyson Bolton killed his own sister?

FOURTEEN

Talking with Patty had Amanda's mind tossing around the possibility that someone from Woodbridge had taken advantage of Michaela's return. And it made sense. Otherwise, why here and why now? Or had the killer counted on Michaela having rivals in her hometown and wanted to muddy the investigation?

The background on Tyson Bolton was clean, and they got his address before leaving Patty's driveway. Then she and Trent stopped for a quick bite from a drive-thru and guzzled coffee as fast as the hot liquid would allow. The clock on the dash reminded her that time continued to march on oblivious to death. It was approaching midnight, and all this had started around three thirty that afternoon. In some ways, it felt much longer given how much they'd done.

Trent yawned as he drove.

"Coffee not working?" she asked him.

"Not in the least. I even slept in this morning."

"Lucky you. Then again, you don't have a nine-year-old who sometimes rises before the sun." She smiled at him.

"Thank heaven for small mercies."

He parked in the driveway of a house that had seen better

days. The white siding was peeling, and some boards had slid out of place giving the house a helter-skelter appearance. It was in a rundown neighborhood but cheap, so it drew people who lived below the poverty line. Amanda took the front porch stairs with tentative steps.

"From the looks of this place, Tyson could use a good payday," he said.

"To boot, it's probably a rental. Someone's home and awake though." She pointed at the light coming through the curtains in one of the street-facing windows.

The door flung open just as Trent was poised to knock a second time. A man in his twenties came out flailing his arm in the air. "What do you— Oh. Are you police?" He scrunched his brow as if he were struck with an instant migraine as he tried to focus on the badges they were holding up.

"Detective Steele, and Detective Stenson. Are you Tyson Bolton?" she asked, though she had no doubt. He looked just like his license photo, though it was disturbing he could legally drive given his addiction.

"Yeah," he dragged out and leaned toward the doorframe but missed. He lost his balance but caught himself before falling and waved it off like it was nothing. "Just had a few beers after work." He stepped back and gestured for them to come inside.

This guy was drunk off his feet. Nothing indicated he was a high-functioning alcoholic. Had he hit the bottle harder than usual due to guilt over killing his sister? "Do you have some-where we could sit down?" She spotted the living room through a doorway on the left. Its small footprint was shrunk further by oversized furniture and clutter. Dirty dishes and empty beer bottles littered any flat surface.

"You'll have to excuse me. I wasn't expecting company," he deadpanned, then laughed as if he were a stand-up comic giving time for his joke to land.

"It's fine," she said, grateful that she had a store of patience to pull from. Even if the day had already taxed it. "A place to sit?" she reiterated, a tight smile and raised brows.

He tossed some throw pillows from two chairs across the room. "Have at it." He gestured to the now vacant seats and dropped onto the couch. "What do the police want with me?" He reached for a beer bottle on the table, put it to his lips, and tipped it back. Afterward, he wiped the back of his hand across his mouth, and then belched unapologetically.

"Mr. Bolton, we have some bad news about your sister, Michaela," Amanda started. "She died this afternoon at Woodbridge Arena."

"I heard." He swigged back the bottle again.

She let seconds tick off in silence to allow him time to elaborate. When he didn't, she said, "How did you hear?"

He flailed an arm toward the television. "It's all over the news. How could I not have heard? It doesn't explain why you're here though." He met her gaze, and the distant coolness of it had her drawing back.

"Michaela was your sister, Mr. Bolton. We wanted to inform you that she is deceased and—"

"Consider your job done then. I know. And don't call me Mr. Bolton. Just call me Ty. Everyone else does."

She refused to call him Ty as it felt far too casual for a police interview, and he was treating the news about his sister with nonchalance. Was it to deflect grief or did he truly not care? "It doesn't seem you're too broken up by Michaela's death."

"People die. Fact of life." Another swig, which emptied the beer bottle. He set it back on the table.

Her career gave her a close up to the many facets of humanity. There was kindness and love, but there was also cruelty and evil. Some people did unspeakable things to their own flesh and blood. She was trying to figure out if his indifference originated from a psychopathic mind. "We've spoken with your aunt. You and your sister weren't close?"

"Nope." He lifted his bottle again and groaned when he noticed it was empty. He moved to get up. "Just getting a new one."

"Please, don't." Amanda bit back the urge to add that he'd had quite enough already, realizing that wouldn't work in their favor. "We shouldn't be long. You can have another once we leave. If that's all right?" She framed it as a question, but she hoped he'd relent.

"Okay, fine."

She was relieved her appeal had worked. "Why weren't you two close? To me, it would seem life circumstances would have brought you together."

"We were completely different people." Again, Tyson looked at his bottle. It was like his crutch for moving through life, and Amanda felt for him. He was only twenty-five years old and digging himself an early grave.

"How's that?" Amanda wanted him to spell it all out. She saw how Michaela's ambition had her using her background to propel her to do better. In contrast, Tyson seemed to use it as an excuse to give up.

Tyson shrugged. "We just were."

"Did you see her since she came back to town?" she asked.

"Nope. No reason to."

Amanda would raise Michaela's refusal to give him money in a moment. "Then you never caught the show?"

"Nope." He popped the *p* as he said it this time.

"Wow. Nothing could hold me back if my sibling had that much success. I'd be so proud of her unless... Were you jealous of her?" Trent asked.

Tyson turned to Trent with narrowed eyes. "You bet your ass I was. She had the freaking golden touch. Meanwhile..." He widened his arms to gesture around. "I'm here in some hovel. It's not fair."

Tingles ran down her arms and anger constricted her belly. "Life takes hard work. Fact of life," she added to mock his earlier comment. She couldn't resist. "Is this the real reason you weren't close? You were jealous of her?"

"Isn't that enough? It wasn't just her success, the sponsorships, the money, but it goes further back. Our grandmother had a soft spot for her. She gave her everything. I spent most of my teen years grounded and sneaking out. Goody Two-shoes, Mick, would tattle and I'd wind up in more trouble than before."

Tyson was making this interview easy. Two minutes in, and it was clear Michaela was the family's golden child while Tyson felt invisible. Her going on to become financially successful would have only added salt to the already gaping wound. "Did you kill your sister?"

"Did I... *what?*" Tyson hopped up from his chair. "The news didn't say anything about murder." He raked a hand through his hair, and his eyes became wild. That look usually manifested seconds before a suspect ran for it.

She stood. "Please, Mr. Bolt— *Ty*," she said firmly. "Sit down, and let's talk."

"No, no, I need some fresh air." He stepped toward the door. He stumbled over his footing but made it outside.

"Here we go," Trent said, jumping up.

Tyson took his few seconds' head start and tore through the back door. They followed him into the yard, which was dark except for pale moonlight to illuminate their steps. "See him?"

"No."

They stood still, listening closely. A rattling chain followed by the scraping noise of metal against a steel-sided shed.

"Is he grabbing a bicycle?" She had her answer a second later when Tyson was pedaling straight toward her. But in his drunken state, he would have benefited from training wheels.

His balance was off-kilter, and he wobbled wildly and overcompensated. He spilled to the ground with a loud curse.

"All right, Lance Armstrong, let's move our chat down to Central." Trent hauled Tyson to his feet, and she called for a squad car.

FIFTEEN

Tyson was set up in an interview room, and Amanda handed him a coffee. Hopefully it would help sober him up enough to make their conversation easier.

She sat down next to Trent across from Tyson. "So why did you run?"

"You're kidding right? I picked up how you were looking at me, like I had something to do with my sister's death."

She'd done more than that. She had actually asked him if he had. Obviously, his intoxicated head kicked that memory out. "Did you?"

"No! But, yeah, it pissed me off she had everything handed to her. Who could blame me? Grandma paid for all that training that set her on the path. There was no money left for me. It didn't seem to matter that I would have liked to pursue basketball."

His words stirred to mind the ones from the note. *You'll be sorry you turned your back on me after all I did for you.* Was it closer to truth than fiction that Tyson viewed his sacrifices as supporting Michaela's success? Did his warped mind justify a cut of what she earned? "I can see how that would cause resentment." She empathized with him, but it was a trap too.

"Right? I mean how could we be close? We weren't even treated the same."

"Which wasn't Michaela's fault, if that was the case," Trent pointed out.

"Trust me, it *was* the case," Tyson was quick to respond. "And she could have stuck up for me, but she didn't."

"It sounds like you sacrificed a lot for your sister's success." Amanda was strengthening the foundation for a case against him. She didn't care for his attitude, thinking it wouldn't take much to push sibling rivalry over the edge in a case such as this one. Michaela had the world at her fingertips, and Tyson from appearances and his own admission was stuck barely able to make ends meet.

He blew out a breath. "I guess you could say I did."

That response made Amanda feel like she fed her words to him. Any defense attorney would pluck this interview apart and accuse her of doing just that. She reframed things in her mind before proceeding. "I was just saying that might have been how you felt. Then again, maybe not." She shrugged, throwing off an indifferent air.

"No, that's exactly how I felt."

"Though I'm sure Michaela took care of you, gave you money when you needed help," she said, laying out a trap.

"She used to but hasn't in a while." Tyson scowled.

"Oh, she turned you away?" She thought it best to treat this as news.

"A couple of times."

"Recently or...?" Amanda asked.

"I haven't seen her since she got to town, and I wasn't at the show."

It didn't escape Amanda's notice he hadn't answered her question. This was also his second time saying he wasn't at the event, which to her rang as a lie. "Then we won't find your name on a ticket sale?"

Tyson sighed. "Fine, I was there."

In this line of work, dishonesty wasn't a surprise. She was more concerned with his reason for doing so. "Why lie to us?"

"I was scared, all right? I didn't want you pinning this on me."

"You're coming off rather defensive," Trent said. "Also you don't seem too broken up about her death."

"Why would I be? We weren't close. What don't you get about that?"

"She's still your sister," Amanda pointed out.

"Biologically maybe. But you're missing the point here, Detectives. *Why* would I kill her?"

"We covered that. Jealousy over her success and her refusal to give you money. That sounds like enough reason in my mind." She tossed out another shoulder shrug.

"I wouldn't kill her over that, and tell me why I'd risk prison."

"From your own admission, it doesn't seem you have a lot to lose," she replied. "But it could have come down to pride. You probably didn't think you'd get caught either. Prison is full of cocky killers."

"I learned that she died on the news. I don't even know how! If I had done it, I would."

She resisted making a snippy response to the effect he could say whatever he wanted. "We found a note with her body. It read, 'You'll be sorry you turned your back on me after all I did for you.'"

"Okay, so...?"

"You just told us that you gave up a lot for her success and admitted she refused to share any of it with you. It fits. You could have written this note." She watched as she laid out the insinuation.

"I didn't though. I swear to you. Besides, I left at intermission, went home, and knocked back some beers."

"Intermission?" Trent volleyed back. "That was around the time she was killed."

"You've got to be shitting me." Tyson slumped back in his chair. "Do I need a lawyer?"

"Up to you. Besides seeing her perform, when was the last time you saw your sister?" Maybe if she finessed her approach, he'd let it slip when Michaela last turned him away.

He bunched up his face in concentration. "It would have been two years ago. She was in town for Gram's funeral."

Amanda's earlier theory circled back. Was the killer's motive rooted further in the past as she thought before? "Do you know what else she might have done when she was here?"

"Aunt Patty might know. As I said, Mick and I don't talk much."

If he was interested in handouts, Amanda could understand how the adult Michaela wouldn't want to speak with her brother. "We heard about her ex-boyfriend, Wendell Smith, and her former friend Deana Jones. Do you know if they were in touch then or since?"

"I couldn't tell you. As I said, my sister and I weren't close. Not ever."

Amanda found it hard to believe two young children abandoned by their mother wouldn't have been close at one time, but it highlighted another thing. "Yet you still saw it appropriate to ask for handouts?"

"Three times maybe."

"When was the last time?" She'd try again.

"Last month," he let out on a sigh. "I was close to losing my place. I was behind on rent, but she didn't care."

Not long ago he was lamenting how meager his surroundings were, but apparently, he wanted to protect what he had. "How did you contact her?"

"I called her. I have her number," he added.

"Was that the last time you spoke to her?" Amanda wanted to confirm this was his final answer.

"Fine. Last week," he spat. "She was being incredibly stubborn and refused to change her mind."

"You must have found a way to turn things around for yourself," Trent said. "You didn't lose your place."

"The landlord gave me an extension, which is now quickly running out."

Amanda hated the judgment that quickly passed through her mind, but if Tyson got himself together and stopped drinking, he'd have more money. He clearly had enough to support his booze habit. But a monetary hit was just one cost of addiction. "Sorry to hear that."

"What would you care? Why am I here anyhow? You have nothing on me. I still don't know how she died!"

"Anaphylaxis. That's death from severe allergic reaction." She watched as clarity moved over his expression, his mouth slightly gaping open, his eyes widening.

"She ate peanuts?"

That confirmed he knew about her allergy, but that tidbit wasn't a surprise. It stood to reason that Michaela's brother would know this. He'd probably grown up working around it. "It was in her protein shake." She watched him as she put that out there.

"Okay," he dragged out.

She didn't get the sense what she'd said had meant much. She added, "Michaela was found in her dressing room."

"All right."

Amanda was unsettled by his lack of curiosity about the details of his sister's murder. Did he know more than he let on, including cause of death? Or was he honestly not feeling the impact of her death? "Did you visit her in her dressing room at the arena?"

"Didn't know she had one."

Amanda scanned his eyes, reading them. He seemed genuine, but the problem with good liars was they were convincing. "Maybe you figured you'd inherit with her out of the way."

"And why would she leave me money?"

"You were siblings," Amanda volleyed back.

"Trust me, it didn't mean anything."

Amanda bristled at that. She had five siblings. One brother and four sisters, and they all meant the world to her. They didn't always see eye to eye, but they had each other's backs. It was hard for her to comprehend becoming a stranger to any of them, but all families weren't like hers. "If we searched your home, would we find peanut oil?"

"You would. I use it to deep-fry chicken."

"Hmph. What about black ribbon?" she asked.

"Why would I have that? I'm not an arts and crafts kind of guy."

"You tell us you didn't hurt your sister. Would you be willing to give us a sample of your handwriting?" she asked.

"If it makes you leave me alone? You bet."

Amanda gave him a notepad and a pen and told him what to write out. It wasn't the note verbatim but included some of the words for an easy comparison. As she watched Tyson put pen to page, with his left hand, he seemed to have a hard time writing. His hand was steady, but he was hesitant and seemed to be struggling to spell out the words. Her guess was he was dyslexic. She was starting to think Tyson fit the frame from a broad perspective but not necessarily upon magnification. She sat back in her chair and glanced at Trent, who subtly shook his head. She took it to mean he was of the same opinion as her. She stood.

"Wait. Where are you going? Can I leave?"

Amanda considered. They didn't have solid evidence

against Tyson, and he wasn't exactly a flight risk. Being a runner didn't count. Regardless, Malone wouldn't approve of holding him without some concrete evidence. "Yes, but don't leave town."

"Not like I have the money for that anyway," he mumbled.

She left Tyson and stepped into the room next door with Trent.

"They weren't close, yet he clearly felt entitled to her money. Are you sure you want him to walk?" he asked her.

"We don't have enough to hold him. There definitely wasn't any love lost between the two, but I'm not convinced he killed her. *Yet*, anyway. I keep thinking Michaela survived a visit home two years ago but not this one. Is there a clue in that?" She met her partner's gaze.

"I suppose something could have happened then that triggered Michaela's murder."

"That right there. We need to turn over every stone, Trent. It could prove beneficial to piece that trip together."

"Except Patty didn't seem to know much about Michaela's social life in Woodbridge other than the one ex and a former friend."

"I'll talk to her again and see if I can jolt anything loose." Amanda glanced at the clock on the wall and considered texting Patty right now, but it was approaching one in the morning. Patty was likely still up, but Amanda would give her a reprieve, allowing her the chance of getting some rest. Besides, she and Trent weren't without things to do. Lux Suites was their next step.

SIXTEEN

Amanda was familiar with Lux Suites from previous investigations. The closest to home was a lead she and Trent had followed in the murder of Logan's estranged wife.

The woman at the front desk smiled at Amanda and Trent when they walked into the lobby, but the expression faded at a quick flash of their badges. Behold the power of the gold shield.

"You want room six-oh-seven. There's an Officer Brandt already up there in the hall." The clerk's implication wasn't hard to miss. She would be happy if Amanda and Trent would just go and join him.

"Just a couple of questions first. Was the room cleaned today?" Amanda wagered it likely had been and that this routine thing could have removed potential evidence. It was unfortunate but unpreventable.

"It would have been." The clerk tapped on her keyboard. "Looks like housekeeping finished at two o'clock."

"And do you know if she had any visitors during her stay?" If it came down to it, they'd request surveillance video, but the warrant might be hard to secure without more to substantiate it.

"A man had me call up to her room on Saturday morning.

Ms. Glover came down, and they went out for about half an hour. Maybe less. She returned alone."

"What time was this?" Amanda asked.

"Around eight thirty, nine."

"You must work long shifts," Trent put in.

She shrugged. "They're a little unusual. From midnight until ten AM."

Amanda was just grateful the clerk had a lead to provide. "How old was he? Can you describe his looks?"

"He was Black like Ms. Glover. In his mid-twenties, say. A good-looking man, above average height."

"Could you tell what their relationship was?" Trent asked.

"I didn't pay that close of attention."

"Anything stand out about him? His voice or his gait?" Amanda was fishing, hoping to catch a lead.

"No, sorry. But I'd say he sounded local."

Did Michaela have a secret lover? Had he been the one to kill her? Or was it possible that Tyson had lied about not seeing his sister? He could check all the boxes for the description the clerk just gave them.

"Did you happen to notice what he was driving?" Trent asked, leaning on the counter.

The clerk shook her head. "I didn't see him come from a vehicle. He could have walked here."

"He could have." Amanda glanced at the ceiling. The security camera that had come in handy in a previous investigation was still there. "We'd like to see the footage from that time."

"I would need to run it past the manager, but Mr. Edwin's not reachable until Monday evening."

It was hard to accept anyone as *not reachable* these days. "Surely there's someone taking on the role while he's not here. An assistant manager, perhaps?"

The clerk nodded. "Mr. Simmonds."

"Can we speak with him?" Amanda countered.

"Not right now. He stepped out for a few minutes."

Of course he did... "When he gets back, please send him up to room six-oh-seven."

"Okay."

"Thank you." Amanda smiled at the clerk, who gave her a cold gaze in response.

Amanda and Trent took the elevator to the sixth floor and found Officer Leo Brandt standing vigil outside room 607.

"Good evening, or should I say 'top of the mornin' to ya'?" Leo grinned.

Trent shook his head. "Reserve that greeting for leprechauns or St. Patrick's Day."

It was hard to believe they were now into Sunday morning, and that for the hours they'd already spent looking for Michaela's killer, they had little evidence to help them. They were due for a change in their luck. She pulled out the keycard that Patty had given her.

The light on the lock flashed green, and Amanda twisted the door handle. They were in, and as she stepped inside, her heart pinched on the fact the last time Michaela had set foot in here, she'd been alive and full of ambition to win Olympic gold. Now, a relative handful of hours later all hopes of that were stolen, lost forever.

The room was fragrant with a floral perfume and a citrusy spritz. It was likely sprayed by housekeeping on the linens. The bed was made, and the garbage bins emptied, but there was a spread of paperwork on the long dresser. Cosmetics and makeup bags lined the limited space offered on the bathroom counter. A soft-shelled suitcase was tucked in the corner of the room.

Amanda gloved up, and Trent was standing at the dresser holding a bunch of receipts in his hand.

"It looks like she kept the receipt for every purchase she made," he said.

"Probably for write-off purposes."

Trent shuffled through them. "Could be. They are mostly restaurants and coffee shops. There's also a gas receipt and the rental agreement for the Subaru." He lifted a stapled packet of paper.

She nodded before going to look in the closet. Her mind was on the wood toggle button found in Michaela's dressing room. Would she find the garment it belonged to here? She opened the doors. There was a pink puffer jacket and a few dresses on hangers. She filled Trent in on this.

"I knew it. Had a good feeling anyway," he said in response.

"About?"

"Michaela was young. I'd be more surprised if she didn't have a life Patty knew nothing about. It's also hard to ignore that she had a male visitor. We were told Michaela didn't have time for boyfriends, and Patty had said she cut everyone from her life. That wardrobe suggests otherwise."

Amanda moved the dresses along the rod, inspecting them closer. "Classy dresses, not sexy. To me, these are more what she'd wear for a nice meal out with her aunt rather than anything romantic. Besides we shouldn't leap ahead about this man. He could have been a friend, as easily as something more." *Her brother...?* But she'd keep that to herself for now and wait for the video.

"It still suggests Michaela had a semblance of a social life. If not, well, I strongly admire her commitment. But then why the need for a rental car and hotel room? She clearly wanted some flexibility and freedom. Was it to hide something? Or *someone?*"

His question poked right at what she'd thought hours ago while speaking with Patty. "Hard to say right now. We just need to keep these puzzle pieces in mind as we go along."

"Exactly."

"On another note, there's nothing here with toggle buttons.

The one found in her dressing room may have come off the killer's clothing."

"Possible. Or was a remnant from another time?"

She wished he hadn't said that, but it was possible it had nothing to do with their case. She left the closet and set the suitcase on the bed and spread it open. No clothing, so Michaela must have placed the contents in the dresser. That spoke to a person who liked order, and a spot for everything. Though Amanda wasn't surprised that the young skater would possess that trait. She'd need a decluttered mind to achieve her goal, and they say the outer world reflects the inner one. But *decluttered* couldn't be used to describe Michaela's mind recently. Not when she was frazzled and unfocused.

Amanda peeked inside the pocket at the back of the suitcase. Something was in there, and she pushed her hand in to find out what. She came out with a letter-size envelope, no return address, but the postal stamp led to a Woodbridge mail office dating back to October, so two months ago.

"Whatcha got there?" Trent asked, coming over.

"Still trying to figure that out." She could feel there was something inside and removed it. "It's a necklace with a pendant." She rolled it over in her palm. "A crescent moon and star with an emerald heart."

"An envelope seems like a strange spot to keep jewelry."

"Tucked into the pocket at the back of the suitcase, no less. There's no return address, but it was mailed from Woodbridge to Michaela in Colorado Springs." Amanda was flipping the envelope over in her hand and noticed that there was something she'd missed. She reached inside and pulled out a note. "And what do we have here?" She unfolded the piece of paper and nearly lost her balance at the sight of the handwriting. She held it for Trent to see. "Look familiar?"

His eyes widened. "It looks a lot like the writing on the note we found with Michaela."

"Uh-huh." She looked again at the address on the envelope and saw that handwriting was also similar. *How had she originally missed that?*

"What does it say?"

Amanda read the note out loud. "'You shine like the star next to the moon. I see you, as does the whole world.'"

"From a lover?"

"If so, why keep it where she had it?"

"It's almost like she was hiding it."

"Was the sender someone she was keeping secret? Possibly that man who showed up here for her? Such a gift would suggest a personal relationship. If it was romantic, it may have fallen apart. Maybe she ended it, and he decided if he couldn't have her, no one could."

"Her ex-boyfriend, Wendell? Was it him who showed up here?"

"We are going to talk to him, but according to Patty, Michaela ended that relationship over two years ago, so likely not. But this mystery guy could have been newer to her life. He followed her here and she decided to end things with him when they stepped out. Again, assuming this was a romantic relationship."

"Was she killed over a bad breakup then?"

"Trent, I don't know, but the sooner we find out, the better."

SEVENTEEN

Yesterday ended at 3 AM today. That was when Amanda and Trent slipped by Katherine's place to pick up Amanda's Honda Civic. Before they'd left the hotel, they'd spoken with the assistant manager, Doug Simmonds, and the conversation had been pointless. All he knew was the video surveillance was managed by a third-party firm. He didn't even have their name. They'd have to wait for the manager to return on Monday. They also entrusted Michaela's room, the necklace with its pendant, and the envelope to Officer Brandt for safeguarding and called CSI Blair to fill her in. She sounded tired, but said she and Donnelly would head right over. It was that larger purpose that must have fueled her, just as it did Amanda. The fact that Michaela Glover deserved justice.

It was the same thing propelling Amanda from bed on Sunday morning at seven o'clock, less than four hours after she'd tucked herself in. She lifted back the covers, pacing her movements and being as quiet as possible so she wouldn't wake Logan. She'd already disturbed his sleep when she got home in the wee hours. Not that he'd minded. Or so he'd said. Sometimes the words between them felt loaded with what wasn't being spoken aloud.

She threw her legs over the side of the mattress, and Logan pulled her back against him. He'd caught her by surprise, and she squealed, snapping her mouth shut hoping she hadn't woken Zoe.

"You get over here, lady." Logan wasn't letting her go without a fight, which was apparent. He now had his arms secured around her waist and had drawn them together. Her back to his front and his—

"Good morning to you." She couldn't help that her voice turned husky at the feel of him against her butt cheeks.

"Exactly why you're not going anywhere yet." He nuzzled his face into the side of her neck and flicked his tongue on the tender flesh. The warmth of his breath fired off a million tingles throughout her body. Then he sucked an earlobe that sent her head spinning.

She gently tapped his forearms, but she lost all power to resist and let herself have this moment. After all, life was too unpredictable to squander. She spun and pinned him, but he flipped her on her back again and made love to her.

They'd just finished when the door cracked open, and it had them rushing to pull up the covers.

"I'm hungry," Zoe's small voice cut through the room.

"We'll out in a minute," Amanda told her, shaking her head at Logan and wagging a pointed finger in his face. She whispered, "That's why we always lock the door."

"Don't look at me. You were the last one in bed."

She should have thought that through. Zoe left, and Amanda got up. She pecked a kiss on Logan's lips and told him to stay in bed.

Amanda threw on her pajamas again and found Zoe sitting in the living room watching a cartoon on TV. The roses intended for Michaela were on the coffee table in front of her, resting in a drinking glass with some water.

"I want pancakes," Zoe told her.

"Of course you do." It was only the girl's favorite breakfast, and not typically a tall order for the weekend. Except for today Amanda wanted to get to work. "How about cereal and some apple juice instead?"

"Colored O's? I need *some* sugar," she replied with sass.

"Yes, but just because it's Sunday." Amanda smiled at the girl, appreciating how simplistic her needs were at this age. If only it was possible to halt time, or at least access memories as tangible, breathing recalls that could be relived.

Amanda poured some cereal into a bowl, concentrating on the serving size. Zoe was much like a hound. Left to her own devices, she'd eat until she was sick.

Zoe took her breakfast back to the living room and parked on the floor in front of the TV. It wasn't a habit Amanda encouraged, and she only allowed it on weekends and special holidays. Logan was more lenient with that "rule."

Amanda grabbed herself a coffee and a piece of toast before quickly popping into the shower and getting dressed for the day. By then, Logan was wandering around the house looking about as wide awake as she felt. Which wasn't much. It was one of those days when a beer hat loaded with coffee cups would come in handy.

When it was time to leave, Zoe clung on to her legs. "Oh, please don't go."

"I have to, baby." It broke her heart, but she didn't have much choice. Being a cop was in her blood, not just because her father was the former PWCPD police chief. She couldn't imagine life without her badge. Just as she couldn't imagine not being a mother. It was also an amazing and rewarding job and just as hardwired.

"What if you don't come home?" Zoe stuck out her bottom lip, the telling sign that she was about to cry.

"I'll be home."

"No. You can't promise that. Look at what happened to my mom and dad."

Zoe's story was a heartbreaking one. The family of three tucked into their beds one night, and by morning, Zoe's parents were gone. Murdered. She'd been exposed to the ugly fact of life so early on. "You're right. I can't promise, but I will do my very best."

"Are you going to Grandma's tonight?"

Every Sunday night, her mother fed the entire Steele clan, which made for a packed house with Amanda's four sisters, brother, and all the partners, spouses, and children that went along with them. "I'll do my best." That was as close as she'd get to making a promise. What the day held in store was the universe's best guess. The thing with murder investigations was they could spin in an instant. She and Trent could be slapping cuffs on Michaela's killer just as easily as things could go lopsided and one of them not make it home at the end of the day. But she refused to dwell on that possibility. If she did, she'd have lost her sanity years ago.

"Do you think I can meet Mickey before her roses die?"

Logan walked into the room at that point, and whispered to Amanda, "I'll talk with her. I assume you have to go?"

"Yeah."

"Mandy?" Zoe prompted.

"Logan's going to talk to you about the roses and Mickey."

"Right. You've got work," Zoe grumbled.

"I do."

"Fine. Go get the bad guy." Zoe's eyes sparkled, and the command was clear.

"Yes, ma'am." Amanda laughed and gave a mock salute

before kissing and hugging her goodbye. Zoe ran down the hall
to her room, leaving Amanda facing Logan. "Please break it to
her gently."

"I will. Just do what you have to, and don't worry about us."
He then brushed his lips to her forehead. But her mind
dissected his words. Were they sincere or born from bitterness?

She'd prefer to take what he said and his tender display of
affection as genuine. It smacked close to moments she'd had
with her late husband. The comparison caused her breath to
hitch. She pulled out of the embrace. "Thank you."

"Don't mention it." He brushed a strand of her red hair
from her eyes and tucked it behind an ear. "It's probably not a
good time to bring this up, but..."

Her entire body tensed, fearing what he was going to say
next. Their relationship had traversed a cycle of ups and downs.
Most of the latter were related to her work and how that manifested in her being an absent partner and mother. That was one
clear area where this relationship differed from the one that
she'd had with her late husband. She and Kevin had naturally
found middle ground. He certainly never questioned if her
priority was her family like Logan had in the past. "I'll do all I
can to be at dinner tonight with everyone."

He put a hand on her arm. "It's not about that, but I've been
thinking about something." He licked his lips, pinched his eyes
shut for a second.

"About what?" Her insides were twisting like a coiled vine.

"Would it be so crazy if we had a kid together?"

She stumbled backward, her hips pressing against the
counter. It was the only thing keeping her upright. "We have a
kid. Zoe." She tried to smile, unsure it manifested, but her heart
was beating like crazy because she could sense where he was
going with this.

He smiled at her and shook his head. "Zoe's great."

"She is." She cursed herself for muttering unnecessarily, but her nerves had taken over.

"And we share responsibilities with her, but it's your name on the adoption paperwork."

"Does that matter?" She realized the stupidity of the question once it left her lips and quickly added, "Zoe thinks of you like a father."

"It's probably best I just come out and say what's on my mind. I want to have a baby with you, Amanda."

"A..." She rubbed her neck, imagining her skin there turning red. "You want a... baby?"

"Sure. Why not? Things between us are good. We're committed to each other, and we've been doing a decent job with Zoe. Why not expand our family?"

She could tell him if she could draw a solid breath. But it seemed too late to be telling him the accident hadn't just stolen her husband and daughter. That it had claimed her unborn son and taken her ability to have any more children too. He'd want to know why she had never confided this in him before. They'd get into a huge fight. Her defense that there hadn't been a reason to mention it before now likely wouldn't go over well. And he might have a hard time accepting that she hadn't because she preferred not to acknowledge all this herself.

"Mandy?" he prompted.

She cleared her throat and pressed on a smile. "It's a big decision. Let me think about it."

"Sure, just don't take too long. I want to pick up on the practicing." He pulled her in for a hug and planted a kiss on her.

As she walked out the door, she laid a hand over her stomach, thinking about making love to him that morning. What would their future be now? When she did talk with him, would he be able to move beyond this? Was she even ready to share her secret with him when she hadn't fully processed that loss herself?

She took a deep breath, got into her car, and drove to Central. At least for the next eight hours or so, she'd have something else to keep her mind busy.

EIGHTEEN

It was a lot harder to shake Logan's proposition than Amanda had imagined. She'd even popped by Hannah's Diner for an extra-large coffee and brought one for Trent. It would be cooling on his desk by this point. At least she had the case to help distract her. Too bad much of it was a waiting game. Several warrants were needed, which took time, and were best to knock off before carrying on with much else. That meant speaking to the ex-boyfriend and former friend were in a holding pattern as was tracking down who sent the flowers. Same too for the postmark on the envelope. That was in limbo until Monday when the post office opened. It was unlikely a coincidence that the handwriting on the note with the jewelry matched the card found with her body. Based on their running theory, that meant whoever had given her the beautiful gift had also killed her. She let all this percolate as she looked at the list of arena employees, but they were just a bunch of names that didn't mean anything at this point.

"Sorry I'm late." Trent rushed into his cubicle and hung his coat on the back of his chair.

"It's fine, but your coffee might be cold now."

"Coffee?" He looked on his desk and plucked the to-go cup. "Oh, thanks, Amanda." He snapped back the lid and took a sip. He shut his eyes as he did so, and it made Amanda smile.

"Still good, I take it?"

"It is. I was running behind and didn't want to stop on the way in. So you're a life saver."

"We do have coffee here in the bullpen."

"It's nothing like Hannah's Diner."

She smiled at having successfully converted him. Hannah's Diner was owned by Katherine Graves's aunt, May Byrd, and it was out of Trent's way, but it didn't stop him from going there most mornings. "Okay, so what do you say? We start on the paperwork for all the warrants we need?"

"Sure. Sergeant Malone was taking care of Michaela's phone records so we can mark that off. But that still leaves us with Michaela's financials, video from the arena's surveillance cameras..."

"The network that broadcasted the event."

"I thought you dismissed its importance."

"Better to have it and not need it, then..."

"I get it."

"We also need to reach out to Royal Rentals to see if they'll part with the GPS on the Subaru Michaela rented or whether they require a warrant."

"I'll give them a quick call and find out."

"Great. We'll also need one for the CCTV in the post office where the necklace and pendant were mailed from." It was an assumption the jewelry and note all came in the envelope she found them in. But it felt like a plausible one, and she planned to treat it as fact.

"All right. Sounds like we have our work cut out for us."

"That we do. That's it for the warrants, though, I think. I plan to call Patty shortly to ask if the pendant means anything to her."

"Ask about Michaela's visitor at the hotel too. Though I wouldn't hold my breath she'll know anything about him. Patty seemed to stress that Michaela was a private person."

"I'll give it a try. This is where Michaela's phone records would come in handy. We'd be able to see who she's been in contact with. Speaking of, I haven't heard back from Michaela's coach." That realization soured in her gut, though there could be an innocent explanation. "I'm calling her right now."

"I'll call Royal and start on the paperwork."

"Sounds good." Amanda selected the coach's number from her call history.

"Hello?" A woman answered, groggy, like Amanda had woken her up.

"Jolene Flynn?"

"Who is this?"

"Detective Steele. I left a voicemail for you last night pertaining to your client Michaela Glover."

"Oh, yes. It's been crazy here if you'll excuse my delay in returning your call. What's going on?"

Crazy there? Amanda stifled a sharp comment. "Michaela was killed yesterday at the—" She paused when Jolene let out a strangled gasp.

"Killed? How can I not know about this? What happened? Who...?"

"I'm not sure how you haven't heard about her death. It's been all over the news since her body was discovered yester-day." Amanda understood life could have prevented the coach from being at the event, but she'd have expected her to have kept some tabs on it, maybe even be contacted by the press for comment.

There were a few seconds of silence, then, "I haven't had two minutes to tune into the news or return anyone's calls. I'm in Washington with my family. The only reason I missed the show was my grandmother passed away. It was expected as she'd been sick for a while, but that isn't making it much easier to say goodbye."

A death in the family was certainly a good reason not to be present for her client's hometown performance. It also explained why she might not be up on the latest news. "I hadn't heard. Condolences for your loss."

"I appreciate that." Jolene sniffled, and Amanda wasn't sure if she was upset about her grandmother, Michaela, or both. "I'm sorry that I didn't call you back. I listened to your voicemail, but that's as far as I got. I didn't realize how urgent it was."

Amanda said that she was calling regarding Michaela Glover but hadn't gotten into specifics. Still she had identified herself as a detective with the Prince William County PD.

"What happened to her?" Jolene's voice cut across the line.

"She ingested peanut oil. We have reason to believe the person responsible added it to her protein shake. It happened sometime during intermission, and Michaela was found in her dressing room after the show."

"Just... Wow. I'm at a loss here. That girl had the entire world at her feet and now she's just gone. Such a waste of tremendous talent."

That seemed to be a recurring sentiment. "It is. Will you please tell me about your relationship with Michaela?"

"I was her coach. That's all. I find it's much better to have that defined line. It keeps things professional and focused. Her goal was Olympic gold, and my job was to equip her with the skills to attain that."

"Understood. We found a note with her. It said, 'You'll be sorry you turned your back on me after all I did for you.' Any idea who might have reason to send that?"

"I'm sorry, but I don't. I don't know of anyone who hated Michaela. Maybe it was someone from Woodbridge who had an issue with her. She didn't strike me as too excited about heading home."

Amanda sat back in her chair. The security guy had said Michaela lacked her regular focus and seemed flustered. She and Trent had speculated that someone local was behind her murder. "Did she say why?"

A deep breath traveled the line. The response was in what wasn't being said.

"Right. Asking her would have been crossing into her personal life. We were told by Henry, the security guy traveling with the show, that she seemed flustered and unfocused before taking to the ice yesterday. He thought she'd been that way for a while. Did you notice that?"

The coach didn't respond immediately, but eventually offered, "I'm sorry, but I couldn't tell you why."

It wasn't exactly a direct answer to Amanda's question, but it sounded like she had observed a difference. Otherwise there would be no reason for her to speculate on a reason. "Did you get the impression she was nervous about performing in her hometown?" It was possible Henry mistook honest nerves for flustered preoccupation. Though he'd mentioned seeing this in her for a couple of months.

"Not possible. That girl was a born performer and had a ton of confidence."

But it was possible that Michaela wasn't looking forward to seeing someone specifically. Whoever that was. There was also another theory she and Trent had bounced off each other yesterday. "Speaking of confidence, she might have gained some from having you as a coach. As we understand it, you're in high demand. You have a line of skaters wanting to work with you."

"I do, but what about it?"

"Could any of them have reason to kill Michaela? After all, if she's gone, you'd have an opening. Who is set to take her place?" It pained Amanda to present such a cold and calculated motive for murder, but it was what it was.

"There's no way that happened. Potential clients are confidential. Some will even approach me without their current coach's knowledge. Anyone I consider taking on isn't in a queue, as such, either. I pick based in the moment weighing several factors such as who shows the most potential and who I feel I can help most. That could be someone who's wanted to work with me for years, or a skater who just contacted me."

At least they could scratch Jolene's potential future clients off the suspect list. "Do you know of any admirers or stalkers she may have had?"

"She had tons of fans, but none that struck me as dangerous. Michaela certainly never mentioned such a fear to me. If she had, I would have suggested she employ a bodyguard immediately."

Amanda noted that the coach never abbreviated the young skater's name. True to her earlier words, she drew a distinct line between the professional and personal. She had to ask a question anyhow. "Do you know if Michaela was seeing anyone recently or turned down anyone's advances? Broke up with someone or if she was planning to?"

"I don't. Again, I had one focus with Michaela and that was getting her Olympic gold."

Amanda admired the woman's confidence and resolve. Every athlete deserved someone in their corner who was that supportive of their professional goals. "Michaela had a silver chain with a moon pendant, a little emerald heart in its center. Do you know anything about it? Who might have given it to her?"

"I never saw her wear one. As I said—"

"You didn't get involved in her personal life," Amanda cut in. It seemed a convenient line to barricade behind.

"Correct, but she didn't have much time for a social life. That girl worked hard and even gave more than I asked of her. At least most of the time."

"What do you mean by that?"

"I wasn't going to say anything. Don't like speaking ill of the dead, but if it helps you figure out who killed her... I noticed she's been off her game for a month or two. She got her act mostly together after I told her my skaters need to have one mindset. Gold."

"How was she 'off her game'?"

"She canceled a couple of practice sessions. That's something a serious athlete just doesn't do. She also placed second and third in some recent competitions when she should have been winning comfortably. I found it highly unusual."

Amanda wasn't even going to ask if the coach suspected the reason for the change in Michaela's performance. She knew what Jolene's answer would be.

Jolene added, "I'm going to miss her though. Overall she had an incredible drive and work ethic."

"I'm sorry for your loss, Ms. Flynn, and thank you for your time."

"Don't mention it. I hope that you..." Jolene's voice lowered, and she cleared her throat before continuing. "Please find out who did this to her. She deserves justice."

"We're going to do our best." Amanda ran through the familiar spiel, telling the coach not to hesitate to call her if she thought of something later. She anticipated ending the call when Jolene spoke.

"Actually, Detective, after thinking about it more... Michaela has been *off* since October."

The hair rose on Amanda's arms. October was the month on the postmark for the necklace and pendant. Now more than ever, Amanda suspected the notes, the jewelry, and Michaela's lack of focus were linked and had resulted in her murder.

NINETEEN

Amanda ended the call with Jolene riding a new high. It wasn't a glittering lead, but it was potentially a telling one. They'd still need to dig deeper, but it was a start.

Trent was tapping away on his keyboard when she hung up.

"I assume Royal Rentals wants a warrant?" she asked him.

He raised his head, his forehead and eyes above the partition between them. "Yep."

"So I just got off the phone with Michaela's coach. She said Michaela's focus has been off since October."

"The date on the postmark."

"Uh-huh, and get this, Jolene Flynn got the strong impression that Michaela wasn't looking forward to returning to Woodbridge."

"Hmm. That could explain why she seemed flustered and preoccupied before the show."

Amanda nodded. "And I bet it all ties in with whoever sent the necklace. Technically, someone could have flown into town to send it, but it was more likely someone local who mailed it."

"I'd say that's a safe assumption. Either way, it seems undeniably connected to her murder."

"With the matching handwriting? Yeah, I agree. This person might even be the mystery man who showed up at her hotel. Except for one thing..." It just struck her as she spoke. "If he was the reason she wasn't looking forward to coming home, why step out with him?"

"Good point. The coach didn't ask Michaela once what was bothering her?"

Amanda shook her head. "She was very clear that she draws a line between professional and personal when it comes to her skaters."

"Too bad. And speaking of skaters, did you ask about others wanting to work with her?"

"I did. It's doubtful any of them bumped off Michaela for her spot with Jolene. Apparently, there's not a list per se. Jolene picks based on potential, among other things."

"Okay, one step forward, one back."

"Yep. You continue with the paperwork, and I'll call Patty."

"Aye." Trent smiled and started tapping on his keyboard again.

Amanda selected Patty from her contacts. It was eight forty-five in the morning, not exactly late if Patty had finally gotten to sleep, but her friend would be eager to answer questions if it might help find her niece's killer.

Patty answered during the middle of the second ring. "Mandy? Tell me you know something."

Amanda pinched her eyes shut for a moment. She should have known that would be Patty's initial response to seeing her name on Caller ID. "We've uncovered a few things I need to ask about."

There was a brief silence on Patty's end, then sniffles.

"Were you able to call someone to come stay with you?" Amanda slipped into friend mode for a second.

"I don't want company right now. My thoughts are loud

enough. How did you ever—" Patty stopped talking there, her voice turning thick.

"Time. It's all that helps to ease the pain." Not that she was any sort of mentor to emulate when it came to grieving. After losing her family, she had moved through life like a zombie, half alive, though mostly dead inside. Even the job she loved lost its shine. It had taken years and the murder of the drunk driver who smashed into their car to awaken her. She cleared her throat, wishing to banish the thoughts altogether, but then a new one entered in. Logan wanted a baby with her. The one thing she'd never be able to give him.

"Mandy? What do you need to ask?"

"Sorry, my mind drifted. Trent and I went to the hotel where Michaela was staying. Apparently, a man visited her on Saturday morning. He was in his twenties, but the clerk wasn't sure of their relationship. Did you get any inkling she was in a romantic relationship?"

"None. As far as I knew she was far too busy pursuing her goal."

"I thought so but had to ask."

"Can't you get security video to see who he is?"

"It's in the works." Amanda wasn't going to point out that even if they saw his face, it didn't mean it would give the investigation traction. But there was something else that struck her as she'd asked Patty about this guy. Michaela hadn't invited him up to her room. Rather she met him in the lobby. But she had left with him for thirty minutes. Would she do that if he made her uncomfortable or afraid? Unlikely. "When we searched her hotel room, we found a silver chain with a crescent moon and emerald heart pendant. It was in an envelope with a Woodbridge postmark dating back to October. Do you know who might have sent it to her?"

Patty was silent for a few beats, then, "I don't. But she loved crescent moons and emerald is her, or *was*, her birthstone. She was born in May."

Her friend didn't need to say one more word, as Amanda could feel her heartache leaching across the phone line. There was nothing Amanda could say to soften the blow of her loss. *Her birthstone though...* That suggested whoever sent her the necklace had known that. It reinforced the sender had a close bond with Michaela. "There was also a note with the gift," Amanda began. "It said, 'You shine like the star next to the moon. I see you, as does the whole world.' That mean anything to you?"

"No."

"The handwriting looks to be a match to the card found with Michaela." Amanda had debated sharing this tidbit with Patty, but settled on the possibility it might jog something loose.

"That horrible card that said she'd be sorry? Are you telling me the same person who gifted her that necklace also killed her?"

This was the very thing Amanda was afraid might happen. With Patty's hope spiked, disappointment may be inevitable. "All I know for sure is we're doing what we can to find this person. When Michaela was home for her grandmother's funeral, do you remember anyone from that day who made her uncomfortable?"

"We're talking over two years ago, and *that* day? My mind was in such a blur."

"I can appreciate that, but I had to ask."

"And it's not the first time. Do you think something happened then to lead to her... *her*... now?"

Murder... "It's just one possibility."

"What do you want me to say, Amanda?" Patty snapped. "I didn't track her every step." Her friend broke down crying.

Amanda didn't say a word, as she understood anger partnered with grief.

There was a deep intake of breath and a staggered exhale. "I'm sorry. I shouldn't have…"

"It's fine." Amanda took a few beats to build herself up for her next question. She didn't want Patty to take her words and twist them into something personal. "I just spoke with Michaela's coach, Jolene Flynn, and she got the impression Michaela wasn't looking forward to returning home for the show. Did she seem preoccupied or unhappy to you?"

"Not at all. We shared lots of laughs."

"I bet you did, and I didn't mean to imply her apprehension had anything to do with you."

"I get it. Do you have more questions for me?"

With the desperateness ringing in Patty's voice, Amanda wished she had. "Not right now. Try to get some rest. I found that sleeping aids were all that worked for me." She wasn't about to add that she'd relied on them for years and was even desperate enough to score them from a street dealer when her doctor stopped prescribing them.

"Thank you, Amanda. I'm sorry for having a short fuse. All this is just so hard to cope with. I keep thinking she's going to walk in the door."

"I'm here if you need me."

"Thank you." With that, Patty hung up.

Amanda was left holding the phone and staring briefly into space. Life was so fragile and fickle. Both an adventure and a horror ride. She'd best sink into work before her thoughts got too carried away. Doing all she could to catch Michaela's killer should help. She'd find out where Trent was with the warrants and roll up her sleeves to help.

TWENTY

Amanda was immersed in warrant paperwork when Malone called and asked that she and Trent join him and the police chief in his office. Clearly things weren't moving along fast enough for his or the public's liking.

She led the way, and they found the sergeant behind his desk. He waved them in, and they sat in the chairs across from him. Chief Buchanan was perched at the wall of filing cabinets, arms crossed.

"Good day, Detectives," Buchanan said to them in way of a generalized greeting.

Amanda made brief eye contact with Malone. The police chief didn't often get himself involved with their investigations, but he was known to step in when they were high profile. Though whatever the media was saying now, Amanda didn't have a clue. She refused to get sucked into that quicksand. One, she didn't want it to taint her view with the investigation. Two, she didn't need to be reminded of how horrible and tragic Michaela's murder had been. She was already living in that aftermath.

"Good day," Trent parroted, and Amanda smiled at the chief.

"I'm sure you've gathered as much, but I'm here because I'd like to discuss the Glover case. As I understand you two are working on it."

"That's right, sir," Amanda said.

"I understand the skater was the niece of one of PWCPD's own. And I don't feel I need to point out that her death is causing quite a sensation with the media. It's only going to explode from here. I plan to direct the PIO to disclose her death is being treated as suspicious. Now more than ever, I want to get in front of where things stand. So, where is that?"

Amanda understood his viewpoint and respected how the chief typically got right to the point. He also had a way of wearing his authority that commanded respect. "We're still sorting through a lot of potential leads."

"Leads are good. What about suspects?"

"We had one but let him go," she said.

"That's news to me." The chief narrowed his eyes and flicked a look at Malone.

"We didn't have enough to hold him," Amanda rushed out to save the sergeant from further reprimand. She also squared her posture, just enough to denote confidence not arrogance. It was a fine line but with Buchanan it was necessary to remain grounded. The chief was watching her though, and she got the sense he wished for her to elaborate. "It was the victim's brother, Tyson Bolton. Apparently, the siblings weren't that close, and there's a vast difference between them. He doesn't have much, is living below the poverty line, or so I surmise from his home. Meanwhile—"

"Michaela was living it up. Top-notch sponsors with money to burn," Buchanan put in.

Amanda stiffened. "Which she worked hard for."

The chief raised his hand in surrender. "I never meant to

imply otherwise. So you believe the brother may have killed his own sister because of jealousy?" His tone was coated in skepticism.

"Why not? It's a solid motive strengthened by the fact Michaela turned him away the last few times he asked for money. He was even at risk of losing his home." She chose to leave out Tyson's lying because she felt Buchanan would want him dragged in again. At this point, she felt there were better ways for them to spend their time.

"Can you place him at the arena?"

"He admitted to being there for part of the show but not in her dressing room where she was killed." She shoved aside the fact that Tyson had lied before and that his denial could be another one. But there was still the fact his handwriting wasn't a match to either note.

"I see."

"We'd want to build a solid case before we'd bring him in," Trent said.

Buchanan nodded. "Good call there. Better to have no arrests than one that comes back to paint the PWCPD as incompetent."

Hearing that from the chief's lips was a relief. "Exactly, sir."

"What are these leads you mentioned?" Buchanan tilted his head like a curious bird.

Amanda inched forward to the edge of her chair. "A man visited Michaela at her hotel on Saturday morning. They have surveillance video, but we're in a holding pattern there."

"How so?"

"The security is handled off site, and the manager is the only one who knows who the contractors are. He's out of town and not able to be reached." Even as she reiterated this, she found it irritating.

"That's unacceptable. What do you mean he can't be reached?"

She shrunk slightly. "Just that, unfortunately."

"How absurd." Buchanan huffed. "If you don't hear back on this tomorrow, you let me know and I'll step in."

As if he'd get further... But she pressed on a smile and nodded. "Will do. The largest lead seems to be finding a note in her hotel room with handwriting that matched a card found with her body."

"You should have started there. Did you have the brother give you a sample of his writing?"

"We did, and it's not a match." She'd leave it there without getting into her suspicion he was dyslexic.

"Your plan of action?"

"The note in her room was with a necklace and moon pendant. Both were inside a mailed envelope with a Wood-bridge postmark dating to this past October."

"All right, we'll look at the video from inside that mail office."

"Already on the warrant paperwork for that. But seeing as it's Sunday, even if an on-call judge signed off today, there's no one to serve it to until tomorrow."

"Right. You have any issues with that warrant, see me. What else?"

"We'd like to nail down where that card came from," she said. "To me, it's the strongest link we have to the killer. There was a card stick in the bouquet, but it was empty. Maybe if we can find out who sent them..."

"Right. Malone told me about the flowers. Tracking the delivery should be easy enough if the arena has a security camera on the door."

"And they do," Amanda told him.

"It sounds to me like you two have this well under control. Keep me posted if any major developments arise. I'll feed what I feel appropriate through the PIO to at least give the illusion of transparency to the public."

"Understood," Amanda said firmly.

With that, Buchanan wished them luck and left the room, closing the door behind him.

"Well, that was a surprise," Malone said.

"You weren't expecting him?" Amanda had assumed that the chief would have given the sergeant a heads-up.

"It wasn't a scheduled meeting if that's what you're getting at. He called me in from home. I guess he figures he's got that right, and I'm not going to argue. Is there anything else that you wish to share with me? Maybe something you didn't mention to Buchanan?"

"Michaela was home two years ago for her grandmother's funeral. We're considering that something might have happened then to motivate her murder." As Amanda voiced this again, she saw it could be seen as a stretch. Those around Michaela had said she'd been flustered the last couple of months. Not for years. Though in conflict to that, the event was announced around that time. "Her coach told us Michaela wasn't looking forward to coming back to Woodbridge."

"Huh. Well, there could be something in that."

"Exactly what we thought," Trent said. "And the necklace and pendant suggest it came from someone close to Michaela."

"You ask the brother about it?"

"Not yet. We found it after we spoke with him," Amanda pointed out.

"Sounds like you should have another chat."

Amanda nodded. "We'll get back to him, I'm sure."

Malone nodded in turn. "His handwriting doesn't match."

"Which is enough for me to move on for now. Any update on when we should expect Michaela's phone records?"

"I'll apply some more pressure. All right, out of my office and get the job done."

"Will do, Sarge." Trent was the first to stand, and Amanda trailed behind.

"Actually, Detective Steele, one more minute of your time."

She told Trent she'd catch up with him.

"You are doing all right?" he asked her.

"Just doing the job, Sarge." She used his title to draw on objectivity and an even emotional keel.

"Amanda, I have no doubt. It's just cases that touch close to home have a way of chipping away at us over time. You've had so many that are rather personal recently."

There was no sense denying that. It was the truth. This sounded like a talk her father had with Malone in the past. Her father passed the wisdom on to her. Focus on preventing future crime, not the past and what couldn't be undone. "I appreciate your concern, but I assure you that my head is in the game."

"What if one day it just gets to be too much?"

"I'll deal with that when, and *if*, it happens."

"Just think about it, Amanda. And when was the last time you took a vacation? Actually got away?"

It had been the summer of last year. Since then she'd been going nonstop as one case stacked onto the back of the next. "I'll think about it," she eventually said and saw herself out of his office. His concern weighed on her mind. Had she done a poor job of compartmentalizing? The investigations she worked often did spill into her personal life with a devastating toll. Broken promises and fractured relationships. But that was to be expected when a person set their career as a... *priority*. Had Logan been right all this time? That she cared more about her job than him and Zoe? Standing on its own, her track record could support that. Yet he still wanted to have a baby with her. As she thought about her life, sacrifices made for her career, she drew a comparison to Michaela. What if someone hadn't been so understanding with her?

TWENTY-ONE

The paperwork for the warrants were off to a judge, and Amanda had put away three coffees since she'd arrived at Central. It was ten o'clock, and her entire body was jittery, and her stomach couldn't handle another drop of java. Her phone rang, and she pulled it out, "It's Blair," she told Trent after catching the caller identity.

Trent left his cubicle and joined Amanda in hers. She answered, "Good morning, Blair. I've got you on speaker. Trent's here too."

"Good morning, guys. Well, I'm going to get right to the point. I'm too tired to do anything but."

"We get that." Amanda hadn't missed that while she'd been downing coffee, Trent had been doing the same and yawning almost nonstop.

"It was certainly a late one. We collected the envelope, necklace, and pendant, and we'll process all of them. Otherwise, the hotel room didn't give us anything informative. Prints and forensics that we lifted tied back to Michaela Glover or were old and degraded suggesting that they were from previous guests. I confirmed that housekeeping wears gloves."

"Then she never had company in her room," Trent concluded.

"Nothing to support that from a forensics standpoint. But speaking of, the vomit and the protein shake were tested, and both showed high amounts of peanut oil. I don't think that's coming as a surprise to any of us, but we also tested the black ribbon and the note. Both had a finite trace."

"Then they likely came together," Amanda reasoned. "Did you ever find a second card, marked with a florist stamp?"

"No. Now, I did swab the vase and there was no trace of peanut oil. But that doesn't necessarily mean anything. Michaela could have gotten the card we found from the delivered flowers and transferred peanut oil from touching the black ribbon earlier on."

"Or vice versa. Which doesn't help us determine where the card came from," Amanda said.

"Unfortunately, not based on these findings alone. As I said the peanut oil on the ribbon and card were faint. The original transfer could have even come from the killer."

Amanda had already considered that. "Anything else?"

"We still have the garbage bags to look at, and there was nothing but smudged fingerprints on that toggle button we found in the dressing room."

"We can't expect to hit the jackpot every time. Thanks for the updates though. Keep me posted if anything else turns up," Amanda said.

"You know it, but don't be waiting by the phone. There is still a lot to process."

"As always, I trust you have it fully under control," Amanda said.

Blair ended the call, and Amanda turned to Trent. "We need to track down where that card came from once and for all, as I said to Chief Buchanan. I'll call Judge Anderson right now and see if he'll rush approval on the arena video. We might get an eye on who delivered the bouquet. Fingers crossed, it breaks the case wide open." She placed the call, fingers crossed in her head.

TWENTY-TWO

Getting fast approval from Judge Anderson had been a breeze, though the fact the paperwork was in his office hadn't hurt. It didn't appear that Ron Hampton had arrived at the arena yet. Amanda had called the manager at home, and he was to meet them here. The parking lot was empty except for one PWCPD police cruiser and thankfully there wasn't a news van in sight.

Her phone rang as she was about to get out, but it was the caller's identity that stopped her. She answered on speaker.

"I'm wrapping things up here, and I thought I'd call to confirm cause of death," Rideout said. "I can say with confidence that it was anaphylaxis. Not sure if you've heard from CSI Blair yet, but the shake and vomit both showed a high concentration of peanut oil."

"She called not long ago," Amanda told him. "Thanks for the call though."

"Don't mention it." And with that, Rideout was gone.

She pocketed her phone, and she and Trent got out of their car and walked over to the uniformed officer, who was still in his.

It was Officer Tucker, an up-and-comer among the

PWCPD, who she didn't cross paths with often. She first met him when he was a rookie, though he wasn't one anymore. He'd earned his own car. Malone had made it clear years back that Tucker held promise, and apparently, he knew how to spot them.

"Morning," he said, after lowering his window to greet them.

"Good day," Amanda replied. "How long have you been watching the place?"

"I relieved Officer Wyatt at seven this morning and have been here since then."

"Anything happen?" Trent asked.

"Not a thing."

A Chevrolet sedan pulled into the lot cutting off their brief conversation, and Ron Hampton was behind the wheel. He parked next to the cruiser.

"Detectives. Officer," he added with a butt of his head toward Tucker. Back on Amanda, he said, "You're interested in that video?"

More prompt than inquiry. He knew the surveillance footage brought them back to the arena. "We're ready when you are," she said.

Ron assumed the lead and unlocked the front door. He took them to a small office with humming computers and buzzing fluorescents and flicked on some monitors. "Video records twenty-four hours a day, and it's all stored on the arena's server."

"We're interested in seeing the footage from yesterday between one and two o'clock," she said, pinpointing the time when the bouquet had been delivered.

"Sure, and you have the warrant? You mentioned you had one over the phone. Can I see it?"

Trent pulled out his tablet and brought up the signed warrant. He held the screen toward Ron.

The manager leaned in, squinted, then nodded. "Good enough." He pulled out a wheeled chair and dropped down and looked at her. "You gave me the time, but which camera do you want to see first?"

They'd come here for the purpose of seeing the flower delivery, but they could use this opportunity to fully verify the alibi of Lilian Berry, Wendy Nicholson's coach, beyond all doubt. "Let's start with the footage from the smoking area in the back of the arena."

"Ah, sure. Same time or...?"

She told him between one forty-five and two fifteen.

He brought up the video, and they watched. Lilian came into view, lit up and puffed away. When she was almost finished, Henry the security guy turned up. This video fully cleared them both.

"Thanks," Amanda said. "Now, if we could watch footage from the front entrance for between one and two PM."

"Whatever you need." Ron turned around to face the computer, wriggled the mouse around, clicked a few times, and announced his success with, "Voila."

She appreciated his exuberance, but she'd withhold hers until she saw what there was to see. They watched it play out in real time for a few minutes, then she had Ron speed up the playback to one and a half times. An older-model beige Nissan Sentra parked, and the driver got out and retrieved the bouquet from the backseat.

"Stop, right there!" she said.

Ron reacted immediately and frozen on the one monitor was the person who had delivered Michaela's flowers. Plain Jane, and much the way Cindy had described the woman. Small stature, wearing a hoodie without any florist logo. Her face was angled toward the pavement. It was hard to know if it was intentional or if she was watching her steps while carrying a glass vase. But there was a card in the middle of the display. It was tucked down, but the corner was visible.

"Can you zoom in on the card?" she asked Ron.

He did as she requested, but it didn't help clarify things much. "Okay, play it again, but in slow motion."

The woman's face never met the camera on her path to the front door. She returned to her car and got in.

"Zoom in again. This time on the license plate," Trent said.

"One second." Ron punched in.

The digits were clear to see. It took all of Amanda's self-control not to run from the room to follow this lead.

TWENTY-THREE

The license plate led them to Nicole Holland, twenty-two, resident of Woodbridge with no criminal record. Her driver's license photo showed a studious-looking young woman with chestnut hair and brown eyes. Her place of employment was Rosebuds & More, a flower shop in town. It was closed on Sundays, so they decided to pay Nicole a house call.

"There was a card in that arrangement," Amanda told Trent as they drove. "Nicole might know what it said or who ordered the flowers."

"Even if she confirms the card, are we really thinking it's the one we found with Michaela? The one with no florist stamp and regular copy paper?"

"We'll ask about all of that. At least we have a jumping point."

Trent parked in front of a gray-brick bungalow. There were a few vehicles in the driveway including the older beige Nissan Sentra that had led them here. They both got out and made their way to the front door.

"Looks like a full house," she commented and wondered if

Nicole shared the home with other people her age, all of them splitting the rent to make it more manageable.

Trent rang the doorbell twice before steps padded toward them. The door was swung open by Nicole wearing a pink cotton robe cinched tight around her waist by a belt. Her makeup was smudged, and it was apparent she'd slept with her cosmetics on. Her eyes were bloodshot, and her brown hair was sticking up in places.

"Ah, yeah?" She made talking sound like a chore, and Amanda would guess she had a whopper of a hangover. Considering that it was almost noon and they seemed to have just roused her from bed helped her reach that conclusion too.

Amanda held up her badge and stepped up closer to Trent. "Are you Nicole Holland?"

"Yeah," she dragged out the word, coated with confusion as if she was uncertain as to her identity.

"I'm Detective Steele, and this is Detective Stenson. We have questions for you about a flower delivery you made to the arena in Woodbridge yesterday afternoon." While Nicole was the right age to be Michaela's peer, Amanda didn't suspect her of the murder.

Nicole shrugged and flailed a hand as if to tell her to go ahead.

"It would be better if we could have this conversation inside," Amanda suggested, though it was more direction.

"Okay." Nicole stepped back and signaled for them to enter. "Just ignore the mess. My roommates thought it was a good idea for us to drink a shit ton last night." Her eyes popped when she seemed to realize she'd let a swear word slip to cops. "I just meant..." She attempted to backpedal, but Amanda smiled at her.

"It's fine. We get the picture." And Amanda most certainly did. The kitchen was immediately behind the entry, and the counter was littered with empty tequila, lime juice, and triple sec bottles, along with dirty margarita glasses and a blender.

"Looks like quite the party. What were you celebrating?" Trent asked.

"Being young enough to bounce back. Apparently." Nicole met Amanda's gaze, and the girl had dark shadows under her eyes. Amanda would guess that's what one of her roommates gave as an excuse to overindulge. "What is it you want again?" She rubbed her forehead with the sleeve of her robe.

Upon seeing that Nicole was leaning against the counter to support herself, Amanda suggested they take a seat in the living room. Nicole didn't argue and sat on a couch, while Amanda and Trent remained standing. The other options were beanbag chairs.

"We have questions about the flowers you delivered for Michaela Glover," Amanda started.

"Right, that's why we were drinking." Nicole blanched, and Amanda thought she was going to vomit.

"Why is that?" Amanda wanted to be clear.

"Oh, Thad said she died yesterday, and we should live while we can."

Thad was a rather unique name, and Amanda recalled it from the list of arena employees. "Did he know Michaela? She grew up here." Assuming Thad was the same age as the young woman in front of her, it was possible they had crossed paths during elementary or high school.

"I don't think so, but she was our age. Just a wake-up call, I guess. What happened to her?"

Amanda wanted to chat with Thad about what he knew. To Nicole, she said, "It's an active police investigation, so I'm not at liberty to say." Though soon the world would know Michaela was murdered. "Did you know Michaela?"

"No, but I had heard she was from Woodbridge. That's cool."

Amanda nodded. She didn't get the feeling that Nicole was hiding anything from her. She pegged the girl as too hungover to have the bandwidth to do so. "Do you know who ordered the flowers that you delivered for her?"

"I couldn't tell you a name off the top. I remember that the order came in online overnight on Friday, and a rush delivery was requested."

"Rush delivery?" Trent said. "For when?"

"Had to be dropped off between one thirty and two PM yesterday."

"That seems rather specific," Amanda said. Did the sender want the delivery to coincide with intermission for a sinister reason?

"That's what I thought. I ended up getting there closer to one thirty."

"Do you remember if a card was requested?" She'd caught a glimpse of one but wanted to set the foundation for further questions.

"There should have been a card with it. I wrote it up myself, but..." Nicole rubbed her forehead. "After last night, I couldn't tell you what it said."

"Are your cards normally a thicker stock of paper, and do you stamp the back with the name of the flower shop?" Trent asked. He had his tablet out and was pecking notes into it.

"Ah, yeah. They're graphic too and occasion themed."

That confirmed the threatening card wasn't delivered with the flowers. But where was that one now? It was also interesting that someone saw the need to send flowers to Michaela at the last minute and at such a specific time. "We need to know who ordered the flowers," she told Nicole matter-of-factly. "Will we need to contact management at Rosebuds?" Just the thought of the delay settled like a stone in Amanda's gut.

"No, I'll have the order form around here somewhere. I had

it when I delivered, and the arena was my last stop. The paper-work should at least show the sender's name and number."

"Please, go get it for us," Amanda requested.

Nicole got up and staggered around the house for what felt like an eternity. When she returned, she had a piece of paper clutched in her hand. "The person who ordered the flowers was Deana Jones. That mean anything to you?"

Michaela's former friend. Why would she be sending flowers if their friendship had ended some time ago? And did any of this pertain to Michaela's murder?

TWENTY-FOUR

Amanda and Trent had a quick talk with Thad before leaving the party house, but he had nothing to offer the investigation. He had known Michaela in public school but not well. There was no apparent reason to suspect him. He didn't even know she'd been murdered, and they hadn't told him. Before going to speak with Deana Jones, they grabbed a cheeseburger each with extra onion from Petey's Patties. It wasn't everyone's preference, but it was for her and Trent. When they'd finished up, Trent took out a tub of fresh mint Tic Tacs.

"Want a few?" he asked her.

Onions tasted good but didn't do any favors for one's breath. "I'd better."

He tapped out a few into her waiting palm, and she savored the minty candy as he took them to the address on file for Deana Jones. It was an apartment in a middle-income Wood-bridge neighborhood.

After Amanda knocked, the unmistakable sound of metal scraping against wood told her the peephole cover was slid open. She held her badge up to the viewing porthole.

Rather quickly, the cover clicked back into place, and the

door was opened the amount the security chain would allow. In the crack was a beautiful young woman with a dark complexion.

"Deana Jones?" Amanda asked her, and she nodded. "We're detectives with the Prince William County PD. We have some questions pertaining to Michaela Glover."

The door was shut softly, and the chain was undone. This time Deana opened the door wide and gestured for them to come inside. Her place was the opposite image of what they saw at Nicole Holland's. What was utter chaos there was complete organization here. It was apparent that Deana assigned a place to everything. She took them to the kitchen table and invited Amanda and Trent to sit down. The living parts of the apartment were visible from here, and many of the walls were decorated with abstract paintings. While Amanda's knowledge of the art world was rather limited, they were eye-catching and vibrant, and each piece conveyed emotion.

"I'm going to assume that you heard about your friend Michaela Glover?" Amanda was basing this on Deana's willingness to open her home upon mention of Michaela's name. She also purposely framed it to sound as if the friends hadn't had a falling out.

"I did." Deana rubbed her arms. "I can't believe she's gone."

"You sent her flowers yesterday," Amanda said nonchalantly. "That was nice of you."

"I guess."

That response had the skin tightening on the back of Amanda's neck. "What do you mean by that?"

"Just that it was too little too late." A tear snaked down her cheek, which she let drip off her jaw unabashed.

"You two have a falling out?" Amanda was curious if she'd admit to as much.

"You could say that. She just didn't have time for me anymore. She had dreams, and they didn't include me."

Amanda hadn't expected this admission would come so easily or so quickly. "That must have hurt."

"It did. We were friends since kindergarten."

Amanda had a best friend like that. Becky Tulson, who worked as an officer with the Dumfries PD.

"You said it hurt, but you don't sound too upset now," Trent said, as he readied his tablet to take notes.

"I moved on, but it took a while. I was a skater too up until she left for Colorado Springs. When our friendship ended, so did my skating."

"Oh?" Amanda found that curious. If Michaela's actions had discouraged Deana from pursuing her goals, that could be seen as motive for murder. Had she ordered the flowers and a card to give the impression she'd moved on, when in fact, she had killed her former friend? It was possible that Deana saw this as an alibi of sorts.

"Trust me. I was ticked off at first when she left me to pursue her dream. But what hurt the most was she told me if I wasn't serious about skating to give it up and make way for people who were."

Trent winced. "Ouch."

"Oh, it hurt until I realized she was right. That's why I sent her the flowers. I was hoping we could make up or, at least, put the past behind us. But more than anything I wanted to thank her."

"Thank her?" Amanda said slowly.

"Uh-huh. I was skating for my parents and because it was what I knew. But her words challenged me, and once I left the sport, I had time to discover that my true passion was art." Her gaze briefly danced over to a teal and gold painting on the far wall of the dining area.

Amanda nudged her head toward it. "You painted that?"

"Yes. I know it's not very good, but I love it."

"I think it's beautiful." Amanda would proudly display the piece in her home.

"Thank you." Deana's cheeks flushed at the compliment.

While the exchange held a genuine feel to it, Amanda never lost sight of the fact that Deana could have killed Michaela and rehearsed her answers if the police came to her door. "There was a card with the flowers that said, 'You'll be sorry you turned your back on me after all I did for you.' Why would you send that?" She was stretching things somewhat but was interested in the reaction she'd get.

Deana's eyes widened and filled with tears. "What? That's not my note."

"You're sure? It was found with her." Amanda made it sound as if it had accompanied the flowers.

"I had the flower shop send a note, but that's not what I asked for."

"What then?" Trent asked.

"One second." Deana got up from the table and opened a file on a desk in the corner of the living room. "Here it is." She returned and gave a printout to Trent.

He looked at it, then Deana. "Where would I find the message for the card?"

Deana stood over his shoulder and pointed at the page. "Right here."

Trent read it off, "'I wish you gold, love Deana.'" He set the printout on the table and looked at Amanda. His eyes were saying what she was thinking. That message was a far cry from the one that was on the note next to Michaela's body.

Amanda had one theory on where Deana's card might be, but she'd discuss that with Trent back in the car. "Just a few more questions. We found this among Michaela's things." She pulled out her phone and brought up the picture she'd taken of the crescent moon pendant. "Does this look familiar to you?"

"No, but is that emerald? That's Michaela's birthstone."

Since they had been friends, it was understandable that Deana knew that. "Would you know where she would have gotten this?"

Deana shook her head. "As I said, we haven't spoken for over two years."

"Then you wouldn't know if she had a boyfriend in her life?" Amanda volleyed back.

"I don't."

"Did you see her when she came home a couple of years ago?" The grandmother's death was only about six months after Michaela had left for Colorado Springs, and the friends had more recently parted ways. It was entirely possible the funeral could have brought them together briefly.

"For her grandmother's funeral?" Deana sniffled. "No, I didn't go. I was still hurt and angry back then. I know this sounds horrible."

It was said death had the power to help people set aside their differences, but that all depended on how deep they ran. Some could be a tall feat to simply release. Deana's admission didn't make her any more suspect in Amanda's mind, but there were still questions that needed answers. "Why specify the delivery time between one and two PM?"

"I figured that would be around intermission so she could enjoy them before the second half."

"Were you at the show yesterday afternoon?" Trent asked.

"I wasn't. I sat with my neighbor's two-year-old for a bit of cash."

"We'll need her apartment number and name," Amanda told her.

"Sure. Just next door on the left, and it's Karen."

"Thank you, and we're sorry for your loss." Unless Deana was a good actor, Amanda was willing to bet her alibi would support her claim.

They quickly asked Deana if she had any idea who might

want to harm Michaela. The young woman broke down crying and shook her head.

After seeing themselves out, they went next door and found Karen with a toddler on her hip. The child's cheeks were red and tear-streaked. They'd clearly come on the tail end of a tantrum. The woman herself looked rattled. They introduced themselves and asked if she could verify Deana's alibi, which she did without hesitation.

Back in the car, Trent slid behind the wheel and Amanda got situated in the passenger seat.

"That girl didn't do this," Trent said.

"I don't think so either. I got the feeling she genuinely credits Michaela for helping her find her path in life."

"All right, so all this time pursuing the flower delivery was a waste of time, it would seem."

"We had to see it through, and now we know there should have been two cards in Michaela's dressing room."

"Right. So where is the one from Deana?"

"My theory? The killer took it with them."

"Why though?"

"The note we have paints someone who was bitter with Michaela. Now imagine how they'd feel if they read Deana's words, 'Wish you gold.'"

"Pissed off, I'd wager."

"They could have snatched the card in a rage."

"It would further support the killer was in the dressing room after the flowers were dropped off."

"Which I don't think was ever in question. But now we can run on the theory that it's most likely the card found with Michaela's body had accompanied the roses with the black ribbon. We need to figure out where they came from. Whether it pays off or not, it's time to speak with Michaela's ex-boyfriend, Wendell Smith, and see what he has to say."

TWENTY-FIVE

"I heard about Michaela. Now the news is saying it was murder?" Wendell Smith was tall and lean like a basketball player. He might only need to stand on his tiptoes to reach the net. He couldn't be described as merely *above average height* by anyone's estimation, telling Amanda he wasn't the mystery man who had showed up at Lux Suites for Michaela.

Amanda and Trent were in Wendell's living room, where he plucked a toss pillow off a stuffed chair and sat down. He gestured for them to sit as well.

"It's all unbelievable. No one deserves that, least of all Mick. She was a star, not just on the ice. Her eyes sparkled when she put on a pair of skates, though, I tell ya. I feel for her auntie and her brother, but I've moved on. We were over a long time ago. I'm engaged now actually. The wedding is this April."

"Congratulations." She meant it, but his upcoming nuptials alone didn't release him from suspicion. The fact that he pulled out her nickname denoted a familiarity that he still clung to. Whether that meant he was carrying a torch for his old flame remained to be seen. On base value, she'd say he'd moved on, but it was far too soon to conclude that with any certainty. As for being over a long time ago, it was only two and half years ago when Michaela moved to Colorado Springs. Not exactly a huge span of time, but longer in the eyes of a twenty-something.

"Thanks. Anne's a great woman."

"And where is she now?" Trent asked.

"She's out with her girlfriends for lunch."

It felt like forever since Amanda had a girls' night out with her best friend, Becky. Amanda's schedule was stuffed with work and home life, just as Malone had pointed out. That didn't leave time to play. In that vein, what was Logan thinking to suggest another child? At least Becky's life had some semblance of predictability. She remained at uniformed officer rank with no desire to advance from there. She liked her set hours and typically got her dose of chaos through her love life. Though that had settled down in the last few years. Becky was seeing an FBI agent, and Amanda wondered if she'd ever get the call that they were taking the next step. She'd settle for cohabiting. "Nice for her. We found this among Michaela's things." She brought up a photograph of the pendant on her phone and walked over to Wendell. "Does this look familiar to you?" She held her screen so he could see it.

"I've seen it before in a jewelry store. I'm quite sure it was a few hundred dollars. It only stood out to me because I knew that Mick would love it. She always had a thing for crescent moons."

A few hundred dollars... "Did you buy it for her?"

"No, that was more than I was willing to spend."

"Then you were shopping for her?" Trent asked, beating Amanda to it.

Wendell sucked in his bottom lip, then shoved it out. "Yeah, I had this brilliant idea to win her back when she returned for her grandmother's funeral. I didn't end up going through with it. Who knows how things might have turned out for us if I had just bought it for her?"

Amanda would wager Michaela would have turned him away. It was rather insensitive to attempt reconciliation at a funeral, while also understandable. Something about death reminded the living there was only so much time left. "What store was this?" If they had that, they might get a lead on who bought it.

"Sorry, but I can't remember that. Quite sure it was in town though."

There were only a couple of jewelry stores in Woodbridge, so they could follow this through. "What was so special about crescent moons for her?"

"I never really knew. Why? Do you think it matters?" He nudged his head toward Amanda's phone as she pulled it back and returned to the chair she'd been seated in prior.

"I think it matters that someone mailed it to her from Woodbridge." She let that tidbit hang out there, while trying to read Wendell for any visual response. If he had any further knowledge about the pendant, he gave nothing away. "Do you know who might have sent her such a thing?"

"Hard to say. But it seems like something her aunt might send her."

"It wasn't her," Amanda said.

"Then I'm sorry, but I have no idea."

A few hundred dollars... The thought repeated. It was too much to spend if Michaela didn't mean something to the sender. Had it been from a love interest? That could gel with the note it was with. *You shine like the star next to the moon. I see you, as does the whole world.*

"Why did things end between you?" Trent asked, clearly wanting to hear the reason straight from the source.

"She said she didn't really have time for our relationship anymore. Her love affair was with skating."

"That must have stung," Trent said.

"It did for a while. I really thought we were headed toward

the altar. I should have known though. Michaela had always been obsessed with skating and improving her skill. Up against that, I didn't stand a chance. I see that more clearly looking back."

Amanda noted how he'd dropped the abbreviation and returned to using her full name. She suspected he was purposely distancing himself from her. Self-preservation possibly from sensing where the conversation was heading. It did seem like he'd moved on fairly quickly and it was hard to believe all his feelings for Michaela had just disappeared. "Did you catch her show yesterday?"

"No, I didn't get there. I was out shopping with Anne."

Amanda leaned forward. "What time was this?"

"Around one thirty or so. Nothing exciting, just groceries."

She and Trent could go to the trouble of finding out where they shopped and confirming they were there, but he didn't raise her suspicions enough to bother. "Before we go, Mr. Smith, two more questions. When did you last speak with Michaela?"

"When she left for Colorado Springs."

"Then you never tried to convince her to take you back?" Trent asked.

"I thought about it around the time her grandmother died, like I said. But in the end I didn't see the point. Her mind was made up."

"Do you think she met someone new?" The question might provoke a reaction or get her the identity of the mystery man. Either would pay off.

"I doubt that. Her life was skating, and that's all she wanted."

"Do you know anyone who hated Michaela enough to kill her?" Trent asked.

"No, not at all. That's why all of this is such a huge freaking shock. She had a way of lighting up a room. And this smile, ya know, that could just..." His eyes glazed over.

Amanda might be extending too much trust without grounds. "Where did you shop for groceries?"

"Corey's Grocery. Why?" He narrowed his eyes.

"Just due diligence." She gave him a pressed-lip smile but was pleased he was ready with his answer. It struck her as the truth.

"You can't seriously think that I... that I...?" Wendell stuttered. "No way. No way," he repeated and slapped a hand to his leg.

"Why react so strongly?" She counteracted her words with a calm manner.

"You're basically accusing me of killing someone I used to love."

Used to... Even hopped-up on emotion he clarified his feelings for Michaela were in the past. She didn't think there was much point in pursuing this angle any further. Verifying his alibi would be a time drain and pointless. She stood. "Sorry for your loss, and we appreciate your cooperation."

Back in the car, Trent got it started and looked over at her. "For what it's worth, I don't see him doing this."

"Me either. That's why I called an end to our chat. He's moved on, and he was brutally honest with us. He even admitted to seeing the pendant before. A few hundred dollars is a significant value for a gift."

"I'd thought the same thing. Do you think we're looking at another love interest? The mystery man from the hotel or someone else?"

"Either is possible. Whoever it is must have known it would mean something to Michaela with her apparent love for crescent moons and the emerald being her birthstone."

"Except here she is lugging it around inside her suitcase.

She even had it in the envelope it supposedly came in. Why? Was the affection unreciprocated?"

"But then, if it didn't mean anything to her why lug it here?"

"To give it back to the sender when she returned to Woodbridge?"

"Hmm. Or are we looking at this all wrong? It might not have anything to do with romantic feelings. It could have been platonic or professional." Her eyes widened. "Tara Coolidge lives in Woodbridge. She'd have more than enough money to afford such a gift. And if there was more tension between her and Michaela than she let on, she could have tried to buy her loyalty."

"Except you're forgetting her handwriting isn't a match to the card or the note with the jewelry. And we're without a motive for her."

"I still say we go have another chat with her. See if she knows anything about it and where Michaela might have gotten it. On another note, what if Tara Coolidge was the reason Michaela wasn't looking forward to coming home? We might just need to dig deeper to explain the difference in the hand-writing and to discover her motive."

"We might. That fails, and we can also pop into the jewelry stores in town and see if they can tell us who bought the neck-lace and pendant."

"You bet." Amanda's mind was spinning. What if it was Michaela's agent all along? She was the last one seen with Michaela while she was alive, and she even admitted to being in her dressing room within the time-of-death window. Had they rushed to dismiss these things?

TWENTY-SIX

It was mid-afternoon when Amanda walked up the path to Tara Coolidge's front door. Trent was beside her, and their strides were both marked by determination. Their minds were open coming here. They hoped Tara could prove useful to the investigation, but it was entirely possible she had killed Michaela and they had yet to find motive and evidence.

Tara's house was the block over from where Katherine Graves lived in her huge two-story home. She hadn't bought it on a cop's salary, but sadly from her mother's life insurance policy. It was also a purchase in honor of her memory because her mother had always wanted a big home. She was murdered before she realized that dream.

Amanda went to knock, but the door gave way. She glanced at Trent, and they both prepared to draw their weapons. "Tara Coolidge," Amanda called out. "Prince William County PD."

She was met by silence. That contradicted the car in the driveway telling her someone should be home.

Pushing the door open the rest of the way, the faint odor of blood hit her nose. "Oh, this isn't good."

"I smell it too."

They slowly treaded down the hallway going deeper into the house. She repeated her callout, but there was no response. She ducked into the living room. Couch pillows and throws were strewn around the room. Books had been pulled from built-in shelving and littered the hardwood.

But she went cold at the sight in the middle of the room.

Tara Coolidge was lying face down in a pool of deep crimson.

Next to her was a marble-base table lamp covered in blood.

"I'll call it in." Trent pulled his phone.

Amanda took in the scene in front of her. They'd come here considering Tara might actually be Michaela's killer, and now she was dead. What the hell was going on?

She asked that question repeatedly for the next few minutes.

"Everyone's on their way," Trent said after finishing the slew of calls. Before pocketing his phone, he looked at it. A few seconds later, he said, "I've got an email from the judge's office. All the warrants are approved."

She nodded. It was good news, but they were too busy to serve any of them now.

"I'd say that Coolidge didn't go down without a fight." Trent gestured toward the ransacked room.

"Too bad it wasn't enough." Amanda felt faint. The blood was deeply colored, and its surface appeared tacky. She'd been dead for a while. Probably since last night or early that morning. If they had held her longer, would that have made a difference to her fate? "She's dressed in the clothes she was in yesterday when we spoke with her."

"Maybe her rush to leave was because she was expecting someone."

"Could have been. But who and why?"

"And how does this advance either investigation? We

thought Tara may have been Michaela's killer, but how does that result in her murder?"

"I don't really know. I mean, unless we weren't alone in our suspicions. We could be looking at someone who killed her in retribution."

"So you're suggesting someone killed Coolidge for killing Michaela?" Trent blew out a breath. "Convoluted but, yes, it's possible."

"It's just one of those things. We need more before we can attach ourselves to any one theory. Let's take a look around the place before everyone else gets here."

Trent pulled two pairs of booties out of a coat pocket and extended one pair to her, but she shook her head.

"I'm prepared today." She plucked a pair from a pocket and put them on over her boots.

They worked to clear the main level, going down a long hallway past a two-piece bathroom to a formal dining room and a kitchen with an eat-in table and peninsula. The countertops were glistening white granite with a blue marbling that ran across the surface like an ocean wave. It would seem Tara did quite well for herself financially. Amanda commented on as much to Trent.

"She couldn't have been that bad of an agent like Lilian Berry had suggested."

"Or her income was aided by her work as a coach."

She pushed on a door in the kitchen and revealed a walk-in pantry. It was neat and orderly, undisturbed. On the way back to the front of the house, they stopped at another room. It clearly served as a home office, and it was in complete disarray. The bi-fold closet doors were wide open, and papers and stationery of all sorts were spewed onto the floor in front of it.

"I'd say whoever killed her was looking for something," Trent said.

"Uh-huh. But what?" She set the rhetorical question out

there as she walked toward the closet to get a look inside. An organization unit filled the space, but it was empty. The fabric totes from each cube were pulled and thrown into the middle of the room. But it was what was tucked into the corner that caught her attention. "Trent, look."

Trent came up beside her, his shoulder grazing hers, and she stepped aside a few inches. She pointed at the small safe with a combination keypad.

"It could contain what the killer was after," he said. "But would that suggest this was a more random thing? That Coolidge was the victim of a home invasion and robbery and not targeted? It seems like that would be rather coincidental considering how closely connected she is to another recent murder."

"There's that. But if the killer was after something inside the safe, they'd need to know it was there in the first place."

"Was the killer close to her?"

Amanda shrugged. Their first theory had been that Tara was killed out of revenge, but her ransacked house suggested something else. Was it possible they were looking at a few things here? She let her gaze linger on the safe. "I wonder if the killer got what they were after."

"The door's shut, but it's possible. We'll get someone in to crack the safe. Have anyone on speed dial?" He turned to her, a hopeful expression on his face, but she shook her head.

"I'll call Malone." She returned to the hallway and made the call to their sergeant.

"Tell me you've got a suspect."

"That's one way of answering the phone," she said. "But not exactly." She brought him up to speed.

"What do you think we're looking at here?"

"Still not entirely sure. Trent and I were starting to suspect the agent again. We tossed around the possibility of a revenge killing, someone getting payback thinking she took out

Michaela. But then there's the ransacked house and that safe..."

"You're thinking a fatal home robbery then?"

"I'm not sold on that either. It just feels too coincidental. I suppose it could have been staged to make it look that way." This revelation hit as she was speaking to Malone, and it had Trent turning to look at her.

"You need in that safe," Malone said.

"We do. Know anyone who could help with that?"

"I'll find a locksmith and send them your way."

"Thanks."

"Don't mention it. I'll be over soon myself."

"Talk later then." She ended the call and told Trent that Malone was on his way.

They continued their tour of the home, heading to the second story. Three bedrooms and two bathrooms. One was an ensuite to the primary. None of the rooms were tossed. The intruder had limited their search to the main level and stopped when they found the safe. Or had they gotten inside and taken what they were after? And how did any of this result in Tara Coolidge's murder?

TWENTY-SEVEN

Amanda could only watch helplessly as time flew by. They had found Tara Coolidge mid-afternoon, but now it was going on four thirty. Ever since the CSIs showed up, things were kicked into high gear. They were processing the living room around Tara's body while Amanda and Trent talked out possibilities. They had already confirmed that there were no obvious signs of forced entry.

"Maybe this is like we thought earlier. Coolidge was expecting someone, and that's why she was in a hurry to leave the arena," Trent suggested.

"But this person showed up, killed her, then ransacked her house? For what purpose? What were they after?"

"It's hard to know what Coolidge was into. She was acting rather secretive and coy yesterday."

Amanda was about to respond when Malone stepped into the entry.

"Detectives," he said as a greeting, followed by, "How does this keep happening to you guys? You follow a lead and find a fresh body."

"I wish I had the answer to that one." They did seem to get their fair share of surprises during their investigations.

"The locksmith should be here soon. Show me the scene."

She walked the few steps from the entry to the living room and gestured for him to look through the doorway.

"Cause of death appears obvious," Malone said. "And the place is a mess. It could have been a home invasion."

"Except for now we know there are no signs of forced entry," Trent countered, sharing what the CSIs had told them paired with their own observations.

"Do you think her murder is connected to Michaela's?"

"It feels like it should be." Even as Amanda said this, she questioned her resolve. Aside from the fact both victims had a relationship, a striking similarity wasn't plainly obvious. One had ingested peanut oil and from the looks of this murder scene, blunt force trauma was responsible for the agent's death.

"Yet, you don't think they are?" Malone asked, raising his eyebrows, and Trent looked at her.

"I feel they must be, but I'm not sure how they connect yet. Trent and I felt Coolidge was withholding from us when we spoke with her yesterday. It's hard to say if that's what resulted in her murder."

"Someone called for the A-team?" Rideout said from the front door.

Amanda turned to see the medical examiner and Liam decked out in protective gear ready to get to work. "She's in there." She pointed toward the living room, and Trent and Malone filed out of the doorway.

"Thank ya, thank ya very much," Rideout said, putting on a poor Elvis impression as he brushed past. "You ready for me?" he asked CSI Donnelly, who was still in the room.

"You bet." Donnelly walked past him and Liam approached Amanda. She was holding a cell phone in gloved hands. It was inside a blue case, worn some on the spine. "I found this under the couch. I'm thinking it fell under there during a struggle."

"It's Tara's." Amanda recognized the frayed edge from when the agent took it out to show them her EpiPen. She remembered being surprised she didn't have a shiny new one. But if Tara and Michaela shared the same killer, why take one phone and not the other? She had considered there might be something on Michaela's phone the killer didn't want police to find, but maybe it was just about cutting off that lifeline. Then again, maybe the killer couldn't find Tara's or ran out of time. Regardless, they needed access to Tara's communications. "Can we get into it?"

"I've tried a few tricks." Donnelly made a squeamish face, and Amanda could guess what one was.

"You tried the vic's fingerprint?" she asked.

The CSI nodded. "But it requires a passcode."

Amanda turned to Trent. "We'll need to get it to Digital Forensics, see what they can do with it. Could you get a bag for it?" she asked Donnelly.

"Sure can." Donnelly set out across the room to her collection kit.

Digital Forensics was a division of the Prince William County PD that handled all things technology. They had wizards on staff who conjured deleted data, unlocked devices, unblocked numbers and tracked them. Their expertise probably entailed more than that.

"You guys want to take it over, or would you like me to handle it?" Malone asked.

"Hey, if you want to drop it off, go for it. Just request that Detective Jacob Briggs process it and ask that he send me updates." She had a lot of respect for Jacob, and he'd helped her and Trent many times in the past.

"Uh-huh."

She might have pushed it by asking so much. At least Malone took the bagged phone from Donnelly.

Amanda looked at Rideout, who was now hunched next to Tara's body.

"She's been dead less than twenty-four hours, but her body is well into rigor," he said, as if he could sense her questioning eyes on him.

"She left the arena last night at approximately ten thirty," Amanda told him.

"Then I'd wager it wasn't long after that. Probably no later than midnight."

Amanda turned to Trent. "So she came straight home and had a visitor."

"Which I've been thinking about more since we've been hanging around," Trent began. "It looks like she was killed by being hit on the head—"

"I thought cause of death was a determination that was mine to make," Rideout cut in.

Trent held up a hand. "Not an official call, just a hunch based on what I see."

Rideout mumbled something and put his gaze back on the body.

Trent turned to Amanda and added, "I was just going to say that it looks like she was killed with a weapon of convenience."

"Good point." Amanda wished she'd landed on that herself. "It's also possible this person didn't intend to kill Tara. It could have been an argument that got out of hand. The person struck her and what…? Took advantage of her being dead and thought they'd see if they could make off with something of value?"

"I still think they came here for something," Trent said. "If the struggle took place here, that may explain why it's tossed upside down, but that doesn't account for the home office looking like a tornado cut through."

"There's no question she was hit with a blunt object," Rideout interjected. "Most likely this bloody lamp, if you ask me." He smiled at his own poor imitation of a British accent. "And the wound is deep, possibly enough so to cause death. She was struck on the back of the head."

"Caught unaware?" Malone asked.

"I'm not sure about that. She does have scratches on her hands indicative of defensive wounds. We better bag them. If she did fight back, we might get epithelial." Rideout gestured for Liam to handle that, as he got to his feet.

Amanda pieced together a possible scenario in her head. Tara and her assailant got into a physical struggle. The scattered items in the room supported that. Then at one point Tara goes to make a move on her visitor, who then grabs whatever they can to defend themselves. They snatch the marble table lamp and hit Tara on the head. If it had ended there, it would have been a possible case of self-defense. Unless this person had no right to be in Tara's home. They had assumed the search of the house came after, but what if Tara had interrupted a robbery in progress? Though how would that explain the fight taking place in the living room, not the office?

There was a knock on the front door as it swung open. Amanda, Trent, and Malone turned toward a man dressed in black jeans and a winter coat. He had a baseball cap on his head with the logo of H&M's Locksmith embroidered in gold thread.

"Sergeant Malone called for a locksmith..." The man's brow creased as he took them in.

"That would be me," Malone said and looked at Amanda and Trent for directions.

"This way," she said. "Just don't look into the—"

"Dear God." The man stopped walking outside the living room doorway. He covered his mouth, but it didn't stop his cheeks from puffing out like he was going to be sick.

Her warning had apparently been too slow coming.

"Let's just keep moving." Trent put a guiding arm on the man's shoulder.

The locksmith didn't move for a few beats but stood there drawing deep breaths. Finally he straightened up. "Okay, I'm good now." He shook his shoulders and stretched his neck.

They showed him to the safe in the home office. "How long do you expect it should take?" she asked him.

"It's not high-end, so not too long."

"Which translates to?" Everyone had a different idea of what *not too long* was.

"An hour maybe."

"Okay." That answer was rather disappointing. Especially when it seemed like Tara's killer had been searching for something and had made their way all the way to the safe, if not inside. Amanda gave the man her business card, and she, Trent, and Malone stepped into the hall.

"You planning to step out?" Malone asked her.

"Yeah. Tara Coolidge told Trent and I that she grabbed drinks yesterday afternoon at the Tipsy Moose Alehouse. I think it would be a good idea for us to verify that alibi. Last steps and all..."

"You back to thinking she killed Michaela, and someone took her out for that reason?" Trent asked.

She shook her head. "I'm not convinced of that. In fact, it's too soon to know motive. But if we can confirm she went out for drinks, it's just one thing checked off our list. We need to find out what exact time she was there."

"Though she already put herself in Michaela's dressing room around her time of death," Trent pointed out.

"Minutes count." She wasn't saying as much out loud, but her own conscience wanted appeasement. Proving Tara hadn't hung around the arena waiting for Michaela to die would go a long way.

"Sure, if you think it would help. Let's go."

"Why not just drop off the phone on your way by?" Malone held out his arm, and she took the bag from him.

As she walked away, she was thinking when it rains, it does indeed pour. They started the day with one homicide to solve, and now they had two.

TWENTY-EIGHT

Amanda went into Digital Forensics while Trent waited in the car. She introduced herself at reception and added, "Could you see that this gets to Detective Briggs the minute he gets in?" She lifted the evidence bag with Tara's phone inside. Briggs was a pleasant man who was always eager to help, but he typically worked the night shift, and it was only four forty-five in the afternoon.

The woman sitting there looked at it. "Sure. Not a problem."

"And pass on the message that it belongs to a murder victim."

"Will do."

"What time do you expect him tonight?"

The woman tapped on the keyboard in front of her. "Seven."

"Okay. Thanks."

"If you're in a hurry, I can have another detective take a look at it."

"That's fine. Detective Briggs is worth the wait."

"You bet."

Amanda turned to leave, confident in her decision to let it sit for Briggs. He was masterful at what he did, and her gut was telling her not to chance it with someone else. She got back to the department car and spotted Trent through the windshield. He was on the phone and smiling. She caught the last few words of his conversation as she got in the car.

"It's going to be great... We're going to love it. Love *you*."

He had ended the call by the time her butt touched the passenger seat.

"Kelsey?" she said, feeling her cheeks heat and hating herself for it.

"Yeah." He smiled at her.

"She seems to make you happy. It's nice to see." She tried to smile, but she was quite certain her mouth wasn't cooperating. It felt like her words, though offered in sincerity, fell flat.

"She does. We seem like a good match." He put the car into gear, and got them on the road toward the Tipsy Moose Alehouse.

Just when she didn't think her mind could entertain any more random thoughts, some took her back to when Trent had shared taking Kelsey home to meet his family for the first time. He'd been beaming as he told her. Often there was an underlying darkness in his eyes, but it was completely gone when he spoke about this relationship. He'd been so happy to announce that everyone loved her too. *Too.* One powerful little word, and it clung like a burr to the back of her brain. She wanted him to be happy, to find love, but she couldn't ignore the twinge of jealousy she felt. Despite having no right to feel that way.

"You're awfully quiet over there. What happened anyhow?"

"Where? Oh, at Digital Forensics?" He nodded, and she said, "Nothing much. Briggs is in at seven, and I asked that the phone be handed over to him."

"Cool."

Cool? Maybe her awkwardness was latching on to him. She didn't remember ever hearing him say that word before.

Trent pulled into the packed parking lot for the Tipsy Moose Alehouse. If the doors were open, the place was busy.

"Pity us for coming close to the dinner hour," Trent said as he squeezed the car in a slot between a dually Ford pickup on the passenger side and a Mercedes G-Wagon on the driver's side.

"Yeah, just watch your door." She credited her older brother, Kyle, for knowing this Mercedes was rather upgraded and probably encroaching on a value in the mid six-figures.

"You're telling me. That thing must be worth a lot."

"You don't want to know." They walked toward the restaurant, and something Trent said sank in. *Dinner hour.* She looked at the time on her phone. *4:50 PM.* She'd told Zoe she'd do her best to make it to her parents' house tonight for the family meal at six. In fairness, that promise came before another body turned up, but still, she'd like to keep her word. At worst, she'd slip over to eat and return to work after.

Trent got the door for her, and the two of them entered the restaurant. Music poured out of the speakers but didn't drown out the possibility for conversation. It was one aspect of the place that kept Amanda returning. The other was they had great food, and she respected the owner, Alex Hurley aka Moose.

"Hey, Amanda, Trent." Mallory, a young server, came to the host stand and plucked two menus. "Just the two of you?"

The simplicity and ease of her inquiry had Amanda feeling like she'd stepped into another reality. One where she and Trent were a couple out for a meal. They'd eaten here together before but always as partners.

Trent looked at Amanda. "We weren't eating, right?"

She shook her head, contradicting her previous advice to him. As she put it to him, being a customer first made it more likely servers or management would talk. Tonight, she had her mother's roast beef dinner ahead of her. Even still, the smells of garlic and pasta and burgers were tantalizing.

"Oh, police business then?" Mallory had just returned the menus to their slot as the door chimed with new customers. She looked around Amanda and Trent. "Just let me seat them, okay?"

"Sure," Amanda said.

Mallory set off with the group of four and returned a moment later and let out a deep exhale.

"Busy day?" Trent asked her.

"When isn't it? So, if you're not eating, what can I do for you guys?"

"Were you working yesterday afternoon by chance?" Amanda thought she'd give it a try.

Mallory pressed her lips and shook her head. "The one day I wasn't working."

"All good. And the person who was...?" she asked.

"Not in today."

"What about the bartender who was working then?" They could ask to see their video too, but Amanda was hoping someone here would identify Tara from her photograph and save her and Trent the trouble.

"Bud is here. You can go on through."

"Thanks," Amanda told her. She was cringing inside though. Years ago, when Bud was new, Amanda had put on the act of damsel in distress. It wasn't a moment she was particularly proud of, but needs must. She had to find Logan to back up her alibi. At that time, Logan was nothing but a nameless one-night stand.

"Don't mention it."

The door chimed again, and more people filtered in.

"How many..."

The noise of the dining patrons and the music crowded out

Mallory's voice as Amanda and Trent moved toward the bar. Bud was behind the counter with a woman who was running around making sure the bottles were topped up and garnishes were ready to go. She wasn't familiar to Amanda, which meant she was probably new. That hunch was supported by the fact she ran into Bud's back and flushed red at the misstep.

Bud saw Amanda and smiled, showing off his deep-set dimples. She and Trent had just claimed a square at the counter. Bud set down two cardboard coasters advertising some local brewery and put out a small bowl of mixed nuts.

"What's your poison, guys?" he asked.

"Duty calls." For years after losing her family to a drunk driver, Amanda wouldn't touch alcohol. In the last year or so, she drank the occasional beer or glass of wine but never on the clock.

"I had a feeling you were going to say that." Bud cleared the space again. "I also suspect you're here to talk to me. So hit me."

Trent had his tablet pulled out already and Amanda caught Tara's license photo on the screen. He showed it to Bud. "Do you recognize her?"

"Tara? Yeah, of course. She comes in fairly often. What about her?"

Trent put his tablet away. "Was she in yesterday afternoon?"

Bud bunched up his forehead and pressed his lips, then shook his head. "Not yesterday."

"You're sure about that?" Amanda asked. "Say in the afternoon from about two or so?"

"Don't know what else to tell ya. She wasn't here."

"Maybe she sat at a table or booth?" Trent said.

Bud shook his head. "Not possible. It wasn't that busy yesterday afternoon between two to four. I would have seen her in the dining room." His gaze traveled past them, but Amanda didn't need to turn to see where he was looking. She had the layout of the place memorized. The bar area extended out and met the dining area. There weren't any walls to block the view.

"Excuse me." Bud's coworker came up next to him. Her blond hair was pulled back, and she had that healthy glow of youth. She was maybe twenty-two years old. She smiled at Amanda and Trent.

Bud turned to her. "Yes, Claudia?"

"That guy over there needs his check." She leaned in closer to Bud. "Apparently, yesterday."

Bud smiled, and told her, "Tell him, I'll be right there."

"Okay." The woman left, and Bud jacked a thumb over his shoulder.

"Unless there's anything else...?"

"Nope, that's all. Thanks." The expression of gratitude was relatively flatline. He just gave her and Trent another mystery to solve.

They returned to the car, and Trent got the heat going. At least they weren't gone for long, so it hadn't fully cooled down yet.

"So if Coolidge wasn't here, where was she?" Trent asked.

"And does this mean she did murder Michaela?" So much for appeasing her conscience by coming here. The trip just confirmed it was possible Tara was a killer. "And if it wasn't that, what really had her leaving the arena before the show ended?" It was just a burning hunch in Amanda's gut that getting this answer was imperative to solving both murders. Amanda's phone rang, and she caught the time on the dash before picking up. It was getting closer to six when she would be expected at her parents' table.

"It's Logan. Just a heads-up. I had that talk with Zoe about Michaela, and she handled it quite well."

"Did she go quiet or start playing in her room?" Both were telltale signs she wasn't dealing well at all.

"She was quiet for a bit and pulled out her coloring book."

So she's quite upset... "I'll talk with her as soon as I can. See if I can help her feel any better."

"That's soon, I hope. I'm currently in one of the bathrooms at your parents' house, and your mother is going a little nuts. She says an investigation is a poor excuse to miss dinner with everyone, and she expects you here in fifteen minutes."

Amanda laughed thinking about Logan hiding from her mother. Her call waiting notified her there was another incoming call. She didn't need psychic abilities to predict who was on the other end of the line. "She's calling me now. I'm not going to answer."

"Mandy, don't do this to me. Tell me you're coming."

"I'll be there in Mother's mandated fifteen minutes. See you soon." She ended the call. Sure enough the screen was flashing her mother's name. *To answer or not to answer...* She smiled at the silly turn of phrase that ran through her head. "Mom," she answered, and Jules set off into an excited babble. Amanda interrupted. "I'm on my way now." A slight exaggeration, but her mother didn't need to know that.

"You're... You are? Good." Her mother hung up, and Amanda was left holding the dead line.

She pulled her phone down and was smiling.

"I don't need to be a detective to figure out what just happened there." Trent was grinning.

"All right, wise guy, by all means..."

"First, it was Logan. Though I admit I could overhear him. He sounded rather amped up. Something to do with your Sunday family dinner?"

"Uh-huh. Keep going."

"The second call was your mother. I'm guessing Logan was worked up because she was on his case."

She laughed. "Something like that. You heard her too?"

He shook his head. "It was how you answered—"

"Mom," they said in unison.

"Right. I gave that one to you. And as much as I'd like to compliment your impressive detective skills, this little mystery was rather easy to untangle."

"It was. Now if only finding Michaela's and Tara's killer was that easy."

"Sadly, that's going to take a lot more work." Her phone rang again, and she let out a swear word but relaxed some as she screened the call. "It's Malone," she told Trent and answered on speaker. "Detective Steele. Trent's here too."

"Two things. Rideout finished up at the Coolidge crime scene, and he's doing the autopsy tomorrow morning first thing at eight."

"Okay, good to know." She was holding her breath anticipating what else he had to tell them. "And the second thing?"

"The locksmith got into the safe. There is a hundred and fifty K in cash in there."

Malone might as well have detonated a bomb. "You said a hundred and—"

"One-five-zero thousand."

"Holy hell." The house and neighborhood spoke to luxury, but that was still a lot of money to have just lying around. Amanda looked at Trent and found he was gazing back at her.

"What the hell would Tara Coolidge need with all that money?" he said.

"I'm quite sure that's your job to sort out," Malone volleyed back. "But CSI Blair found a banking slip in the office showing the withdrawal."

"When was it taken out?" Trent asked.

"Yesterday afternoon."

"That could explain where she really was," Amanda said to Trent. Then added for Malone, "She told us she was having drinks at the Tipsy Moose, but we just checked that out, and she never showed up yesterday at all." She caught the minute change over on the clock on the dash. *5:51 PM.*

"Sarge, I've got to pop out for an hour or two, but I'll pick up afterward."

"You better catch the Steele clan dinner, or you'll never hear the end of it," he said.

Apparently, everyone knows of the tradition... "You're telling me." She ended the call, and Trent had thankfully taken the initiative to get them on the road. Basic deduction told her she'd be really late if he took her to Central for her car. "Could you drop me off at my parents' place? That is if it's not a big deal. I assume you're going to break for dinner too. You could pick me up in an hour or so?"

"Yeah, I can do that." He smiled at her and got them headed to her parents' place.

Her mind was at the furthest possible point from making chitchat with her family. She had two murders to solve, both layered with mystery. And she was quite certain she lacked the puzzle pieces to see why a sports agent had a hundred and fifty K in her home safe.

TWENTY-NINE

Amanda had her hand on the car door, ready to leap out, as Trent pulled up in front of her parents' place. It was six ten, and her mother was going to give her grief. She ran Sunday night dinner like a military drill. Punctuality was demanded and expected. Trent hadn't fully stopped the vehicle when she unclipped her belt.

"Just wait until I come to a complete stop before parachuting out," Trent said, mimicking a ride operator. *Keep your arms and legs inside the vehicle at all times...*

He parked on the street behind Logan's truck. From the looks of it everyone had come tonight. The driveway was full. Even her sister Megan with her husband, Ray, were parked out front. They had a baby, Gabe, and sometimes life came up and they missed family dinner. But a packed house might mean she'd be able to sneak in unnoticed at first and surprise her mother.

"I want to get this over with so I can get back to work." She winced, realizing how horrible that sounded. In her defense, though, they'd just landed a second homicide in two days. Also the first twenty-four hours of an investigation were crucial. Her family, aside from her mother, might excuse her, but she'd essentially made a promise to her little girl.

"The investigation will be waiting for you. Just enjoy this time with your family."

"Thanks. What are you going to do?"

"Not sure. I'd pop home for an hour, but no one's there and my fridge is empty."

She looked at her partner, her friend, and had this nudge. But she wasn't so sure it was one she should listen to. Logan wasn't exactly a fan of Trent's, and he wouldn't be too happy to see him encroaching on personal terrain. Though surely, he could appreciate Trent needed to eat too. "Why don't you come in with me?"

"What? No." Trent shook his head, a silly smile touching his lips. "I'd be out of place."

"Nonsense. You're family to me." The words slipped out and shocked her as much as it must have him. His eyes widened slightly, and it felt like the air in the car grew thick and still. Quiet, so very quiet.

"If you're sure? I mean I could eat." He winced. "You don't think anyone would mind? Your mother?"

"She'll adjust." That's what she told Trent, even though she wasn't quite so confident in her mother's abilities to go with the flow. It wasn't exactly her strong suit. And maybe asking Trent to come inside with her was a tad selfish. With her partner at her arm, her mother would need to be nicer. She wouldn't be as likely to lash out at her for being late.

"All right." Trent turned off the car and beat her out of it.

They walked up to the front door, and she let them in. The door was unlocked, which Amanda should pick at seeing as her father was a former cop and should know better.

Inside the foyer, Amanda held a finger to her lips admonishing Trent to keep quiet as much as possible. As if they could just slink in unnoticed... But she'd prefer the next few minutes play out on her schedule. It was honestly surprising that no one came to the door yet. They must have been immersed in dinner, but it also sounded like little Gabe, the baby, was cranky. His cries were interspersed with the adults chipping in with advice on how to settle him down.

She shucked her shoes and coat, and Trent did the same. "Just don't look anyone straight in the eye," she teased, and he laughed.

"My God, it smells amazing in here."

"Do lots of that. Mom loves compliments on her cooking. It might help her forget I'm late and also brought another mouth to feed." She smiled at Trent and led the way deeper into the house toward the dining room.

Everyone froze and fell silent when she and Trent hit the doorway. Even Gabe had quieted. Her stomach sank at the sight of Logan standing next to her sister holding on to the baby. He had been rocking him in his arms, side to side, but upon seeing her and Trent, stopped. He met her gaze, and his jaw clenched. He handed Gabe back to his mother and sat down.

The tension was palpable. Asking Trent might have been a bad idea, after all. But she was just being a good person by inviting him to dinner. Asking him was the nice thing to do, the *right* thing. She'd repeat that until it sank in.

"Trent!" Zoe popped up from her chair and ran across the room to hug him. She had been seated at the kids' table with Amanda's three nieces and one nephew, though they were all teenagers.

Amanda cringed inwardly at her daughter's reaction to Trent. The betrayal played across Logan's face, but the subtle twitch of his lips revealed another emotion. Anger. Possibly jealousy. She turned away, hating to see he was feeling either when it wasn't necessary.

"Hey, Zoe." Trent met the girl with equal exuberance and hugged her back, mussed her blond curls.

She was giggling despite not being a fan of that anymore. Her mood there could be hit or miss. Sometimes when Amanda did it, she'd get a scolding for messing up her hair. It gave her insight into what Zoe might be like as a teenager. But the way time flew by, she'd find out soon enough.

"Excuse me," Amanda said. "What about me?"

Zoe started to skip back toward the kids' table but swiveled around. "What about you?" She chuckled and hugged Amanda and gave her a big wet and loud kiss on the cheek.

The girl started to pull back, but Amanda held on just a few seconds longer. At least she seemed okay for now. She'd save the talk about Michaela for a more suitable time. "Okay, off you go," Amanda told her.

Zoe returned to her meal, picking at the beef with her fingers.

"You're here, but you're late," her mother said, with far less animosity than would have been the case if she'd been alone.

"I got here as fast as I could. I hope you don't mind that I brought my partner, Trent. But we caught a new case this afternoon, and if I was going to make it tonight, well..."

"The more the merrier," her brother, Kyle, chortled.

He was the royal shit disturber of the family, with Amanda a close second. They all knew their mother didn't adapt well to last-minute changes.

"I'll get you a setting. It might be at the kids' table," Amanda offered.

"That's fine, Mandy. I'll handle it." Her mother pushed out her chair and pointed at the empty chair between Logan and her brother. "Sit."

Like I'm a dog... But like that obedient canine she did as her mother asked. To get there she had to go to the other side of Logan. As she took her seat, she felt him stiffen, but he leaned in toward her.

"Are you going back to work after dinner?" Logan spoke so quietly that she was certain only she could hear him.

She nodded, and his gaze hardened.

"So you're Mandy's partner..." her sister Megan said.

The Steele family would associate Trent with a case against one of their own. At least it seemed her brother had forgiven Trent.

She looked at the spread before her, though it was never in question what was on the menu. Roast beef was sliced on a platter, a huge mound of mashed potatoes, beans, and carrots were in bowls, along with a gravy boat. Her family had already dug in, but it was hard to tell from the remaining feast. As delicious as everything looked and smelled, it still might prove challenging to eat and keep it down. Her stomach was tossing, just feeling the tense energy coming off Logan. She'd really messed up inviting Trent. She could see this from Logan's perspective. But from her viewpoint, she really hadn't done anything wrong. There was no ulterior motive. It was strictly motivated by kindness. If she'd worked with a female partner, she'd have invited her in tonight too. It was convenient and made sense.

Trent's stomach growled loudly from where he was standing next to the table.

"Guess they don't feed you in your line of work?" her sister Kristen teased.

"Who has the time to eat?" Trent responded, letting the jest roll off him.

"Well, despite Mom's attitude—"

"Hey," her mother cut in as she returned to the room with a plate and cutlery.

"We're happy you're here, even if you are both late." Kristen had carried on like her mother hadn't interrupted and laughed.

Everyone thinks they're a comedian...

Trent was set up with a chair at the kids' table but first loaded his plate, leaning over the main table between Amanda and her brother. He grabbed a generous portion of beef, a spoonful of mashed potatoes, and some beans. He even patted a tab of butter on top of the already creamy potatoes and then showered them with gravy.

"Save some for the rest of us, champ," Kyle teased.

Amanda shook her head at her brother but was smiling. "Just leave him alone, would you?"

"It's all right. I can handle Kyle after growing up with two sisters myself," Trent said.

"Oooh." Kristen started laughing. "Looks like you've met your match, Ky."

"Just watch yourself," Kyle said to Trent, putting on his gruff voice, but it was all an act.

"Ignore him," Amanda told Trent as he backed away from the table with his heaped plate.

"He certainly packs an appetite," her mother said.

"Jules, let the boy be. The same goes for everyone. You're going to give him indigestion," Nathan, Amanda's father, said, shooting her a smile while he was at it.

Her mother pushed a forkful of potatoes into her mouth, and it was likely to keep her from saying more.

Amanda shook her head and dished some food onto her plate. She took a bit of everything, even gravy but kept it light. She had a decent metabolism but knew if she didn't watch it at her parents' Sunday dinners, she'd pack on the weight. Logan had put on a few pounds in the first month. And that's a man whose job was physically active. Now even he was careful about how much he served himself.

The meal passed in a blur of chitchat and catching up. Trent didn't seem affected in the least, and after the initial hazing, they seemed to lay off him. Logan wasn't saying much of anything. Zoe and Trent were riotous at the kids' table, laughing like they were getting away with something.

Amanda kept catching her father's eye. He was seated at the head of the table, and Amanda couldn't imagine him anywhere else. He had always been someone she looked up to, even somewhat idolized growing up. He was why she was PWCPD and had Cop running through her veins. For many years, she'd wanted to climb the ranks and go for police chief. Something she hadn't given thought to for a while now actually. She'd just been so busy.

But every time their gazes locked she felt her father trying to read her mind. Knowing him, he was probably doing a pretty good job of getting it right too. At least some of it. She hoped he didn't pick up on her attraction to Trent, no matter how far she'd tamped it down. If he did, she'd trust he'd keep it to himself.

After dinner and dessert wrapped up, her family started clearing out. They all had jobs or school to get to the next day. She had a case to get back to now and was putting her boots on in the entry. Trent had already slipped out to get the car warmed up.

"Zoe and I are headed home," Logan said to her, shrugging his last arm into the sleeve of his coat. "Do you know when you'll get there?"

She shook her head, and before she could say anything to him or to Zoe, her mother squeezed in and demanded one more cuddle with her granddaughter. Amanda tried not to laugh out loud at the look she caught on Zoe's face. It was a cross between terror and surrender.

Get used to it, kid...

Amanda mussed her blond hair as she turned to walk through the front door and received a stank face for her trouble. But then Zoe giggled and hugged her. At least she wasn't holding the fact against her that she'd be home late. Or she didn't realize it yet.

"We'll see you when we see you." Logan left, and Amanda

felt a cold breeze gust in from outside. It matched the vibe he was putting off.

"Yep. Drive safe," she told him.

"You be safe too," Logan said without looking at her.

Her father shut the door behind them and faced her. A man of few words, he didn't need to say anything now. She got his message that he was there if she needed to talk. Out of everyone present tonight, he would understand her the most. He had walked in her shoes. Sadly, not just on the job, but he had been torn by feelings for another woman for a brief time too. His had led to him having an affair, and Amanda was determined not to become *that* person.

"I see you're heading out too," her mother said, reminding Amanda that she was there. How she'd been able to overlook her strong energy was surprising. "At least you made it to dinner." Her mother smiled. "But maybe a heads-up if you're bringing a guest next time."

"It was last minute, Mom."

"I know that's what you said."

Amanda didn't know what to make of that response or how to reply.

Her mother went on. "I know you do important work, sweetheart, but your family needs you too."

"That's why I'm here." It wasn't likely her mother's intention to dredge up how Amanda had cut them from her life for a few years while she was deep in grief, but there were times that decision drowned her with regret.

"And it was great to see you." She gave Amanda a hug and a kiss on the cheek. "Now, I'll get out of the way because I sense a *talk* coming on." She waved her hands when she said *talk* as it was her way of referring to pep talks Amanda would get from her father.

"Thanks, Mom, and dinner was delicious."

"If I mess up a roast beef dinner after all these years, there would be something wrong with me." She waved a hand over her head as she walked deeper into the house.

"So, what is it, kid?" Her father leveled his gaze at her, his eyes warm, his body language more relaxed than she ever recalled. Retirement suited him, but she wouldn't go so far as to say he was getting soft.

"A friend of mine lost her niece yesterday, and I was there. I found her body."

"The figure skater?"

"How did you know?"

"Logan let it slip before you got here."

"At the dinner table?" The back of her neck stiffened, thinking how insensitive that would be within earshot of Zoe.

"Not like that. I should have been clear. Just to me."

She let out the breath she was holding on the one score. On another, her mind was back on the young skater, her friend's niece. She felt a knot of anguish ratchet her chest. "It's all pretty awful," she admitted.

"Murder is. Any leads?" He was obviously caught up on the news.

"Nothing solid yet."

"You'll get there, I have no doubt."

To hear her father's faith in her abilities had her heart swelling.

"Scott doesn't have any doubts either," her father added.

The one downside to having her sergeant and father being long-time friends was they talked about her too much. "He has no reason to."

"That's right, but it doesn't stop him from worrying about you."

That sounded like the highlight reel of the conversation she'd had with him that morning. "He doesn't need to do that either."

"The cases you work do tend to touch close to home quite often."

She shrugged that off. "Small county. It's bound to happen."

"Not sure about that, but whatever the case, you always carry yourself with grace. But you were mentored by the best."

"Sergeant Malone is pretty great," she said with a wink and a smile.

"Very funny."

"You know I focus on the outcome more than anything, like you taught me. On saving future victims."

"You got it. And you said you caught another case today? Related?"

She nodded. "We just need to figure out how it all links together still. Speaking of, I better get going."

"Take care, kiddo." Her dad kissed her forehead and hugged her before she left.

She closed the door behind her, making sure it was sealed shut. The temperature had dipped tonight, and it was rather cool out there.

The trill of her phone cut through the night air, and she fished it out of a pocket. Detective Jacob Briggs was on the caller ID.

"You get the phone I left for you?" she answered.

"Possibly. Is this Detective Steele?" Jacob said, a lightness to his voice.

"You know fair well it is."

"Then, yes, I did. I even got it unlocked, and there's something you'll want to see for yourself. Could you meet me in half an hour?"

"Let's make it fifteen or less," she said getting into the passenger seat and ending the call. To Trent, she said, "That was Detective Briggs. There's something on Tara's phone we need to see." She cautioned herself not to get too excited, but what if this was the solid lead they'd been waiting for?

THIRTY

Amanda and Trent were led back to Jacob's cubicle, and the man greeted them with a beaming smile. He loved his job and viewed mining out digital leads as a personal mission. That was the main reason Amanda trusted him and his work so much. He even came through when he wasn't on the clock.

"You weren't kidding about fifteen minutes or less." Jacob clicked on his keyboard and the printer on his desk whirred to life.

"I try to keep my word." She smiled at him, but the expression faded as it sank in as a bittersweet admission. She'd followed through by making family dinner tonight, and it had ultimately bitten her in the ass.

"I promise you won't be disappointed." Jacob snatched the papers and handed them to her.

"And what am I looking at?" she asked as Trent came up beside her to catch a peek too.

"I might have gotten a little carried away, but I knew the phone belonged to a murder victim. You left that note at reception for me. I poked around and recovered some deleted text messages from an unknown number."

"That's what this is?" Trent pointed at the printout.

"Gold star for Detective Stenson." Jacob laughed. "But go on, read them."

Amanda held the papers in such a way that Trent could see without being quite so close to her. They both read in silence. Page one was an exchange of messages that took place the same day from this past October.

Unknown number: You're going to do as I ask if you don't want the truth to come out.

Tara: Who is this? And what do you want?

Unknown number: You're a liar and fraud. Michaela does drugs. You will send me 50k if you want me to keep your dirty secret quiet. Otherwise, your star will be exposed for who she really is!

Amanda stopped reading there and looked at Trent, but he kept his eyes on the page.

"We'll discuss when I'm done here," he said.

She didn't respond to him, but her mind was going crazy. *Michaela does drugs...* Her thoughts were locked on that and *star*. She put her focus back on the page.

Tara: You have no proof.

Tingles raced down Amanda's arms. The reaction was defensive, making it sound like this person's accusation was the truth. The unknown number countered:

Are you really willing to take that chance?

An hour passed before Tara replied, asking where to send the money.

The unknown sender requested a cashier check and provided a postal box at a Woodbridge mail office.

The address was one she was familiar with. "Trent, I don't know how far along you are—"

"Just finished, and is that the same postal office where the necklace was mailed?"

"Yep." Her heart was pounding. "There is no way that is a coincidence. Whoever is behind this number is connected to Michaela and likely responsible for her murder too. You did pick out the blackmailer's reference to Michaela as a star like in the note with the necklace?"

"You bet," Trent said.

"I didn't know anything about a note," Jacob began, "but I knew you'd want to see these messages."

"One thing standing out to me though, is I know you can block your caller ID when making a call from your cell phone, but I didn't know texts could go without the sender's number," Amanda said.

"There are ways around it, namely certain apps and such."

"Learn something every day," Trent put in, and Amanda nodded.

"But is that something you can track?" This lead was ripe with the potential of blowing the case wide open, and she hoped they hadn't hit a roadblock.

"Of course." Jacob was grinning again. "At least with the power of a court order. Put simply some of these anonymous texting apps retain records of their users' actual contact info. Thankfully, this was one of those cases. I was able to confirm these texts link back to a Woodbridge number. In turn, it's attached to a prepaid SIM card serviced by Universal Mobile."

"And were you able to track the number?" she asked.

"Tried that, but the phone must be off. Its last known location was the skating arena in Woodbridge on Saturday afternoon."

Amanda looked at Trent. "That can't be a coincidence. Okay, can you keep a trace open on it? If the phone becomes active again, let us know?"

"Of course."

"Do you know where the SIM card was sold and activated?" Trent put in.

Jacob looked at him and smiled. "I'm good, but not quite *that* good. Or at least not that fast."

"We'll need to get a warrant over to Universal, asking where they sent the batch of SIMs with the number we're after," she told Trent.

"Shouldn't be hard to do."

"There is more from this number too." Jacob snatched a fresh printout.

"You split it up, so it was more dramatic?" Amanda asked.

Jacob shrugged. "Maybe."

She started reading again. The first message at the top was from that past Friday afternoon to Tara.

Unknown number: Your time is running out. Michaela is going to fire you and you'll never work again once you're exposed for blackmailing your client. Because that's what you must be doing.

"Okay, hold up." Amanda lowered the page she was holding. "Tara was being blackmailed, but apparently also blackmailing Michaela? Over what?"

"The other text alleged Michaela did drugs, and the sender accused Tara of keeping Michaela's secret. Maybe she was doing so at a cost too," Trent suggested.

"Would that even be necessary?" Amanda countered. "If she exposed Michaela, it would hurt her bottom line."

"Keep reading. It will be worth it. Trust me." Jacob's encouragement had Amanda excited. What she'd read already was enlightening.

She lifted the page to continue reading.

Tara: I haven't done anything!

Unknown number: We both know that's not true. You are keeping secrets, and I will expose them.

Tara: Leave me alone or I will go to the police.

Unknown number: I think we both know that's not true. 150k CASH in one hour or the truth will come out.

Tara: The banks are closed tonight.

Unknown number: When then?

Tara: Tomorrow night.

Unknown number: 9 PM. Final deadline. I'll come to you.

Amanda barely had enough patience to read the exchange through to the end. She glanced over at Trent, who met her gaze before she lowered the page. "That explains Tara's rush to leave the arena and the hundred and fifty K we found in her home safe."

"Only the money never made it to the hands of the blackmailer."

"So why go to the trouble of taking out the cash if she wasn't going to hand it over?"

"Things changed since Tara withdrew the money. Michaela

died," Trent pointed out. "With her gone, so was the leverage for the blackmailer."

Amanda considered that and shook her head. "Not entirely. The blackmailer could have threatened to expose Tara. As the text implied this person thought Tara was keeping Michaela's secret. If the blackmailer had proof of that, Tara would have gladly paid." She shook her head. Her entire speech circled right back to the original dilemma. Why didn't Tara hand over the money when it could have saved her life? Which now led her to something else. "Why didn't Tara tell us any of this?"

"Maybe she didn't feel threatened. The blackmailer's words 'I'll come to you' imply they knew where she lived. So maybe Tara knew her blackmailer's identity by that point. She could have thought she could handle the situation on her own."

"Or she planned to get rid of them, but it backfired?" Amanda said.

"Could be. After all, if she could get rid of the blackmailer, her problem would be solved."

"Just more to back up the blackmailer's accusations as the truth." Just the thought of Michaela doing drugs hit hard. She didn't look forward to telling Patty and wouldn't unless absolutely necessary.

"Whatever the case, the blackmailer seemed confident Tara wouldn't go to the police. There was something Tara stood to lose, and it was high enough stakes she may have been willing to kill for it."

THIRTY-ONE

After leaving Digital Forensics, Amanda decided she and Trent should call it a night and get some rest. For all the good that ended up doing though. She woke up the next morning feeling like she never slept. Her mind kept replaying what they'd found on the agent's phone and Trent's words, "she may have been willing to kill for it." What was *it* that demanded protecting at all cost? Though if word got out about Tara keeping Michaela's secret, her reputation as an agent and a coach would be destroyed. Was that enough?

Another thing weighing on her was the high probability that Michaela used drugs. Tara was willing to pay to silence the blackmailer, something she wouldn't do if their accusation couldn't be backed up. Were the drugs recreational or was Michaela doping? Either way, her career would be ruined if she was found out.

She finally gave up on sleep and got out of bed when her alarm clock flipped to 6 AM. It was hardly fair how time had a way of speeding along like a bullet train or creeping like a slug. It felt like the latter right now and that the business day was taking forever to arrive. As soon as the doors opened, she'd be getting over to that postal office, serving a warrant for their video and following up on the mailbox noted in the text to Tara Coolidge. If luck was on their side, she and Trent would get a name. Not that she was holding her breath it would be that easy.

It was tempting to get showered and dressed for the day and sneak out before Logan or Zoe woke up. If last night was any indication, Logan wouldn't be pleasant to be around. It wasn't that late when she got in last night, but he hadn't said much of anything to her. He'd just offered some snide comment about being surprised to see her home so early considering how important the first twenty-four hours of a new case were. She'd let it slide, not possessing the bandwidth to discuss the underlying issue. With the light of a new day, there might be no more putting it off.

She was halfway through her coffee when Logan staggered down the hall. It was surprising that Zoe wasn't up yet. But talking to her about Michaela was another conversation Amanda wasn't looking forward to. She wished that she'd handled the initial one, but it was impossible to turn back the clock.

"Morning." Logan beelined to the coffee machine and snapped in a pod. He stood there while it brewed and didn't say another word.

"How did you sleep?" she asked him, instantly regretting doing so when she saw the muscles in his back tense through his T-shirt.

"Truth?" He spun and supported his weight against the counter. "Not so well. You?"

"Same." She had a feeling their reasons for insomnia were worlds apart though.

He grabbed his brewed coffee and took a sip of it and stood at the other side of the peninsula facing her. "Have you given any more thought to my proposal?"

She wished she had snuck out of the house before anyone had gotten up. It would have been the easier choice. If she'd known he'd want to discuss a baby this morning, she would have. "I've been rather busy." It was a partial lie, because of course she'd given it thought. It wedged in among the many she had about Michaela's and Tara's murders.

"That's a no, then. Is that right?" His eyes took on a steely cool intensity that sent shivers down her arms.

"I'm not sure now is the best time to talk about this." She eased off the stool and rinsed her cup in the sink and then set it in the dishwasher.

"And why's that, Amanda?"

"Please don't be like this." She could feel her fiery temper stirring and wasn't sure she could douse the flames once it fully ignited.

"Are you hesitating about a baby because of these... these feelings you have for Trent?"

"I told you there's nothing there, Logan, but you just won't accept that."

He flailed a hand in the air. "You must think I'm an absolute idiot. I see the way you look at each other. And you invited him to a family dinner? Jeez, Amanda. What were you thinking there?"

"I..." She snapped her jaw shut. She was too furious to form rational thought let alone speak coherently. She imagined words just pouring out in a jumbled torrent. "I need to get to work."

"At seven fifteen in the morning now?"

"As you so accurately pointed out last night, the first twenty-four hours in a case are crucial. So, yeah, I'm going to work." She stormed down the hall, showered, got dressed and left the house without saying another word to him. She couldn't. And Zoe hadn't shown any signs of stirring awake, so she left her girl blissfully unaware of the hell that had just taken place.

Are you hesitating about a baby because of these... these feelings you have for Trent?

Logan's question kept replaying on an endless reel and was quickly driving her mad. If he had any idea why she didn't want a baby, or more like *couldn't*, he wouldn't be so quick to judge and leap to conclusions.

She pressed her foot to the gas pedal of her Civic and got to Central in record time. She was so full of rage, she hadn't even noticed that she skipped stopping at Hannah's Diner for a coffee until she got to her desk.

It was only 7:45 AM, and Trent wouldn't likely be in for another forty-five minutes. They hadn't gotten much sleep on Saturday so when they parted ways last night, they hadn't made any promises about getting a fresh, early start today. Before they called it a day though, Trent was to gather the necessary paperwork to support a couple of warrants. One for Universal Mobile to disclose where the blackmailer's SIM card would have retailed. The other for the post office to hand over the renter's information on the blackmailer's postal box.

She got to her desk and opened her email. Several filtered in but two caught her attention. One confirmed the reports were on the server from canvassing officers in Coolidge's neighborhood, and the other was from CSI Blair. The subject was *Coolidge Investigation*, and she opened that one first.

"Good morning." Trent came into her cubicle and set a coffee from Hannah's on her desk.

She looked from the cup to him. "You must have read my mind. Thank you."

"Don't mention it."

She peeled back the tab on the lid and took a generous sip. "Heaven. You're here early."

"Could say the same to you."

"Had a hard time sleeping and figured I'd get a start on the day."

"Same. Hey, I really hope it wasn't a big deal that I crashed your family dinner last night."

"No, it was fine." She smiled but buried it at the edge of her cup and disguised that by taking another drink.

"Fine?" He hooked an eyebrow.

"Seriously, it was fine." She would shoot herself in the foot if she used that word one more time. "My family loves you." *And why did I say that?*

"That's why I felt like I was under fire?"

"Something like that." She laughed taking in his comical expression that was a cross between disbelief and confusion. "My family can be strange. What can I say? Don't give it another thought. You needed to eat, and it was convenient and efficient."

He dipped his head. "All right. Well, you should know that I got the signed warrant for Universal Mobile and forwarded that along. Did that before I left home," he added as he must have anticipated she was about to ask when he'd had a chance.

"Awesome. Hopefully it doesn't take them too long to get that info back to us. I had just opened an email from CSI Blair when you came in." She flicked a finger to the screen. "Do you mind?"

"Not at all, but I've read it already."

"You— How?"

"I was CC'd on it and read it on my phone before leaving home."

"Wow, did you sleep at all?"

"As I said, not much." He took a drink of his coffee.

"I'll take the highlights then, wise guy." She leaned back in her chair, swiveled.

"A couple of things. They collected Coolidge's laptop and got it to Digital Forensics last night."

"Did she say who they left it with?"

"She did not."

"Okay. I'll text Detective Briggs and have him look for it."

"No need. I already did."

"Let me guess, from home?" He pressed his lips, and she went on. "What else did her email say?"

"Coolidge has a Beretta Tomcat registered to her, but it seems to be missing. Blair found the case for it in her dresser nightstand. It was unlocked and empty."

A Tomcat was a compact and concealable weapon, something easily tucked into a purse. "Huh." She took a sip of her coffee, her mind on the crime scene. "We thought Tara might have planned to get rid of her problem, that being the blackmailer. So she goes home, gets her gun, and waits for them to show up."

"Only there turns out to be a struggle, during which maybe Tara loses hold of the gun at some point...?"

"Then the blackmailer gets the upper hand. They smack her on the back of the head with the lamp base. After looking around for the cash, they eventually give up and leave with Tara's gun."

"That all makes sense to me, which would mean the blackmailer is not only dangerous but now armed."

"Yep. Just what we need."

"Detectives." Chief Buchanan was taking fast strides toward her cubicle.

At the sound of his voice, Trent straightened his posture, and she set her cup on her desk and squared her shoulders.

"Good morning, Chief," she said.

"Update in Malone's office." He didn't wait for them to follow but tore down the hall at a quick pace.

She and Trent made eye contact, and it wasn't often that Buchanan lost his temper, but the skies were darkening and the storm was drawing near.

The chief knocked on Malone's doorframe, and he looked

up from where he was seated at his desk. Apparently, everyone was in before the crack of dawn.

"Come in." Malone straightened out some papers on his desk that he had been reading prior to the interruption.

"Sit if you'd like." Buchanan gestured toward the chairs in front of Malone's desk. Even when the man was angry, he had manners, but the offering felt like a test.

"I'm good to stand." She smiled politely at him, and Trent turned down the offer too.

"Very well," Buchanan stated coolly. "Two days, two murders, and zero suspects. Do I have that right?"

She wasn't going to correct him with the technicality that Michaela and Tara were both killed the same day. The agent was just found the following one. "Chief, we're doing all we—" She snapped her mouth shut at the sight of him holding up his hand.

"The media is going to need something, Steele. What can you give me?"

She was the last person he should be asking for fodder to feed the wolves, but this was the top dog for the PWCPD. It was only a matter of time before the texts got back to him and the sergeant. It was best they heard about it from her. "Texts were recovered, and it seems that Tara Coolidge was being black-mailed on account of something her client Michaela Glover did."

"Which was?" Buchanan popped his eyes.

"Drugs." It pained her to verbalize this, but it was fact for the case. She still felt the need to defend the girl. She then told him the details of the money requests and added, "But aside from these messages between Tara and her blackmailer, we haven't found anything to support Michaela having a drug habit."

"Okay, but you mentioned a demand for fifty grand in the fall, which I assume Coolidge paid them?"

"As far as we know." She knew how damning this admission looked for Michaela's character. "I see how that would lend credit to the accusation."

Buchanan pointed a finger at her. "Precisely. But the one-fifty was left in her safe?"

"That's right," Amanda said.

"This all seems rather straightforward to me. The agent stopped paying up and got killed for it."

"Or it's more complicated than that. We believe the black-mailer killed Michaela and Tara," she said.

"And what leads you there?"

Under his intense gaze, she was happy she had more than her gut to support her. "There was similar phrasing between a note given to Michaela Glover and a text sent to Tara Coolidge. The blackmailer referred to Michaela as a star in both cases. Then there is the postal box the blackmailer provided in the fall for the fifty grand. It's at the same postal office where someone mailed the necklace to Michaela."

Buchanan grimaced. "That can't be a coincidence. Have we tracked this number down yet?"

"In the works. Digital Forensics found it's a prepaid number serviced by Universal Mobile. A warrant has been signed off by a judge and sent over to find out where that SIM was sent for retail," she pointed out.

"And the warrant for the postal office? Where does it stand? Before you were after video, but we should find out who rented the postal box."

She nodded. "Another was submitted. Once it's all in our hands, you can bet serving them will be our priority."

"Good to hear it, but I'm still failing to know what we can tell the media. An Olympic hopeful *and* her agent were murdered. We can't remain quiet."

"How about the PWCPD is taking the matter seriously and considering several suspects?" she offered.

"Rather vague, don't you think?"

"It's the truth without giving too much away. We need space to do our jobs."

Buchanan's eyes narrowed, and the room became silent.

She retraced her words and felt her cheeks heat. "I didn't mean to imply that you're... that you are micromanaging us or anything."

"You sure about that?" the chief asked.

"I only have the utmost respect for you, sir. It's just you're right. There is a lot of pressure on the PWCPD with this case and most of that weight lands on myself and Trent. But I assure you that we are on top of all the leads coming our way."

No one said anything for several beats. The chief eventually broke the silence.

"Very well, Detective. But I'd like to hear that you have brought someone in by the end of the day."

"The end of the..." Trent's voice was strangled, and she could appreciate why.

"With all due respect, Chief, we can't promise that," she said.

"I don't need your words, Detective. Just bring me someone." With that, the chief swept out of Malone's office.

"Just bring me someone?" she repeated, looking at Malone. "Are you kidding me? Like anyone will do? Does he want a sacrificial lamb to serve up to the media or justice?" She'd never witnessed this side of the chief and didn't care for it one iota. Her respect for the man dipped to an all-time low.

"He's under pressure too," Malone said. "We all are. Just keep your head down and do the job. That's all we can ask."

What does he think we're already doing? "You got it. Any word on when we should see Michaela's phone records?"

"Matter of fact, I was about to let you know they're on the server."

"We're off." She led the way from Malone's office, but Trent quickly caught up with her. The mail office might not be open yet, but they had their work ahead of them.

THIRTY-TWO

Amanda dropped into her chair, and Trent wheeled his into her cubicle and sat down. There was a definite sense of anticipation in the air after seeing the types of messages recovered from Tara Coolidge's phone. Would they uncover something on Michaela's that would more strongly link the two murders?

She opened the file on the server, and they read the results on screen. She first went to the texts section and found what she was after. "That's the number, isn't it? The one that was unknown on Tara's phone."

Trent pulled out his notepad where he'd scribbled the unblocked number and nodded. "Yep, that's it all right."

"So why did the blackmailer block their number from Tara, but not from Michaela?"

"I can understand why given the blackmail, but we don't know what they had to say to Michaela yet."

"Let's get on with it then." She turned to the screen, and Trent leaned in next to her. His warm breath cascaded over her arms, and her skin tingled. *I see the way you look at each other…* Logan's words from that morning returned as an assault, and she repositioned herself and started to read the messages. She noted the date on the oldest and had to comment before she carried on any further. "The first message was sent a week after the postmark."

"I caught that. 'I need you in my life. How can you just ignore me?'" Trent turned to Amanda after reading the message out loud. "The person doesn't sound too happy."

"And it doesn't look like Michaela bothered to respond. Look"—she pointed out the date on the next message—"the sender reached out a week later. 'You are who you are because of me! I need to meet with you.' That wording sound at all familiar to you?"

"Same tone as the note found with Michaela's body. 'You'll be sorry you turned your back on me after all I've done for you.' Ask me and it's the same person."

"But Michaela responds to this message. 'Please leave me alone!'"

"She knows who this person is but wants nothing to do with them. Could they be why she didn't want to return to Woodbridge?"

"Since it's looking like this person might have killed her, I would understand why."

"You and me both. Let's hope that Universal Mobile is quick to respond."

"And that the postal box pays off." Amanda looked back to the messages again. The next message came from the black-mailer in November. "'I see you whenever I turn on the TV. You are a star!'"

"The way they keep referring to Michaela as a star is starting to strike me as jealousy not simple admiration."

"Agreed, but the text gives us more than that clue. It's more clear than ever this blackmailer sent the necklace to Michaela."

"And we know the handwriting that accompanied the jewelry is a match to the note with the necklace and the one found with Michaela's body. There's no way the two murders aren't directly linked and tie back to Woodbridge."

"And so far all we have is a number and postal box and no clue if either will get us to this person. On another note, did you pick up that Michaela wasn't swayed by the praise? She didn't respond to that message either. Still, the person messaged again. 'Please, I just want to meet with you when you're in town.' This was sent Wednesday, just a few days before the show."

"Persistent, I'll give you that. You read Michaela's reply to the proposal to meet though? 'No. You poisoned me!'"

"And the blackmailer said, 'Come on... you need to let loose and have fun sometimes. You're young,'" Trent read off the screen.

"'I never want to see or hear from you again.' Holy crap, Trent, I'm not sure if you're thinking what I am but *poison, let loose, have fun...* Did the blackmailer drug Michaela without her knowledge and then use it as leverage to blackmail her agent?"

"Tainting something Michaela would ingest fits their MO."

"True enough. So this blackmailer is all buddy-buddy with Michaela, praising her, sets her up, blackmails her agent when their plan falls apart, then kills both of them?"

"It's a real brainteaser."

"I'd say, but we take this one step at a time."

They finished reading through the conversation thread, and she considered poking around Michaela's communications for longer until she saw the time in the bottom of the screen. It was finally after 9 AM. "How about we take one of those steps right now?" She backed out of the file and flicked off her monitor. She'd been waiting since last night to chase this lead.

THIRTY-THREE

Amanda and Trent served the warrants at the post office. For their reward, they might as well have butted their heads against a wall. It was going to take up to twenty-four business hours for them to get the video together, and the blackmailer's mailbox was available to rent. The record housing the name of the previous renter was stored off site and would take at least the same mandated amount of time.

She kicked the tire of the department car. "Just looking for one little break here." She didn't often let frustration get to her like this, but her morning with Logan kept coming to mind and playing with her emotions. How were they supposed to hold it together? He had said he'd forgiven her for kissing Trent, but it was so clear that he hadn't forgotten. And as long as that was the case, how could they ever truly move forward?

"We're not without next steps. We talked about following Michaela's movements since she got to town. We haven't seen that through yet. We have the signed warrant for Royal Auto Rentals. What do you say we present it and get our hands on the GPS records for the Subaru she rented?"

"Why not?" She should have known better than to get her hopes up that the mail office would be an instant payoff.

They got into the car and were back at Central late morning armed with the GPS records from Royal Auto Rentals.

The GPS showed trips to Patty's house, Lux Suites, and the Woodbridge arena. There were also several restaurants and two trips to Eagle Cemetery. One on Friday and again early Saturday morning.

"To start these are standing out to me." Trent drew her attention to the trips to the arena. One was on Friday night and another Saturday around 10 AM. "I could assume that Michaela was there to get some practice in, but why did no one mention this to us?"

"Patty said that Michaela hated being late for anything and planned to get there early. Her niece must not have mentioned just *how* early. But the manager didn't say anything about it at all."

"I say we find out who was there to let her in and out. We know her protein shake was tainted just before the show or while she was on the ice. So..."

"We can't afford to rule anything or anyone out. You heard the chief, and he's right. Two days and two bodies. Technically it was one day for two bodies and we're starting day three but..."

"I wasn't about to correct him either." Trent smiled at her. "But don't let him get in your head."

"Too late. We need to retrace all her steps." *Even the cemetery...* Not a trip she looked forward to. She couldn't go there and not face Kevin's and Lindsey's gravestones. Or the stone that marked the resting place of her unborn child. It had already been such a long time. Her phone rang, rescuing her from her thoughts. She answered without looking at the caller's identity.

"It's Hans," the medical examiner announced himself, never standing on formalities. "I thought I'd let you know that there was epithelium under Coolidge's nails, and this has been forwarded to the lab. I can also confidently tell you that cause of death was blunt-force trauma to the back of the head. We already covered time of death on scene."

"Yes. Thank you," she told him.

"Don't mention it." With that he hung up.

Amanda turned to Trent and shared the ME's findings.

"We can only hope the bastard who killed her is in the system," he said. "While you were on with him, I was noting Michaela's first stop when she got to town on Thursday." He pointed at the Earth and Evergreen Restaurant on the screen for two o'clock.

"What about it?"

"For one thing, she must have gone with someone who picked up the tab. I flipped through the receipts in her hotel room, and there wasn't one for this restaurant."

"The fact you even remember that is impressive. Well, she couldn't have gone with Patty because she was working that day. She didn't get off until Friday. It could have been a lunch date with Tara, who picked up the check."

"As you're always telling me, we can't afford to make assumptions."

"I'm so wise." She smiled. "What do you say to an early lunch?"

"Is it that early when it will be just after noon when we get there?"

"Suppose not."

THIRTY-FOUR

Earth and Evergreen Restaurant was a rather unnoteworthy building with its cream stucco exterior and wood-shingled roof. It hadn't changed much in appearance in all of Amanda's life. The same went for the interior with its dated green carpeting and dark wood tables and spindle-back chairs. The place honored military and law enforcement. Patches from police departments from all over the world were mounted to the ceiling. Marine Corps plaques were on the bulkheads. Despite being in desperate need of a remodel, it provided a cozy setting to have a meal.

She and Trent were seated by a smiling server with the name Holly pinned to her uniform shirt.

"Just flag me down if you need anything," Holly said before taking off.

Trent was reading the restaurant's menu, which was large enough to hide his face and most of his chest. She could only imagine how small she'd look next to the thing, if she cared about searching the options. Her stomach was a tight ball of stress. No matter how much she wanted to release what had happened at home that morning it was proving near impossible.

It wasn't their first disagreement, and if their track record told her anything it wouldn't be the last. Their spats always circled back to one of two things. Her job with its unpredictable hours or her slip with Trent. The former had caused them to break up at one point, and it was only happenstance that they reconnected and decided to give their relationship another go.

"You not hungry?" Trent attempted to set down the menu but had a hard time finding a spot to accommodate it. He ended up putting it near the edge of the table with a third of it hanging over. "Mandy?"

"Ah, yeah?"

"Penny for your thoughts?"

"I'm not sure they're worth that much." She was preoccupied with Logan but now she was also assimilating Trent calling her Mandy, which wasn't something he did that often. When he did pull it out, it always felt like putting on a cable-knit sweater and snuggling under a blanket next to a fire. *Gah! I'm beyond help.* "It's just the case. We think whoever is behind that Woodbridge number is who we're after, but why kill either one? I mean Tara didn't pay up so that could come across as an apparent motive, but she was taken out with a weapon of opportunity. I'm not sure it was the blackmailer's intention to kill the agent. But we believe they also killed Michaela, so you'd think it would be easier to take a life the second time." As she said all this, she was happy that they were seated in a quiet corner away from other tables and eavesdropping ears.

"Maybe they stupidly thought Tara would simply hand over the money and they would be free to go."

She nodded, filling in the blanks. "Only Tara held a gun on them..." She pulled from their earlier theorizing.

"Uh-huh, but what's creeping me out is how the blackmailer goes from praising Michaela to killing her. It's more than being double-faced. Dual personalities? In the least, this person is mentally or emotionally unstable."

Holly returned with a tablet in hand ready to tap in their meal orders. "Have you decided, or do you need another minute with the menu?"

Trent laughed, and the woman smiled and cocked her head.

"You must admit the size of the menu is rather large," he said.

"You're telling me? I cart them around all day. So does that mean you're ready or you've given up?" Holly was smiling at Trent and flicked a strand of hair behind her ear. She was clearly flirting with him.

"I'll have the fish and chips. One fillet."

"You betcha. And you?" Holly looked at Amanda.

"Just a small order of fries."

"Oh, that's all?" The server seemed shocked by the request.

"That's all." Amanda handed her the menu she'd been given, the spine of it not even cracked open, and the server left.

Trent clasped his hands on the table and looked at Amanda. "You all right over there?"

"Not really, and before you ask, I don't want to talk about it. Let's just get these investigations solved and bring Michaela's and Tara's families some closure." They hadn't had to serve notice to Tara's next of kin because her parents lived out of town. The local police there would take care of that. But Amanda had been so preoccupied with tracking leads and her home life, somehow Patty had slipped to the back of her mind. She picked up her phone and texted her a quick, *Still working the case and thinking about you. Call if you need anything.*

"It will be nice to put them to bed for sure."

"You hear back from Briggs?" She was referring to the laptop and assumed he'd know that.

"I did. He's got it and will let us know if he finds anything worth sharing."

"Great." She pressed on a smile, but it faded quickly. Her phone pinged with a response from Patty, and she said she was working on funeral arrangements for Michaela that afternoon. Amanda tapped back, *XO*.

Their meals came, and they ate in relative silence. Well, Trent ate, and she pecked at her fries. She obviously wasn't a mind reader and didn't know what Trent was thinking, but her thoughts were on Logan. And she hated that they were. Every bit of her focus should be on the investigations, not her personal life and uncertainty about the future.

Holly cleared their plates and stood at the side of the table holding on to them. "Will that be all? Or did you save room for dessert?"

"No dessert. But we would like to ask you a question," Amanda said.

"Sure."

Amanda flashed her badge. "Detective Steele."

Holly, who had been relatively chipper all this time, frowned slightly and her posture stiffened.

Amanda continued. "Were you working last Thursday afternoon by chance?"

"Yeah." Holly dragged it out and suddenly it was like the dishes she was holding weighed fifty pounds or more. She was shifting her footing, clearly uncomfortable by having a cop ask her a question.

"Do you remember serving Michaela Glover?" Amanda asked.

Holly set the plates on the end of the table. "I did." Tears beaded in her eyes, and she swiped them away.

"Did you know her?" Trent asked.

"A little, I guess. We went to the same school. I finished a couple of years ahead, but her name was on everyone's lips even then."

"She was popular in high school?" That would be their first time hearing this, though it was unclear how it could further their investigations.

"Not really. Just people talked about her back then..." Holly wiped her cheek on her shoulder. "Kids can be mean. They'd say things like she'd always be a virgin because she was so obsessed with skating."

Amanda nodded. "So when you served her on Thursday, was she with someone?" They knew another person had picked up the tab, but she wanted the question to be unassuming.

"Uh-huh. A man. He had to be about twice her age. Though it's hard to know for sure. He could have looked older than he was."

Or younger... "Is there anything else you can tell us about him? Accent? Tattoos? Birthmarks? Body shape? Facial shape?"

"He was tall, thin. Black. Though I hate pulling skin color into it."

"I get it," Amanda said. "You're just describing him, though, don't worry. Do you have any video surveillance here?"

Holly shook her head. "If you have someone in mind, I can look at their picture if you like...?"

"We appreciate that," Amanda said, "but we don't know who this man is yet either. Do you know how he paid?"

"Cash."

If it had been a credit card, they'd be able to potentially track him down. That was assuming a judge would see enough cause to sign a warrant. If so, they could forward that to the credit card company for the cardholder information. "Did you catch any of their conversation or grasp what their relationship might have been?"

"I don't have a clue, and I don't make it a habit to snoop on my customers' conversations."

Amanda was grateful for that considering what she and Trent had discussed since sitting down. "Even when that customer was Michaela?" She imagined it would be tempting to listen in on a quasi-celebrity.

"If I heard anything, I would tell you, Detective."

"Excuse me..." A man at a table across the way was waving his arm at Holly.

"I better go." Holly walked off in a fluster, leaving the plates on the table.

Amanda looked over at Trent to find he was watching her.

"Is this really happening again?" he said.

"Yep, we have another mystery man."

He smiled and shook his head. "It seems we get at least one with every case."

"That it does. Though this time it's two. We still don't know who showed up for Michaela at her hotel."

A couple of minutes later, Holly returned and set the check on the table, but Amanda was quick to produce her credit card to cover their food. When Holly came back with it and the receipt, she said, "I remembered something else. Not sure how much it will help, but I think he was driving a blue car."

THIRTY-FIVE

After leaving the restaurant, Amanda and Trent decided they would just stick to the plan of following Michaela's trips on her GPS. That took them to the arena next as they were curious what had the young skater there Friday night and hours before the show. Trent had called ahead to the arena manager, and Ron was going to meet them there.

When Trent pulled into the lot, a PWCPD cruiser, an officer behind the wheel, was there as well as the manager in his sedan.

Once Ron saw them pull in, he got out of his car and came over to theirs.

"We appreciate you meeting with us again," Amanda told him.

"Don't mention it. The owners and management of the arena want to know what happened to Michaela Glover just as much as the police."

That sounded noble, but Amanda suspected optics were also involved. "Let's go inside then. We have questions for you, so it would be best if we hit your office first."

"That's fine, but when will we be able to fully reopen the doors?"

"I wouldn't think it would be too much longer before we release the scene," she told him.

"It's already been a couple of days."

"I realize it's an inconvenience, but a young woman was murdered," she served back.

"Yes, I know. And I must sound insensitive." He left his statement hanging there and led the way into the arena and to his office, where he parked behind his desk. "Fire away." He gestured for either one of them to start asking their questions.

"We found out that Michaela Glover was here on Friday night and Saturday morning," she began. "Why was that?"

"To practice." Ron put that out there like it was a no-brainer.

"Did she come alone?" Trent asked.

"Yes."

"So no agent or coach?" Amanda highly doubted the coach would leave her family who were grieving to come here, but she had to ask.

"Just herself."

"And who was working at those times?" she asked.

"Friday night, just me and Richie who runs the Zamboni."

"Tell us about this Richie," she said. "Was he also working on Saturday?"

"Yeah, of course. As I said he runs the—"

"Zamboni. Right. So did Michaela and Richie interact?" They hadn't spoken to this Richie guy, but it was likely one of the uniformed officers had when taking everyone's information.

"Not that I saw."

"Then you wouldn't say they knew each other?" Trent interjected.

"They definitely didn't. When I called Richie in, he was excited to do all he could to help Michaela and wanted to meet her. He was gushing like she was a real celebrity, and I told him to get a grip."

That hardly made it seem that Richie was the killer they were after. "So just you, Richie, and Michaela?" She was asking the same question a third time, but she wanted to give the manager ample opportunity to correct his statement if needed.

"That's right. But I'm not sure I like what you're implying." He narrowed his eyes and regarded her with distrust.

"I wasn't implying anything. And Saturday morning?" she asked.

"There were probably twenty staff here getting ready for the show."

That was a lot of people to keep an eye on. "Anyone who would have gotten close to or entered Michaela's dressing room while she was practicing?"

"I couldn't tell you."

"Here's the thing, we believe that Michaela's drink was tainted before the show or at least after she took to the ice." Amanda watched as that hit the manager.

Ron was sliding down his chair and appearing smaller every minute. "Okay, but I'm not sure what I can do to help in that regard. Am I going to need a lawyer? I'm starting to feel like I'm under suspicion."

"Just being diligent, Mr. Hampton," she assured him. "Could we take a look at the video from Friday night and Saturday morning to see who came into the lot?"

"Warrant?"

"The one you already received would cover this," she said coolly. "Besides, I thought the arena owners and management wanted to cooperate with the PWCPD to find Michaela's killer."

"Come with me," he mumbled as he got up and headed to the security room.

The exterior footage was loaded first for Friday night. As it played out, they watched Michaela's Subaru enter the lot and park. But she wasn't alone.

A blue car pulled in after her and parked. Shortly later, a tall man unfolded from the driver's seat.

Could this be the man who had lunch with Michaela the day she got into town? His height and the color of his car fit with what the server at the restaurant had told them. "Is there any way to zoom in?"

"On the blue car?" Ron asked.

"Uh-huh."

"I'm assuming you're after the plate, but we're not getting it with the angle he's parked on."

She wasn't a fan when people gave up without trying. "Could you try anyhow?"

He did as she'd asked and shook his head. "As I told ya."

"Okay, resume the video, please," she said to him.

The footage continued to play out on the monitor. Michaela and the man stood face to face. He towered over her. While they were several feet apart, words were exchanged and a few moments later, Michaela's arms were gesturing wildly. Following that, he got back into his car and left. Still not affording them a clear shot of the plate. But they weren't entirely empty-handed. "Go back and zoom in on the man's face."

"Sure." Ron did as she asked.

Staring back at them was an unknown man. Perceivably about double Michaela's age, but Amanda could grant him late thirties. "You ever see this man before?" she asked him.

"Nope. He doesn't look familiar to me at all."

"Okay, please print this off and forward a copy of the video to me." She provided the manager with her card, though she probably gave him one on Saturday. That felt like a lifetime ago.

"You want to see Saturday morning still?"

"Yes. Just for a bit from when Michaela first arrived." She

supposed this video might give them more if they dedicated hours to watching it through. They might even spot someone wearing a coat with wood toggle buttons. *Might.* They didn't have time to squander.

Ron brought up the video. They watched Michaela come into the lot and go down the side of the building.

Right... "She parked at the side toward the back. Do you cover that area?"

"I can try the camera on the rear of the building." Ron set about doing that, but when he brought it up for the corresponding time, it was clear the camera's range didn't take in the Subaru in the lot.

"All right, just that photo of the man and we'll be on our way," she told Ron.

He switched over to the screen where the mystery man was rather clear, pressed some buttons, and a printer across the room started up.

She and Trent left a few minutes later armed with the face of Michaela's lunch date. She was certain of it. He checked the boxes for height, age, and vehicle color.

Trent got the heat running in the car and turned to her. "That guy could be our mystery man." He pointed at the photo in Amanda's hand.

"I think the chances are in our favor. We'll try running his photo through facial recognition databases, but what was his business with Michaela?" She kind of hated how she could take a lead and complicate it.

"Whatever it was, Michaela didn't look entirely pleased to see him show up at the arena. Did you see the amount of space between them?"

"Hard to miss it, and the gesturing of her arms... She didn't want him there."

"And he got the message because he pretty much left right away."

"Yeah." She chewed on this, trying to make sense of what they had seen. Impossible without context. "But is he the black-mailer and killer? That's the real question." Her phone rang, and Blair showed on the caller ID. She answered on speaker and was pleased that some warm air was finally blowing from the vents. She put her hands in front of one to warm her chilled fingertips, letting the photo fall in her lap. "Detectives Steele and Stenson here," she said.

"It sounds like you guys should open a firm, Steele and Stenson," Blair teased, her smile traveling the line.

"Someone sounds like they're in a good mood. Tell me you have something for us." Amanda was daring to embrace optimism even though it typically backfired on her.

"I do, but I'm going to pace myself."

"Don't worry about that on our account," Trent put in, rich with sarcasm.

"All right, all right. Isabelle and I finally made it through all the garbage and recycling bags from the arena. We struck some gold. To start, an EpiPen with a prescription sticker confirming it was Michaela's. There were a few sets of fingerprints on there that didn't belong to her, but no hits in the system. One might tie back to the killer, but we won't know until we have someone in custody. Otherwise, it would make sense some would belong to a pharmacist or anyone else in the medical field who handled it. We also found a card stamped with the Rosebuds & More logo. The card from the bouquet?"

"The right florist," Amanda said. "What was the message written on it?"

"'I wish you gold, love Deana.'"

"That's the one. So the killer popped those in the trash on their way from the arena. But no sign of Michaela's phone?" Amanda asked.

"None whatsoever. Thinking the killer probably held on to it or ditched it somewhere else."

"Well, Trent and I came across some damning messages through Michaela's records, and we think her killer is behind them. They probably didn't want them found."

"They'd have to know you could get them without the physical phone."

"Sure, but it takes longer going about it that way," she griped.

"But that's not all I have for you. The results are back from the tissue and gum found in Michaela's rental car. They are a familial match to a male sibling."

Tyson Bolton. "You should have led with that."

THIRTY-SIX

Tyson was panting like an enraged bull when they dragged him from his work. His nostrils were flaring, and he kept swearing at the officer who wrangled him into the back of a cruiser. An hour had passed and from where Amanda stood on the other side of the one-way mirror looking in on the interview room, he hadn't calmed down much. So far, he hadn't requested a lawyer at least.

They left him for a bit longer and ran the mystery man's face through facial recognition databases only to find no hits. They also got the parts moving that would allow a search of Tyson's home for peanut oil, black ribbon, a garment missing a wood toggle button, and the Beretta registered to Tara Coolidge. He'd admitted to having peanut oil before, but Amanda still wasn't so sure this would all pay off. After all, his handwriting wasn't a match. It was hard to dismiss the lies though. Unless the truth was there and they hadn't fully realized it yet. "Trent, I just thought of something." He looked over the divider, and she continued. "Tyson's writing isn't a match for the notes sent to Michaela..."

"It's bugging me too."

"Not sure it is me anymore. He gave me the impression he is dyslexic. Most people who can't read find ways to work around that. I'm sure it's the same for someone who suffers from dyslexia. Did Tyson get someone else to write the note, the card to Michaela?" Her heart was racing by the time she summed up her epiphany. "We know he has motive. Jealousy."

"And he's also interested in a payday."

"Uh-huh. Now, he could have used voice to text for the messages. He doesn't seem to have a problem with his speech. But even if he spoke the words of the note and tried to hand-write them, copying is often difficult for people with dyslexia. An alternative might be that he dictated his messages to someone else who then sent them."

Trent paled. "Which means he could be the blackmailer and the killer. Or he's in on this with someone."

"Yeah." She mulled that over while she considered the damning evidence against Tyson. It occurred to her when they first found out about Michaela's male visitor at the hotel it might have been Tyson. She never shared this suspicion with Trent, but now she had her answer. The video came through in the last hour too, and it showed Tyson entering the lobby and leaving with Michaela. They were gone for about thirty minutes as the clerk had told them, and she returned alone. They had him caught in a lie on camera. There would be no denying that.

Malone came clamoring over to their cubicles for an update, and they filled him in on why they had brought Tyson in for questioning. He promised to pass this along to Chief Buchanan, and Amanda was happy for the mediator. The chief should be happy too for another reason. They brought someone in before the end of the day.

"I think Tyson's stewed long enough." She got up and walked to the interview room with Trent.

"Are you trying to get me fired?" Tyson roared. "You can't just drag me from work and—"

Amanda pulled a photo out of a folder she had with her and plopped it onto the table in front of him, as she sat down. Trent parked next to her.

"What's that?"

"Looks like a picture of you in the lobby of Lux Suites with Michaela."

Tyson fell silent for several seconds. It might have stretched to a minute or two. Amanda and Trent weren't going to speak first.

"So what?" Tyson eventually said. "She's my sister. I can't see her?"

"Oh, you can, but you told us you haven't seen her in a long time, hadn't spoken to her since last week. But that wasn't exactly the truth, was it?" she said.

He shrugged. "Technically Saturday was last week."

"We spoke Saturday night," she served back.

"So what? I mixed up my days. Talking to my sister isn't a crime."

"That's not. But lying to us is," she pointed out.

"You've got to be kidding me."

"I'm serious. You could face charges for making false statements to police officers." She let that lie out there until Tyson met her gaze. "I might be willing to let it go if you tell us why you lied."

"As I said, I mixed up my days is all."

"Why were you there?" she countered.

He licked his lips, stuck out his chin. "I asked her for a loan."

"You were with her for half an hour," Amanda pointed out.

"We went for a little drive. I got a lecture about getting my life together and how she was helping me more by not giving me a handout."

A drive would fit the timeline, and the DNA results put Tyson in the rental. "You like to chew fruity gum sometimes?"

"That bit me in the ass? Listen, I swear I didn't hurt her."

"Why didn't you tell us about meeting up with her before?" she asked, though she figured the answer would be to protect himself.

"I know it would make me look more suspicious."

"Good that you see it. What about these?" She put the text exchanges sent to Michaela on the table.

He looked at them. "Never seen them before."

Amanda set the texts exchanged with Tara Coolidge on the table. "What about these? Look familiar?"

"No."

"Then this means nothing to you either?" She pressed a finger to the prepaid number used by the blackmailer.

"Nope."

"How well do you know Tara Coolidge?"

"Mick's agent? Not well. Haven't spoken in years."

"Well, Tara Coolidge is dead, murdered in her home. It seems that it was about money."

"About money?"

"Were you blackmailing Tara Coolidge and when she refused to pay up you killed her?"

"What? No way. I didn't kill anybody. Besides, why would I kill Ms. Coolidge?"

It wasn't missed that mention of the blackmail just seemed to be ignored. "So going back to the texts, are you sure you didn't dictate these to someone to send them out? Were you working with another person to blackmail Tara Coolidge about your sister's drug use?"

"What?" he snapped. "Ain't no way Mick used drugs."

His quick and adamant response had Amanda inclined to believe him, but it would take more than that for her to release him. "What about that postal box?" She pressed a finger to the text that included the address. "Will we find your name on the rental agreement?"

"I know nothing about it." Tyson swallowed roughly, his Adam's apple bulging out.

"All right, what about this? Detective Stenson, do you have a photo of the pendant you could show Tyson?"

Trent worked on his tablet and held it toward Tyson.

His eyes barely fell on it when he said, "What about it?"

"Look familiar to you?" she asked him.

"Nope."

Amanda was starting to see that single-worded response was Tyson's go-to. What bothered her more was he hadn't taken his eyes from the screen. "Something else you're seeing?"

"Ah... yeah. Where did you find this?"

"It was among Michaela's things," she told him. "It appears to have been mailed to her from a post office in Woodbridge."

"The one with the box?"

"The same one." It was curious he'd even asked, but she sat back as if she were unaffected by the inquiry.

Tyson worried his bottom lip.

She gave him a few moments, sensing that if she rushed him to speak, he'd say nothing more.

"That's a crescent moon," he said eventually.

"That's right." She wasn't sure what was crucial about that observation. "That mean something to you?"

"To me? Nope."

Amanda studied his body language, and he was making comfortable eye contact. "Do you know who might have sent this to Michaela? Who it might mean something to?" That's if it wasn't Tyson. Though Michaela's ex-boyfriend did say it cost a few hundred dollars. It was possible if Tyson was partnered with someone that they paid for it. The necklace came before the first blackmail request. It could have been seen as an investment to gain his sister's favor.

"No clue."

His answer came far too quickly. And she wasn't sure how to reconcile Michaela telling her blackmailer she didn't want to see them again with her stepping out with her brother for thirty minutes. Not if they were one and the same. "Listen, Tyson, maybe you can help us with something." She softened her approach.

He shrugged and exhaled in surrender. "Do I have a choice?"

"Did you and your sister talk about anything other than money? Maybe she shared with you that she wasn't happy to be home or that she was afraid of someone." If the blackmailer and killer wasn't Tyson, there was a chance he could point them in someone's direction.

"Nope. We weren't close. Not like she bared her soul to me. She just liked imparting lectures about hard work paying off."

"All right. Did she seem upset or distracted?" she served back.

"Actually, yeah, she did. She said she had a difficult day ahead of her without my interference. I had a hunch she wasn't happy with her agent."

"Would you know why?"

"No clue."

Amanda could wager a guess. Tara was keeping Michaela's secret at a cost to the skater. "Detective Stenson, could you pull up that photo of the man from the arena?"

"Who?" Tyson blurted out. "What are you doing now? I swear I don't know anything. And I'm not working with anyone."

Trent was occupied on his tablet, and she answered Tyson. "When Michaela got into town on Thursday, she had a meal with a man not long after. We figure he might be important."

Tyson looked from her to the tablet Trent had placed in front of him. He licked his lips and rubbed his jaw.

"Tyson, do you recognize that man?" she pushed.

"I sure do, but I don't know why he's with Michaela."

"Who is it?" Trent asked.

"It's my dad, Darren Bolton."

THIRTY-SEVEN

Tyson was kept in holding while the search was conducted on his residence by investigators sent from Manassas. Amanda had requested Blair and Donnelly, but sometimes it was the luck of the draw. It was six o'clock in the evening when Amanda was ringing the doorbell at Darren Bolton's front door. While Tyson was currently under suspicion, she wanted to find out what had Darren speaking with Michaela.

The plates on the blue Toyota in the driveway were registered to him, so presumably he was home. She amped up her efforts to get an answer by banging on the door. Then finally, footsteps padded heavily toward her and Trent. The door was swung open, and their tall mystery man stood there, towering over her and her partner by several inches.

"We're Detectives Steele, and Stenson," she said while showing her badge. "Are you Darren Bolton?" she asked, though it was a mere formality. His own son had ID'd him, and he matched his license photo on file with the Department of Motor Vehicles. They had gotten that when they pulled a background on him. It was clean.

"I am, but it's really not a good time right now." He started to close the door.

"We're sorry to hear that," she rushed out. "But it doesn't change the fact we need to speak to you about Michaela Glover."

The opening widened again. "I just can't believe that beautiful young lady is dead."

"Would you let us in so we can talk?" Trent said this, standing firm.

A few beats passed before Darren complied with the request and welcomed them into his home. He took them to the living room where they sat down.

"What was your relationship with her?" Amanda put up a wall around her emotions, determined to retain her objectivity. Patty had warned her that Darren was a liar, but that opinion could have been colored by the way she'd seen him treat her sister. She had no recent contact with him, and people could change.

"I'm her father." He nudged out his chin, exuding pride for the flicker of a moment. Then it dulled, leaving his face a blend of shadows.

"The father's name isn't noted on her birth record," Trent said.

"That's because of Cheryl. She just said Michaela wasn't mine to make me jealous, to have me think there was another guy involved."

"We heard there was," Amanda fired back. "Possibly more than one."

"I don't think so."

"Regardless, we have it on good authority, you were never in the picture for Michaela or Tyson, your son," Amanda said.

Darren's eyes widened slightly at the mention of Tyson, though she wasn't sure why. "I was selfish when I was younger. Worse than that, I was a drunk and drug addict, but I've cleaned up my act in the last couple of years." He gestured toward a large crucifix on the wall, as if that was a verified badge that marked him as an upstanding person. "Not only have I found God, but I'm working the program. Alcoholics Anonymous. Making amends. If I am her father, I want to apologize for not being there and make up for that."

Amanda's father had gone through the steps too and broken twenty years of sobriety after Kevin's and Lindsey's deaths. These days, he was back to meetings and off booze. "All right. Good for you. Were you and Michaela in contact?" They had him on video, but depending on his response, it could set up a foundation of trust.

"We were."

Amanda could credit him some points for honesty but penalize him for being vague. "And why was that?"

"We were working to build our relationship."

"For how long?" Amanda would guess a couple of months if they didn't already know about the blackmailer surfacing then.

"Since the summer. Mid July or early August. I was working through my amends at that point, but I had to know, once and for all, if she was my daughter."

The timing was sooner than she would have expected. It had to be the drug use and the person behind the prepaid number weighing on Michaela's mind. "And the program and mere curiosity were your only motivators after all these years?" Amanda could imagine one reason might be that Darren saw the opportunity for a payday, but she kept quiet awaiting his response. Thinking of Michaela's money, she realized her financials still hadn't come in. They could reveal something.

"That is enough, isn't it?"

"Sure. Did you see Michaela when she got to town?" Again, she played it like she didn't know.

"I'm guessing you know the answer to this question, and it might be why you're here in the first place."

She shrugged, choosing the action and nonverbal response intentionally to prompt an answer to her question.

"We met up for lunch on Thursday at the Earth & Evergreen Restaurant. That's not against the law."

Like father like son with a defense like that. *Had they worked together?* "I never said it was, but it has you wound up."

"Because it feels like you're attacking me."

"No one's attacking you, Mr. Bolton, but the fact is Michaela was murdered. We're tasked with finding out who killed her. Since she was your daughter, I'm sure you want that answer as much as we do." She wasn't even broaching the subject of Tara Coolidge quite yet.

"I do, but..."

"What did you discuss at lunch?" Trent asked.

"I wanted to know beyond a doubt if she was my daughter. I asked her if she'd take a paternity test."

"And what did she say to that?" Amanda asked.

"She said she'd think about it, but she really didn't need a father. She said she'd lived this long without one, what difference would it make?" Darren's face contorted in anguish at this recollection. "But she said she liked me and our chats."

"How did her other words make you feel though?" On second thought, she wasn't even sure if she could believe him. Like any smart liar, he'd pick and choose when to be honest to build rapport. It made people less suspecting when the fabrications started coming.

"Hurt, but I got it."

"Did you though?" Trent leaned forward. "We have you and Michaela talking on video outside Woodbridge arena on Friday night. There were a lot of arms flailing."

Darren looked from Trent to Amanda and back to Trent, like he was at a loss for words.

"Mr. Bolton," she prompted him.

"I wanted to ask that she reconsider the paternity test."

"Seems a rather odd choice of location considering you had lunch on Thursday." Amanda brought the video imagery to mind with its dimly lit parking lot. "Are you sure there wasn't more to it?" She didn't think it was about paternity at all but extended the benefit of the doubt to get him to talk more openly.

They sat there in silence, using it as a mind game to compel Darren to speak to fill the void. It worked after a few moments.

"There was more. It was a conversation that started at lunch on Thursday, but she swore me to secrecy."

The word *secrecy* had Amanda sitting up straighter. Was it to do with drug use or something else? "You need to tell us everything. Whatever you are holding on to might help us find who killed her."

A tear splashed the man's cheek. "I just can't shake that she's gone. She's really gone."

"Mr. Bolton, we appreciate that you must be reeling from your loss." She said this with genuine sentiment, but there was an edge to her voice she was unable to hide. If his plan was to dissuade her from pushing for answers, he'd be disappointed. "What had she confided in you?"

"I wanted to get involved in her life, but she told me she'd handle it on her own. Maybe if I had been more persistent..." He sniffled and snatched a tissue from a box on the table next to him.

Amanda empathized with the man, but she balanced this with Patty's caution. He was being evasive with his remarks now, and he kept trying to steer them from this secret he was holding on to for Michaela. "Tell us, Mr. Bolton, or we'll have no choice but to move our discussion to Central Station."

The tears stopped, and he leveled a cold glare at her. "My daughter is dead."

"*Murdered*," she corrected to frame it properly. "I won't ask again. What is this secret you're holding on to?"

"Someone has been blackmailing her for a few months." The words came out stacked on top of each other. He took a deep breath afterward.

Amanda glanced at Trent, who was looking back at her. They'd discussed Tara withholding Michaela's drug use for her own benefit. Was this what Darren referred to now? "Did she know who was doing it to her?"

"Her agent. Tara Coolidge."

They had the texts to back up Tara being blackmailed. There was nothing solid against her to prove she was exploiting Michaela. "What was Tara holding over Michaela?"

"Ah, information that, if it got out, would have crushed Michaela's Olympic dreams before they were even realized."

"Drug use?" Amanda put out there, using the blackmailer's one message as a springboard.

"You know?" He frowned. "But she wasn't a drug addict. It was just the one time. Michaela ate pot brownies at some point last fall. Not that she knew that before she ate them. But whether it was on purpose or not, it wouldn't matter. If it got out, it would create a scandal. For athletes bound for the Olympics, it ruins their reputation. She might not have been able to compete. Marijuana is seen as a performance-enhancing drug. They'd blow it up into some testament to her character."

You poisoned me... One text message that Michaela sent to the blackmailer's number. Amanda could see from Michaela's perspective, drugs would be poison. "Did Michaela tell you if she suspected who laced the brownies?"

He shook his head. "If she knew, she didn't share."

But Michaela must have known. Not once had she asked the identity of the person behind the blackmailer's number. There was just the blatant accusation. But there was another side to that if running with the assumption this all tied back to the pot brownies. It told Amanda that Michaela had trusted the person enough initially to eat them. That could fit a brother or a father. Before she could speak, Trent did.

"From what I'm gathering then, Tara kept quiet about this in exchange for money?" he asked.

"In a roundabout way. Tara was losing sponsorship deals and failing to sign new ones. Michaela was quite sure she wasn't going to get Active Spirit, and she wanted a new agent. But Tara said if she left, she'd expose Michaela for marijuana use. Guess she had some picture or video of Michaela high as a kite. Ask me, and I doubt she had a thing on her. But it was enough to scare Michaela for a while."

Amanda pieced together all they knew. Tara was being blackmailed for Michaela consuming drugs, while she herself was also exploiting the situation. "So she wasn't going to put up with it anymore?"

"No. Michaela was going to fire her and report her to the ethics committee. She'd be finished in the world of sports. That's why I'm really starting to think that Tara killed my daughter."

That sounded like a strong enough motive to kill Michaela if Amanda didn't have the broader picture. And she wanted to put faith in what Darren was telling them, but she also had Patty's warning pinging around in her head. They hadn't uncovered evidence that Tara was extorting from Michaela for keeping her secret. Withholding it though could be selfishly motivated in itself. Michaela made her money. But if Michaela was planning to turn on Tara, that could change things dramatically. Would they find the damaging photo and video on Tara's laptop? They still needed to look at it. But in the meantime, there were two connected murders, and the man in front of her could know more than he was telling them. "Why didn't you report this to the police?" She had to wonder if the reunion with Michaela hadn't gone as blissfully as he painted it.

"Are you suggesting that I might have had something to do with my daughter's murder?"

"Did you?" She hadn't even brought up Tara's murder yet. She saw clear motive why Darren might want to kill her. To start, he'd just admitted he thought she killed Michaela.

"Absolutely not."

"Where were you on Saturday afternoon?" she asked.

"I was at the arena. There was no way I was going to miss her performance."

"Huh." The guttural sound slipped out and had Darren angling his head and watching her, seeking an explanation.

"I was at the show too and went straight to her dressing room after. You didn't go to see her?"

"I wanted to, but I saw Patty and left. That woman's like my kryptonite. She never liked me, and the feeling is mutual. I saw you there with her actually. You friends?" He narrowed his eyes as he tossed out an implied accusation, as if her relationship with Patty might in some way jeopardize justice for his daughter.

Yet he never said a thing until now... "That's not relevant to the investigation, Mr. Bolton. But revisiting our earlier concern. You never really said why Michaela seemed upset with you on Friday night. What was the real reason?"

"I wanted to tell her I'd handle Tara if she wanted me to, but she insisted she had the situation under control."

"Huh, that's interesting because Tara was found murdered in her home yesterday afternoon. Anything you can tell us about that?" Amanda watched as Darren folded in on himself and started rubbing his temples. "I think it's time we take this conversation to Central."

THIRTY-EIGHT

Amanda watched Darren's Adam's apple bulge out as he greedily gulped the bottle of water they gave him. She was seated across the table from him with Trent in an interview room. Malone and the police chief were watching in from the observation room next door.

Darren put the bottle down once it was empty. "I'm still coming to grips with this. You're telling me that Tara Coolidge is dead."

She'd seen killers and suspects react in all sorts of ways and denial and shock weren't new. "It's hit the news."

"I haven't tuned in," he said drily.

"She was killed in her home. Is there anything you'd like to say about that?" she asked.

"Is there..." His mouth gaped open as he reached up and pinched the collar of his shirt. "I'm... I have no idea. Who... How?"

If Amanda were swayed by playacting, she might buy his performance. But in her line of work, she rarely gave anyone the benefit of the doubt. Especially when they could have motive. "You told us that Ms. Coolidge was blackmailing your daughter, threatening to reveal information that could have destroyed her future as an Olympic figure skater. As Michaela's father that had to make you angry." Until someone had a child of their own, they couldn't fully appreciate the lengths one would go to in order to protect and defend them. Maybe in Bolton's case, get revenge for them.

"You bet it did," he said, the words rushing from him. As if realizing the attention that reaction attracted, he sat back.

"You even voiced your suspicion about Tara killing Michaela. You didn't come to us. Did you get your own revenge?"

"Absolutely not! I didn't kill her. I swear that to you."

"Then why not pass on your suspicions about Tara to the police and let us sort it out?" She was starting to feel like a parrot repeating the same question so many times.

"Trust me, I really wish I had now."

And still no answer... That told her he was holding back. Was it to avoid incriminating himself for murder? "Where were you on Saturday night, Mr. Bolton?"

His hands began to tremble on the table, and his eyes pooled with tears. Slowly, he raised his gaze level with hers. "She was alive when I left her."

A stone sank in Amanda's gut, and her entire body became cold. "Who was alive?"

"Tara Coolidge."

Goosebumps laced down her arms. "Are you admitting for the record that you were in Tara Coolidge's home last Saturday night?"

"I was there, but it's not what you think."

"I'll tell you what I think. Michaela didn't want anything more to do with you, but somehow you convinced her to meet you for lunch on Thursday." She was playing off the text exchange between Michaela and the prepaid number. She produced a printout of the texts received from the blocked number to the agent's phone and slid it across the table.

Darren picked it up, his eyes scanning it, and he flicked back toward Amanda. "No. That wasn't me."

"Then you'd have no problem letting us look at your phone," she countered.

"None at all, but an officer took it from me."

"That's fine. We'll catch up with it. You painted your reunion with Michaela as blissful." She put it out there as if that were in question.

"It's the truth."

She set the printout of text messages sent to Michaela on the table in front of him. "From the same number, and by the sounds of it, you poisoned her."

"I didn't send her any texts. I prefer to talk to people. And I certainly never *poisoned* her."

"Well, the person who was messaging her did, or at least she thought they had. What sickens me is the two-faced nature of this person. They came hard at Tara but buddied up to Michaela."

"Hey, if you're thinking that's me, forget it. I certainly didn't write any of these." He pushed the page away. She pushed it back.

"My partner and I have reason to suspect that the person behind this number and these messages killed both Michaela Glover and Tara Coolidge."

"Then you're really off the mark. I wouldn't hurt Michaela."

"I find it rather convenient that you wanted to reach out to Michaela after all these years and try to play father," she said.

"I told you. I was working through the steps and wanted the matter answered once and for all."

"You're sure that's all? You never turned up because you

wanted something from Michaela? You played the long game, but she only ended up sending you away?" Trent put in.

"None of that happened." Darren's voice was a strangled cry as he made this claim, and it had Amanda stiffening. It sounded like the protest of an innocent man, but she'd seen convincing performances before.

Amanda continued. "But she ended up deciding she didn't want you in her life and sent you packing. You snapped and decided you'd kill her. You see, we still haven't eliminated you as the person blackmailing Tara Coolidge. You told us you found out about her holding something over Michaela on Thursday. What's to say you didn't know long before that? Say back in the fall when you put things into motion. You sent the pot brownies with the plan to use them against her. Only when the scandal didn't break, you jumped on it. Decided to make some money through Michaela's agent."

Darren was shaking his head. "This is ludicrous. All fiction."

Amanda continued. "But after you killed Michaela, you still thought you could get money from Tara. You went to her house, but Tara had plans of her own. She held a gun on you, there was a struggle—"

"No! None of that's true. Was I angry as hell with that lady? You bet. Tara was taking advantage of Mick. And Mick thought of her as an older sister." Tears were falling down Darren's cheeks now, and he swiped them away. "Then my girl was killed." He served that word with darkness and malice. "She did this. I know it. And now you tell me she's dead? Well, good riddance."

"Why did you go to her house?" she asked.

"I wanted to talk to her face to face."

She pressed her lips and shook her head. "I'm not buying it."

"It's the truth!"

She gave it a few seconds, letting Darren cool down. Then she said, "I can't help you if you're not going to be honest with us."

Darren took a few deep breaths, clearly steadying his temper. A pulse tapped in his left temple. "Fine. I was right pissed off. She denied everything, even the blackmail."

"So what did you do?"

"Nothing. And I swear, she was very much alive when I left her house."

Darren's interference in the case could be enough reason why he hadn't come forward with his suspicion about Tara. But the secrecy and his covert mission to try to handle things himself didn't bode well for him. He had motive to kill the agent, and if he was lying about his reunion with Michaela, he potentially had motive there too. Just how did both motives fit together? Was it as she laid out and Darren had orchestrated the potential scandal from the start and then exploited it for his own monetary benefit? If so, though, what had pushed him to kill his daughter and stop the flow of cash? Had he gotten greedy and asked Michaela directly for money when she got to town? Then her refusal pushed him to murder? It was all possible, but there wasn't enough proof yet. Between lack of evidence and all the questions, she was getting a headache. Hopefully, the answers weren't far off.

THIRTY-NINE

"Malone filled me in on Tyson Bolton and your suspicion he was working with someone. I asked for one suspect, and you brought me two. Great job," Buchanan announced with pride the second Amanda and Trent entered the observation room. "I say we proceed with murder charges and get an announcement drawn up for the media."

The chief's bold statement had Amanda glancing over at Malone for interference.

"Chief," Malone said, grabbing his superior's attention, "before we rush ahead, the detectives still need to build the case against them."

"He was there the night the agent died. The man's known to be a liar. Who knows if he and Michaela got on as he said they did?"

Amanda didn't know how he'd heard about Darren's character, but she let that go. "As you said at the onset, we'll want an arrest to stick if we go public. Let Trent and I continue to do our jobs."

"What else is there?"

"To start, we get a search warrant for his home. We see if we can find peanut oil, black ribbon, a garment with wood toggles, and Coolidge's Beretta."

"Consider that done. I'll get on the phone with a judge myself." Buchanan pulled his phone but made no move to make the call right then. He was watching Amanda with expectation.

"We still need a sample of his handwriting to compare with other instances in our investigation. We also need to take a look at his phone to see if it's the prepaid number that ties back to Tara's blackmailer."

"That one's easy. It would have been taken from him when he was brought in."

"Yes," she admitted.

"All right. But even if it's another phone number, that doesn't mean Darren Bolton is innocent. He could have the prepaid phone hidden in his home or have tossed it by now."

"Either is a possibility," she said.

"I'll make sure that's included in the search warrant for his home." The chief pushed a button on his phone, put it to his ear, and left the room.

They hadn't even gotten into the fact that they couldn't tie him to the postal box or the necklace yet. Her phone rang before she could say anything to Malone or Trent. "Detective Steele," she answered.

"It's Patty. Are you seeing this?"

"What's that?" Amanda was hesitant to even ask given the somber voice of her friend.

"The news."

"Patty, it's probably best that you avoid it for a while. You might think it's helpful, but—"

"You don't get it. She's on the news right now with that Diana Wesson of PWC. *That bitch.*"

The term could apply to the reporter, but Amanda got the impression Patty was referring to the other *she* Diana was talking with. "Who, Patty?"

Both Malone and Trent moved in closer to Amanda, likely to eavesdrop.

"Cheryl."

"Michaela's mother?"

"Uh-huh. She's playing grieving mother. Give me a break. She has to have some end game here." Patty fell silent, and Amanda made out voices in the background. "Oh my God, she's claiming that she shared a special bond with Michaela. Amanda, what the hell is she talking about?"

Amanda was stunned into silence as she tried to decrypt what Patty had told her. She assembled it with things she'd said before. How Cheryl was immature and selfish. She was probably just out for her fifteen minutes of fame. "I don't know, Patty, but we'll talk to her." The thought of tracking her down while working to build a case against Darren and Tyson Bolton seemed overwhelming. But she might have something to offer about Darren. That's if she was around more than Patty believed. And if Darren and Cheryl were still drawn to each other like they had been when they were younger, what's to say they didn't recently re-enter each other's lives? After all, Darren was working through his amends, and he surely owed Cheryl at least one apology for leaving her pregnant and alone. "You have any idea where I can find her?"

"No, I've told you before."

"Okay, I'll figure it out."

"Thank you." Patty hung up.

Amanda was left holding her phone, but she turned to Trent and nudged her head toward his tablet. "Bring up the *PWC News* website and see if you can go back and watch the news from the start. Apparently, Wesson interviewed Cheryl Glover."

"Michaela's mother? Okay. Wow." Trent hurried to do just that, and she and Malone huddled around him. Within a few seconds, they were watching a tearful and heartbroken mother laying out her grief for the world to see. A bubble of rage rose in Amanda's chest at the hypocrisy, and she couldn't keep it to herself.

"How dare that woman step forward now? She wasn't in her daughter's life for most of the last two decades, but suddenly they had a special bond? It's disgusting," she spat and shook her head. She looked at her phone and plucked Diana's number from her contacts though she'd blocked it several years ago. She hit the call button and listened to the line ring and ring. She landed in voicemail. "This is Detective Steele, Wesson, and I need you to call me back as soon as you get this message." She ended the call and licked her lips. Her fiery temper was alive and well. "This woman harasses me every chance she gets, and now she's not answering her phone." *Now I have to unblock her...* The action pained her.

"Probably because she's still live on the air." Trent angled his tablet more toward her and pointed at the *Live* caption. Diana was currently interviewing Wendell Smith, Michaela's ex-boyfriend.

Amanda left the room. "I've seen enough, if you have. Let's follow up with the chief, make sure the execution of the search warrant for Darren Bolton's home gets started. I'm sure he requested it be open-ended so anything that might incriminate him in either Michaela or Tara's murder is admissible. But we'll want to make sure." They'd done that with the warrant for Tyson's home, and it was rather common not to limit a search to specific items. "Actually, how about you get on that, Trent, and I'll get a sample of Darren's handwriting for comparison purposes?"

"And his phone?" Trent asked.

"Let's go check it together quickly." She had this swirling sensation in her gut. It was telling her they were closing in on a killer.

FORTY

It was a late night by the time the warrant had been executed on Darren Bolton's house. Neither his house nor Tyson's had turned up anything that incriminated them in either Michaela's or Tara's murders. The phone that Darren Bolton had on him when they brought him in was not the prepaid number belonging to the blackmailer. Another strike. And Darren's handwriting looked nothing like the notes. Amanda could see no clear reason to continue holding them. Thankfully they hadn't rushed to publicize the PWCPD's interest in them or it would have cast a shadow on them for shoddy police work. It still didn't make for a happy police chief though. Buchanan wanted someone to serve up to the media *yesterday*. Amanda would rather get it right.

Conveniently, Michaela's financials came in too, but nothing about her banking history flagged as a potential payoff leaving her accounts. If Darren Bolton was right and Tara was holding the pot brownies over Michaela's head to keep her job, she wasn't also asking for money on the side.

Amanda and Trent still had leads to follow and warrants to be fulfilled, but they put some effort into finding Cheryl Glover.

In part to have a chat, but mostly to make good on her promise to Patty. As Patty had told them, the last address on file was a bust. They had asked the Bolton men about Cheryl before letting them go, but both claimed they hadn't been in touch for a long time. Diana Wesson wasn't helpful either. She had returned Amanda's call and refused to disclose Cheryl's information.

So in the end, it had been a long and frustrating night. She finally tucked into bed around midnight, and Logan was already asleep. Or at least he pretended to be. When she said his name, there was no response, but she swore she heard him roll over when she cracked the door to their bedroom.

But all that was hours ago now, and she woke up to an empty bed. The smell of coffee drifting down the hall beckoned her to her feet. The alarm clock told her it would be a good idea as it was already 7 AM.

She made a pit stop first and then padded to the kitchen. Logan and Zoe were on the couch in the front room. He was reading a novel, and she was watching television. It was a week-day, but she let it go. "Morning, guys."

"Hey, Mandy." Zoe barely took her gaze off the TV.

Logan didn't say a word but set down his book. "Zoe, why don't you go get ready for school?"

"Oooh, please, just five more minutes."

"Now." One word, one look from Logan, and she huffed and flicked off the television.

"She eat already?"

"Yep." Logan was clearly in a mood, and she wasn't ready to deal with his attitude.

She made herself a coffee and took a few long, desperate pulls from the cup. He came up behind her and made another for himself.

"I'd like to talk," he said.

A pit formed in her gut. Nothing good usually came from those words. "Sure. With Zoe here?"

"Why not? She's always going to be around, but she's occupied right now."

"What is it?" She squared her shoulders, tried to project confidence and strength but her legs were like jelly. She wasn't a fan of confrontation or defending herself, but she'd do it without hesitation if provoked. But this sick feeling was washing over her. The look in his eyes warned of an impending storm. "If this is about Trent, I assure you that you have noth—"

"It's not about him, and I shouldn't have said what I did yesterday. I'm sorry about that."

"Oh, okay." She was genuinely surprised by his apology. "I appreciate you saying that."

"But I do want your answer about having a baby."

"Logan, it's—"

He held up a hand. "Please don't tell me it's not a good time. Things have been going well for the most part."

For the most part... "Babies are a huge responsibility and not the right move to bring us closer."

"I disagree. Our own baby, Mandy." He set down their mugs and took both of her hands into his. "Let's do this."

"I'm thirty-nine." She was grasping for a defense, all so she could avoid the real reason. That she couldn't have babies. But that wasn't all if she were being truthful. This relationship wasn't solid enough to bring another child into it. She wasn't even sure if it could withstand another disagreement. She'd known this for a while, first as little whisperings in her mind that she desperately wanted to ignore.

"Women have babies into their forties these days. You're fit and healthy. I don't see why not." His eyes were wide and bright, while a fire burned in her gut. "What is it? Your hands are trembling. Are you okay?"

"I'm..." She pulled her hands back. "A baby isn't something

I can give you." She swallowed roughly, treading as close to the truth as she dared. And just when she thought she'd processed the loss and had accepted it...

Logan let go of her, and his face shadowed. "Can't or won't? Is this because of your job or does this have to do with Trent? You do still have feelings for him. I thought we moved past that. We were building a future together."

He certainly didn't waste time smacking her with a double whammy. She also didn't miss the past tense used to describe their future. Tears filled her eyes, and her heart shattered. All she likely had to do was deny her feelings for Trent and come forward with her truth. She couldn't have a baby. Her injuries from the accident made that physically impossible. She could have suggested they adopt a baby together, but it was the fragility of their relationship that had her taking pause. The rage swirling in his eyes reinforced her silence was the right decision. Besides, he was still jealous of Trent. Clearly, he continued to hold resentment against her job too. He'd never understand what she did or why she did it. How many more years would they burn pretending what they had was working? "Logan..." Tears snaked down her cheeks. "I think we want different things in life, and if we're being honest with ourselves no matter how badly we want it to be each other, it isn't anymore."

Logan's mouth set in a firm line, and he shook his head as if clearing his ear of water. But in this moment, she felt all anger dissipate and a calmness move in.

"You feel it too, don't you?" she said gently.

He licked his lips and nodded. "I'm so sorry."

"Me too."

They fell into an embrace, and she held on for as long as she dared because when she let go, Logan would be gone from her life forever.

.   .   .

Amanda was nauseous as she drove to work. Her mind just kept replaying that morning, her breakup with Logan. How Zoe burst into the kitchen a moment later. Her timing had allowed her and Logan just enough time to decide they'd hold things together until the weekend when they'd break it to Zoe and explain why he was moving out. Until then, Logan promised he'd take care of Zoe like always. If she was running late, she didn't need to call. He'd run on the assumption she would be and leave leftovers in the fridge for her to eat whenever she did come home.

She parked in the lot at Central and cut the engine. A few tears snaked down her cheeks, and she swiped them away. Her mind accepted their breakup was for the best. Her heart was having a hard time catching up. And Zoe was going to be devastated. The girl loved Logan, and he'd been a significant part of her short life so far. But Zoe was hers from before she and Logan got together. How was she going to break it to Zoe that Logan wasn't going to be a part of their everyday life? Was he going to want to play any role in Zoe's life after he walked out the door? He had no parental claim, but she knew he loved the girl.

A knock on the driver's window startled her. She turned to find Trent standing there waving with a goofy smile on his face. *Someone's in a good mood...* Hopefully, it would rub off on her.

She got out of the car, plastering on a smile. *Fake it until you feel it...* "Good morning."

He looked at her, narrowed his eyes. "It doesn't sound like it is. Wanna talk about it?"

"Not at all, but you look happy this morning."

He didn't say a word but placed his hand on her wrist. They both stopped walking, and he peered into her eyes. "You can talk to me about anything."

"I know." She bobbed her head and pressed her lips, doing her best to suppress the tears that wanted to flow. "Why are you so chipper anyway?"

He pulled back his hand and smiled. "I wasn't going to say anything until the logistics were worked out, but Kelsey and I are moving in together. It won't be until the new year, but she practically lives at my place already anyhow. It makes sense."

She saw the words spilling from his lips, but the sound of his voice struck her as if coming from the other side of the world. Then they landed, thrusting into her like a punch to the gut.

"Amanda, you heard what I said?" He was grinning like he'd lost his mind.

He's in love... She put a hand on her stomach, removed it hoping that he hadn't seen. "That's great, Trent. I'm happy for you."

"You are?" His question hinged on an arch.

"I am." The truth, and a lie.

"Thanks." He got the door for them, and they headed straight to their cubicles.

On the way, Amanda's phone chimed with a text from Briggs. She shared the gist when she got to her desk. "Detective Briggs got into Tara's laptop, and he found some things we'll want to see. Apparently, it's on the department server."

"Coming right over." Trent left his coat in his workspace and stood behind her chair.

She popped back a quick thanks to Jacob, and then opened the folder from the server. There were a couple JPEGs, a video file, and some email files. She clicked on one of those first.

This message was between Tara Coolidge and Active Spirit. As Amanda read, her neck tightened. When she finished, she summed it up. "They turned down Tara's proposal to sponsor Michaela. They said they heard the athlete was off her game recently and to contact them in the future if her stats improved."

"So Tara had lost the deal."

"Not her doing though. It was the fact that Michaela was drugged that likely led to her lack of focus and placing poorly in recent competitions."

"When did the email come in?" Trent leaned in for a better look. The timestamp was in a smaller font for some reason. "Friday, the day before the show."

"Yet she told us she was still working on it."

"She might have been planning to go back to them. We might never know for sure."

She opened the other email files, and they were of a similar tone. All were from athletic equipment and fashion companies rejecting sponsorships. Next, she opened the photos, and they showed a spaced-out Michaela.

"Tara did have leverage on Michaela," Trent said.

"Yep." It was disgusting how Tara had used this situation to exploit Michaela. Even more so considering the girl was already a victim. She hadn't taken drugs of her own volition.

Trent pointed to the video file, and Amanda opened it.

They watched as Michaela spoke to the camera, clearly high with red eyes and dilated pupils.

Amanda shut it down before it ended as she'd seen enough. "The only reason for Tara to keep proof of Michaela's drug use was to hold it over her head. We haven't found any written conversations about this, but it's easy enough to fill in the blanks. Tara was using it to manipulate Michaela to keep her on as her agent, as she told Darren Bolton."

"It's unsettling for me that Tara took photographic and video proof of Michaela being high."

"You and me both. It's possible Michaela wasn't happy with Tara for a while so when she saw an opportunity to exploit, she did."

"Right. What Tara didn't expect was for the person who

drugged the brownies to turn around and blackmail her."

"Just who the hell is this person?" She flumped back in her chair. The twenty-four hours the post office had required to produce on the warrants wasn't up yet. The way she saw it, there was one logical course of action. Even if she didn't like it all. "We need to continue tracking Michaela's movements. Eagle Cemetery is our next stop."

FORTY-ONE

As Trent drove them under the metal arches of the cemetery, Amanda took a deep breath. Guilt moved in at not visiting more often, but she'd been trying desperately to move forward with her life. Her grief would always remain a part of her, but coming here weighed her down even more. She cleared her throat. "I'm going to stop by their graves first. Alone, prefer-ably," she told Trent. She'd had him stop at a flower shop on the way here, not about to visit her late family without an offering of blooms. She told Trent where to take her, so she was within close walking distance of her family's graves.

"No problem at all." He took them there and parked, then said, "While you're paying your respects, I'm going to call the cemetery office and find out where we'll find the gravesite for Michaela's grandmother. Gloria Glover, right?"

"Yes. Okay, I'll meet you back at the car in a few minutes." She got out of the car, her steps leaden as she walked up the small rolling hill to their graves. The air was cool and damp today, and a slight breeze penetrated her jacket. She tucked her chin into its collar, but it did little good to cut the cold. Her ears took the brunt of it, and she could hardly feel them or the tip of her nose by the time she reached their stones.

There was a dying bouquet in front of each, likely left by her mother or in-laws, who she really needed to make some time for. They had lived out of state for most of her marriage to Kevin, so they had grown apart. After his death and that of their granddaughter, it was easier not to stay in touch. They were all grieving in their own ways.

She removed the dead flowers, and set in the fresh ones she had brought with her. She then stood back and tucked her hands into her pockets, momentarily at a loss for words. In many ways, her time with them belonged to another life. So much had changed for her. It hadn't been easy and moving forward had taken living one day at a time. How quickly they accumulated, morphing into months and then years.

"I never know if you can hear me..." It was the way she often started her conversations with them. A genuine admission and an acknowledgment she just may be a fool talking into space. "I hope you're both happy wherever you are. Just when I think I've found my way, well, I feel more lost than ever." Tears threatened to fall, but she resisted them. She recalled Logan's tender touch from the other day and their embrace when they were saying goodbye. "Zoe's doing good though." *At least until she learns of the breakup...* She'd told her late family about Zoe before. "I just need to know I've made the right decision and that I'm not alone." It was all so silly, she knew, expecting affirmation from the dead. A warm tear hit her cheek, and she turned and wiped it away.

A sparrow landed on Kevin's gravestone. Its little head tilted as it studied her.

She hiccuped a sob, but otherwise didn't dare breathe, caught up in this incredible feeling as she watched the bird, like she wasn't just standing there alone. Suddenly, she was no longer chilled either. If there was an afterlife, she swore she had just received confirmation and assurance.

I'm not alone...

And she suddenly found the strength to acknowledge what she kept pushing away. For the first time in years, if she'd ever really let herself see it, her gaze took in the stone that marked the grave of Nathan James. It was next to Lindsey's, and Amanda never had a chance to meet him. He'd died as a result of the accident. She'd named him after her father and had chosen to bury him, even though he was the size of a walnut. Just the thought...

Her heart pinched, and a tear fell down her cheek. She hadn't spent much time grieving for him, or the fact the accident left her barren. While she'd chosen a small casket and even paid for a plot, her grief was mostly concentrated on Kevin and Lindsey, as if by truly absorbing all that day had cost her, it would tip her over the edge. Whenever she tried to come to terms with it, she felt like such a failure, an unfit mother who couldn't bring her baby to term. As if that hadn't been due to outside circumstances but all her own doing.

"I know you would have been an amazing man, Nathan, if only given the chance." She said this to his spirit, his memory, to her own self.

She turned to leave. If only that was all it took to forget and move on. Once her back was to the stones, the sparrow sang its lovely song, and it put a smile on her face. She'd been so mad with God all these years, but she was really starting to think there just might be life after death. But now wasn't the time for self-reflection or existential thinking. She had a killer to bring to justice.

Amanda found Trent back at the car, but he got out when she approached.

"Ms. Glover was laid to rest just over there." Trent pointed to a spattering of stones, all different sizes and colors of marble. Some were flecks of gray, others black, some a pale pink.

She walked with him, taking his guidance. They took a few turns, but it wasn't more than a three-minute walk. And where he had parked was likely the closest lot anyhow.

"It should be right around"—Trent pivoted on his heels, then proudly pointed out his discovery—"here."

There was a dying bouquet in the holder. "Michaela could have left this for her grandmother. I don't think they've been here long. The flowers are limp and blackened, but the cold alone would do that."

"Could be from Michaela. The GPS put her here on Friday afternoon. Today would be going on four days."

Amanda caught a glimpse of an envelope and bent down to pick it up. There was handwriting on it. "Addressed to *Grandmother*. I'd say that cinches that the flowers are from Michaela. Normally, I wouldn't open such a private missive, but..." She gloved up, and Trent finished her thought.

"This is a murder investigation. We don't have a choice. Whatever is inside might help us." He nudged his head at her, as if giving her further approval to open the envelope and read the contents.

"It doesn't make me feel less invasive, but here goes." She gently pried a fingertip under the seal to release it. She pulled out a small piece of folded plain paper and found a handwritten note on it. She read this to Trent. "'I wish you were here to help me know what to do. You always knew just what to say. I will love you for eternity. Until we meet in heaven, Mick.'" Her voice cracked on the girl's parting words. When she'd written this, she wouldn't have thought that time would come so soon, but it also plucked at Amanda's emotions after her thoughts at her family's graves. Unlike herself, it would seem Michaela had a firm belief in life after death.

Trent dipped into her eyes, as if he read her thoughts and felt the shift in her energy. His gaze communicated concern and inquiry, but he remained silent. She appreciated that because this wasn't about her.

"She came here to pay her respects but also to ask for guidance," Amanda said, realizing how she'd summed up the obvious.

"Yep. Probably to do with her situation with her agent."

"Very well could be." They might never know for sure. She was about to suggest they leave when she caught Trent do a double take at the flowers and squint. She followed the direction of his gaze. "What are you seeing— Oooh."

Another small batch of flowers had been pushed into the holder. A strand of ribbon kicked up in a gentle breeze. *Black* ribbon. Just like the one used on the roses given to Michaela with traces of peanut oil.

FORTY-TWO

Amanda was just processing what this discovery meant when her phone rang. Malone showed as her caller, and she answered on speaker.

"The footage from the post office is in if you want to come take a look."

"Yeah, we'll be there in a minute." She was having a hard time taking her eyes off the black ribbon. At the onset they theorized Michaela's killer had been someone close to her. It would seem this person had reason to visit Gloria Glover's grave. "What about the rental box? Do we have a name?" she asked.

"That hasn't come through yet. Where are you anyway?"

She and Trent looked at each other. "We'll explain when we get back to Central, which should be soon."

"Mysterious but all right." Malone ended the call.

Trent took gloves out of his pocket and collected the flowers with the black ribbon. They put them into an evidence bag once they got back to the car.

"Tyson could have reason to visit his grandmother's grave, but no ribbon was found at his place," he said as they walked through the cemetery.

"He's cleared as far as I'm concerned. This came from someone else."

They loaded into the car after getting the flowers and ribbon into a bag, and Trent drove over the speed limit to get them to Central faster.

Malone was behind his desk and waved them in the second they shadowed his doorway. "Talk."

Amanda filled him in on how they were following Michaela's stops from her GPS and that they were just at the graveyard. "And we found this." She gestured toward Trent, and he lifted the evidence bag with the flowers and black ribbon.

"And I'm looking at what exactly?"

"The same black ribbon used to tie the roses given to Michaela."

"Oh. Okay, then who are we looking at? Do you think we should haul the brother back in for questioning? I know we didn't find ribbon in his home, but he could have thrown any leftovers out."

"Before I answer that, I'd like to watch that video first," she told him.

"Suit yourself. It's on the server as I told you."

She and Trent left his office.

"You sure you don't just want to drag Tyson back in?" Trent asked.

"Not yet. We build a case before we do that again. Your place or mine?" She bobbed her head toward his cubicle, then hers, when they reached the warren for Homicide.

"Yours is fine."

She brought up the video for the day of the postmark. They watched the footage at one-and-a-half speed and at 11:05 AM, according to the timestamp, a woman walked in. But it wasn't just any woman.

Amanda hit stop.

"Cheryl Glover," they said in unison.

She shook her head. "I just knew something was off about that woman re-emerging."

"What are you saying?"

"I'm not entirely sure yet, but we need answers. And we need to talk to her ASAP." She got on the phone with Judge Anderson and stated her case. He gave her the verbal approval she needed to get started. A few minutes after hanging up from the judge, the signed warrant came into her email, and she forwarded it along to Diana Wesson. Then she called the reporter.

"Detective Steele, you finally decide to give me an interview?"

"Not on your life, but I need something from you."

"If this is about getting Cheryl Glover's information again, I can't help you."

"Check your inbox."

There were a few beats of silence, then, "I can't believe you're making me do this."

"Where can I find her, Diana?" Amanda pushed.

"Listen, I only have a phone number that she gave me. My desk at the news station doesn't always show Caller ID by the time it routes through the switchboard."

Unbelievable. Cheryl Glover had contacted the reporter to go on television and play grieving mother. What was her end game with that move anyhow? Was it just for the attention? "And that number would be?"

"Hold on." Diana returned a few seconds later and rattled off the number.

"You're sure?" Amanda's heart was pounding as she looked at the digits she'd written on her notepad.

"Of course I'm sure." With that, Diana hung up on her.

Trent leaned over her shoulder and read what she put down. "Is that...?"

"The prepaid number tying back to the blackmailer? Yes, it is."

"Okay, then does that mean she also poisoned her own daughter back in the fall? Or at least Michaela blamed the person behind the number. What sort of mother would do such a thing?"

"I'm starting to fear it gets much worse than that." Her mother was probably why Michaela didn't want to come home. She could have run into her mother on her trip here a couple of years ago. The mother would also have reason to visit Gloria Glover's grave and it could explain the black ribbon. "And another thing, why didn't we hear back from Detective Briggs that the prepaid phone went live?"

"Detectives," Malone cut in. He stood at the doorway of her cubicle and waved a piece of paper in the air. "Darren Bolton rented the postal box."

FORTY-THREE

Amanda pounded on Darren Bolton's door, harder than necessary. It was partially due to frustration over the fact that a call to Briggs confirmed the prepaid phone never went live. Cheryl Glover must have called from elsewhere but still handed over her number. But why take that risk? She knocked on Darren's door again. "Open up, it's Prince William County Police." No response. It looked dark inside, but his vehicle was in the driveway. She pressed the doorbell, banged again. "Prince William Count—"

Darren cracked the door open and poked his head through. At the sight of them, he let out an exaggerated groan. "Not you again. I had nothing to do with anyone's murder. I'm grieving here. Please leave me alone."

"We're not doing that until you talk with us again," she said firmly.

"I told ya, I don't know anything about anyone's murder. Let me grieve in peace."

"You lied to us, and I will arrest you if you don't cooperate." In fact, she was the only thing standing between him and arrest. His name was on the postal box that received the blackmail money. But something about it felt a little too convenient, which got her thinking.

"You let me go." His voice was weary.

"Mr. Bolton, we're not interested in you." That was the truth in her mind. When she'd explained her thinking to Malone, he wasn't so sure he saw it her way, but he trusted her instinct. He also promised to keep this latest update from the chief.

The door opened. "I don't understand why you're here then."

"Let us in. We just need to talk."

He stepped back to let them inside, and they sat in his living room.

"By this point you're well aware that someone was black-mailing Tara Coolidge," she began.

"Painfully. I believe you accused me of doing that."

"Well, a recent discovery doesn't help your case," she volleyed back.

Darren stiffened. "You said you weren't interested in me, but maybe I should get a lawyer."

"Fully up to you, but I don't think that you need one."

"I'm confused." Darren turned to Trent.

"Where can we find Cheryl Glover?" Trent asked him.

"Cher? I told you already that I haven't spoken to her in a long time."

"And I'm quite sure that's a lie. We believe she rented the post office box and put your information on it." Her gut feeling could be wrong. The two of them could have hatched a plan to exploit Michaela together, but Amanda didn't think so.

"She what? Why would she do that?"

"I'm sure you can piece it together," Amanda said and let the silence stretch out.

Eventually, Darren said, "No, there's no way she could have..."

"Tell us when you last spoke and make it the truth this time. Cheryl would only know your current address if you were in touch. I'm sure you made amends to her..." They had raised this point when they'd first asked if he knew where they could find Cheryl. He had claimed he never tracked her down.

"Fine, we reconnected."

"When?" Trent pushed out.

"Last summer around the time I made amends with Michaela."

"Then you know where to find her?" Amanda grasped on to that.

"I did, but I haven't seen her in a couple of months now."

"Where was she, Mr. Bolton?" she pressed.

He gave them an address. "I'm telling you she's not there anymore, but her friend Deidre Robins might know her whereabouts."

"And where would we find her?" she flipped back.

He gave them the address and cried out, "Did Cheryl actually... Did she...?" He rocked back and forth.

"Talk to us." She had this strong feeling there was more he wasn't saying.

Darren sniffled. "When we reconnected, I told her all about reaching out to Michaela. She seemed happy for me at first but that changed."

"Do you know why?" Her patience levels were depleting and that was saying something.

"I'd say jealousy. I shared how our relationship was growing, and it only seemed to tick her off. She told me to stop rubbing it in her face. Then she ghosted me."

Amanda could fill in the blanks in her head easily enough. Darren was successfully connecting with Michaela while the girl had turned her mother away. The texts supported that. But there was something else Darren could help them with. "Do you know if she ran into her daughter a couple of years ago at Gloria Glover's funeral?"

He licked his lips. "A few days later anyway. Cheryl bumped into her at Gloria's grave. She said Mick turned her away and said she didn't want anything to do with her. I encouraged her to not give up and told her I had a similar reaction at first too. It didn't work out so well for Cheryl though. I should have kept quiet. Is Mick dead because of me?"

His silence up until now certainly hadn't helped. Tara Coolidge might even still be alive. *Maybe.* "You lied to us about a couple of things, Mr. Bolton. You recognized that number we showed you, didn't you?"

He nodded.

"Same with the pendant. You recognized it?" It had been in his fast response at the time that stuck with her.

"Yeah." He sobbed. "She showed it to me before she mailed it. I told her Michaela would love it."

"Why have you been protecting Cheryl?"

"I was in denial. A woman I've loved most of my life doing something so horrible... I didn't want to believe it."

"Instead you didn't say anything." Amanda was the first to stand, and she and Trent left Darren Bolton to his regrets.

FORTY-FOUR

A woman with black hair and gray roots answered the door, and flailed her arms at the sight of their badges. That reaction instantly had Amanda's back up.

"Are you Deidre Robins?" Amanda asked.

"Yeah."

"We need to talk to you about your friend Cheryl Glover," Amanda told her.

She squinted. "What about her?"

"Where can we find her?"

"Not here." She pressed on a dismissive smile.

That strange response had Amanda taking notice. "Why would she be here? Does she live with you?"

Deidre's eye twitched. "So what if she does?"

"We're going to need to come in and look around." Amanda took half a step forward, but Deidre blocked her path.

"Oh, no, you don't. I know my rights, and you can't just force yourself into my home."

"Give us five minutes, and we'll have all the authorization we need." Amanda pulled her phone and made the call to Judge Anderson under Deidre's piercing gaze. When she finished, she said to Deidre, "As you might have picked up, I just called a judge, and that warrant is as good as in my hands."

"Until it is..." Deidre eased back, closed the door, and threw the deadbolt.

Amanda shook her head and faced Trent. "I'm sure she has her reason for hating cops but still. We're here asking about her roommate, and she's playing coy."

"What is it about Cheryl that has people lining up to protect her?"

She thought of the seemingly charismatic woman on TV. "She's a master manipulator." Amanda watched the warrant pop into her email and banged on the door.

Deidre opened it with a whoosh and an elongated sigh. "Warrant?"

Amanda opened it and turned the screen to face Deidre. "That work?"

"Fine. Come in, but don't break anything or I expect the police department to compensate me."

"It doesn't exactly work that way," Trent said.

"Before we look around, we need you to answer some questions."

"Don't I have the right to remain silent?" she jested.

"Sure, if you're guilty of a crime and don't want to incriminate yourself," Amanda pushed back.

Deidre's face scrunched into an ugly mask. "I ain't got nothing to hide." She folded her arms.

"When did you last see Cheryl?" Amanda asked.

"This morning."

"Time?"

"Before work, so around nine."

It was after one in the afternoon now. "You home for lunch?"

"Home for the day. I have a tummy ache."

The woman looked fine to her, aside from miserable. "How has Cheryl been recently? Acting cagey or been moody?"

"Not that I noticed."

"Even after the murder of her daughter?" Trent asked.

"She's fine."

"Fine? Her only daughter was killed and she's *fine*?" Amanda had a hard time swallowing that one even though she'd witnessed the ugliness of the human race as a career cop.

"What's she supposed to do? Dress in black and wail over some brat who won't give her the time of day?"

Amanda stiffened, erecting a wall around her emotions. "Yes, she is."

"I have a very different opinion on the matter. Don't make either of us right. Besides, how's Cheryl supposed to process the girl's death when she's still reeling about the fact she rejected her."

"Michaela didn't owe her anything. Her mother wasn't even in the picture." Amanda was impressed she was able to keep a level tone.

"Agree to disagree. That woman gave her life. And why Cher even bothered to watch that show is beyond me."

"She was at the arena on Saturday?"

"Yeah. That brat gifted her a ticket. Can you believe that? As if it would make everything all right between them."

Amanda had to change direction, or she'd lose her temper. "What do you know about the murder of Tara Coolidge?"

"Caught it on the news. Why?" She pressed her forehead and danced her gaze back and forth between them.

"Do you know who the woman is?" Trent asked.

"That brat's agent. Cher told me about her." Nonchalant.

Amanda resisted the urge to smile. She'd just admitted that Cheryl was familiar with Tara. "Cheryl is of primary interest to the Prince William County PD in relation to Tara Coolidge's murder." She put it out there in a cool, authoritative manner.

Deidre's height seemed to shrink in front of them. "You think she killed someone?"

"We do." *Possibly two...* Amanda refrained from saying this because as strong as Deidre puffed herself up to be, even she would take issue with her friend killing her own kid. "We're going to take that look around now. Show us to her room?"

Deidre took them upstairs to a bedroom not much larger than a closet. There was a futon bed and an old pine dresser with peeling varnish and brass knobs squeezed into the space. The square footage was shrunk further by the fact the bed was unmade and the comforter overflowed to the carpet and dirty clothing was tossed everywhere.

"Thanks," she told Deidre.

"Uh-huh." The woman left.

Amanda gloved up and so did Trent. She took the dresser, and he, the closet. She found newspaper clippings and internet printouts that advertised the ice show and numerous articles that covered Michaela's suspicious death until more recent ones that declared the star skater had, in fact, been killed. And she had a length of black ribbon. She told Trent about the trove.

"That's not all we have." He lifted a coat out of the closet on a hanger. It was missing a wood toggle button. "And then there's this." He exchanged the coat for something else. In his palm was a bedazzled phone case with the letter *M* on the front.

FORTY-FIVE

Amanda had her suspicions but to have them confirmed didn't come without shock. "It really all fits. We figured someone close to Michaela killed her, how they were able to access her sports bottle, her EpiPen... Then the moon pendant that spoke to a gift from someone close. But the mother likely sent it as a bribe to manipulate Michaela's affection. When that failed, she snapped and set out to exploit her daughter."

"And make a payday for herself," Trent put in.

"Probably the primary reason she wanted a relationship with Michaela anyhow."

"I wouldn't doubt it."

"And two years ago, Cheryl ran into her daughter at Gloria's grave. Maybe that happened again. It could explain the flowers tied in black ribbon there. Though I suppose it could have been at another recent point just as easily."

"Deciding whether to welcome her mother into her life could have been what Michaela was worried about in her letter to her grandmother."

"Could be. Though it might apply to Tara exploiting her too as we first thought. Either way, we need to find Cheryl."

Amanda stormed down the stairs and cornered Deidre in her kitchen. "Where is Cheryl?"

"I have no idea."

"Call her right now."

Deidre's hands shook as she put her phone to her ear. "It rang straight to voicemail."

"What number do you have for her?" Amanda asked.

Deidre confirmed, and it was the prepaid number they were aware of. The phone was probably still off.

"What places does Cheryl like to go?"

"I don't know."

"I thought you were friends," Trent put in.

"Sure, but I'm not her babysitter."

Amanda considered having Deidre hauled to Central, but to what end? She was probably telling them all she knew already. "What about Saturday night? What time did she get in?"

"Long after I went to bed, but she woke me up with her thumping around. I think she tied one on at the bar."

Or just committed her second murder of the day... Amanda shoved her card into Deidre's palm, clamped her hands around hers. "You call me if Cheryl gets back here, *the second* she gets back. You hear me?"

"Ah, sure. What the hell though? Cheryl's not some killer. Her head isn't screwed on right, but ain't no way she killed anyone."

"The evidence suggests otherwise. Don't go anywhere, stay out of her room, and don't let anyone else inside." Amanda stepped outside and tried to take some deep breaths. *Tried* being the operative word. "We need to have an officer sent to watch the house in case she comes back."

"Crime Scene eventually too but it's probably best to keep a low profile. We wouldn't want to spook her if she does return."

"Good point." She made a quick call to the on-duty uniform

sergeant specifying the officer park back from the house and be in an undercover car. She hung up and confirmed with Trent that someone was on their way.

"Good. It's not exactly reassuring when the woman's best friend says 'her head isn't screwed on right.'"

"Not really. It confirms my worst thoughts. Cheryl is a killer and murdered her own daughter. I don't think that's in question now. We just need to find her."

"But where...?"

The answer danced on the edge of consciousness, but it would require some work to pull it into the light. "Let's talk this out. Cheryl's selfish, immature..."

"Greedy."

Amanda snapped her fingers. "That right there. She's so driven by money there's no limit on what she'll do for it."

"Agreed, so where does that lead us...?"

"Patty. She stood to inherit Michaela's estate. All two million of it. Cheryl would have to assume that too." Amanda pulled her phone again and called Patty. "It's ringing..." It continued doing so until she landed in voicemail. Panic rose in her chest. "No answer."

"She could be on the phone."

"There's such a thing as call waiting, Trent." Amanda shook her head. "No, I have a very bad feeling." She held up her hand for Trent to toss her the car keys, and she got behind the wheel while he loaded in the passenger seat. CSIs would collect everything later.

She pressed the gas pedal, the worst-case scenario plaguing her, and it hit. "Cheryl's missing but so is Tara's gun. We never recovered it from Cheryl's bedroom."

"Which means she could be armed?"

"Yep." She turned down Patty's street.

"We strongly believe Cheryl killed Michaela and Tara now,

but why would she go on TV and play up the grieving mother?" Trent asked.

"To try to throw the case? She's desperate at this point, and I'm terrified that she's going to do something..." She couldn't complete the thought. At least out loud. Somehow giving it breath would make it real. Patty's house came into view, and Amanda sat up straighter. "Her car's not in the driveway."

"It doesn't mean something horrible has happened to her. She could be at a friend's."

She looked over at Trent's profile, seeking consolation from his strength. "I hope you're right." But the fact all her calls to Patty's phone ended up rolling over to voicemail didn't help the dread curdling in her belly.

She parked in the driveway, and they got out. Amanda jogged to the front door and knocked. The door swung open.

She gave one look to Trent, one that would have communicated all her fears rising to the surface. They prepared to draw their weapons. Slowly, she pushed against the door to open it wider.

"Patty! It's Amanda. Are you home?" Her entire body was trembling as she took one step after another deeper into the house.

It was silent, but the air crackled with an energy that danced over the hairs on her arms, giving her chills. "Just call out to me. Patty? Where are you?" Though even as Amanda asked this, she had this creepy knowing that she wouldn't get a response. No one was home. She kept her gaze ahead as she whispered to Trent, "She'd never leave the door unlatched. Something's happened—" Any further words froze on her tongue as she caught sight of the living room. The area rug was curled up, and one coffee table was uprooted and lying on its side. She searched desperately for something more concrete, knowing Patty was in grave danger.

She kept moving through the house, Trent at her heels. Was

she going to find her friend's body like she had found Tara's? But it wasn't long before they'd cleared the entire house. "No one's here. They're probably long gone by now. Son of a—" She'd never forgive herself if something happened to Patty.

"I'll call it in," Trent told her, pulling his phone.

She nodded, though it felt like her head hardly moved. She tried calling Patty's number again and heard the ringing return to her ears in stereo. Patty's phone was in the house. Amanda let the line ring and followed the sound until she found Patty's device. It was on the dining room table under some paperwork.

In the background, she overheard Trent on the phone, making his requests for officers to come to the house and for crime scene investigators to be sent out. It all felt surreal, as if she needed someone to pinch her back to reality.

He ended his call and told her everyone was on their way.

"Her phone is here. There's no way of tracking her location aside from her car. We need to get a BOLO issued for it." She was breathless. Here she was a veteran detective on the verge of a panic attack. Whatever happened to Patty was her fault.

Trent put a hand on her shoulder. "This isn't on you, or me. We followed the evidence we had as it came to us."

It took time for his words to penetrate, but he'd obviously read her mind. His assurance was still hard to accept. But her one weakness was expecting perfection from herself. She knew it wasn't reasonable or achievable, but that didn't stop her from doing what she could to attain it, regardless. Her eyes landed on the paperwork, and she gloved up and flipped through. Though the gloves were likely overkill and unnecessary. After all, she'd already rummaged through them. The logo on the top of the pages told her all she needed to know. "Patty was in the middle of reviewing funeral arrangements for Michaela when…" She swallowed roughly.

"Let's just take things one step at a time, okay?" Trent spoke to her, level and calm, and it was starting to transfer to her.

Amanda's heartbeat slowed, the ache in her chest eased if only a fraction. "I'll get the BOLO out on Patty's car and APBs on Patty and Cheryl," he added.

"Okay, and I'm going to call Detective Briggs and make sure he has someone watching the prepaid number even when he's not in." She stepped through the back door into the cool air. It worked its healing magic and cleared her head. She called Jacob Briggs on his cell phone, and once he answered, she didn't waste time with pleasantries.

"Come on, Amanda. You know me better than that. Of course I have someone watching it. I told you that last time you called too." Briggs gave her the name of an on-duty detective. She called them and was assured there was no new activity.

Then she called Malone. "We're still looking for Cheryl Glover, but I'm quite sure she has Patty. We believe she's armed with Coolidge's Beretta too."

"Continue to keep me posted. I assume you have a BOLO and APBs out?"

"Trent's working on that now." She looked at him through the window in the door, and he gave her a thumbs up while still holding his phone to his ear.

"Just remember to breathe, Amanda," Malone said, and his gentle appeal and use of her first name had a calming effect.

"I have to find her."

"And you will. I have faith in you, Detective. Just focus on the job." His voice was stern now, and again exactly what she needed to hear.

"Yes, sir." With that she ended the call and reentered the house.

"The all-points bulletin and be-on-the-lookout are being circulated as we speak," Trent informed her as he pocketed his phone.

"Digital Forensics is also watching the prepaid number. If it goes online, we'll be the first to know. Where the hell did she take Patty?"

"We'll figure it out. It's what we do."

"You sound like Malone. But Patty's out there somewhere with her lunatic sister. At her mercy." Fear gripped her spine, and chills ran along her shoulders and arms, standing all the tiny hairs on end. "Deidre said she last saw Cheryl this morning at nine AM. That leaves anytime from then until now for when she turned up here." Amanda refused to think they might be too late to save her.

"Where could she have taken her? We know so little about her. It's hard to speculate."

"But we need to try. So she kills her daughter and her agent, and now she's so desperate that she kidnaps her sister."

"We felt this was about money," Trent pointed out. "I say Cheryl came here and asked Patty for money. I'm not sure how she thought taking her sister would work in her favor. Did she accompany her to the bank at gunpoint? But surely, Cheryl would know it takes time for estates to pay out to the beneficiaries." Trent blew out a breath.

"I don't know." That admission came as a blow. She looked at the mess in the dining room. Papers were everywhere. An altercation had clearly taken place there. It was also where they found Patty's phone. Then it clicked. "This paperwork is from the funeral home. Cheryl would have seen it... What if seeing the burial arrangements for Michaela hit her with remorse? She has to know we'd be getting close to catching her. Maybe she wanted to see her daughter one last time?" Her eyes widened as she met Trent's. "Did she make Patty take her to Angels Eternal Funeral Home?" Theirs was the logo on the paperwork.

"I know the place, but do we even know if Rideout released the body?" Trent asked her.

"I never heard, but let me make a quick call." She called the

Office of the Chief Medical Examiner and had her answer within a few minutes. "She was sent there on Monday."

FORTY-SIX

Amanda was holding her breath as Trent pulled into the back of the funeral home. It was late afternoon by this point, and there were only two cars in the lot. One was Patty's, and it was tucked into a spot near a hedgerow.

"You were right. They're here. We need to call this in." He pulled his cell phone, and she put her hand over it.

Procedure was battling with her instinct. Looking at the building, all she could conjure was the sisters inside, at least one crying over the body of the dead girl. But how long had they been here, and what was Cheryl's current mental state? The scary part was she'd probably feel like she had nothing left to lose. Amanda hated to think what that meant for Patty's fate. It could be just as dark.

"You can't be serious? We need to get backup."

"It might already be too late for Patty and whoever else is in there."

Her comment seemed to prompt Trent to enter the plate from the other vehicle. "Murray Hickman, fifty-five. But if it's already too late..."

She picked up on the implication. Waiting a few minutes

for reinforcements wouldn't make a difference in that case. "I need to check on things. But if you're not comfortable, you stay here. I'm good to go in alone. All I know is I'm not sitting around if there's a chance that I can help Patty and this Murray fella." She may have sounded dramatic, but for good reason. Cheryl's friend said she wasn't in her right mind, and it seemed apparent she had killed her own daughter. How hard would it be to kill a sister? She got out of the car and heard Trent's door echo behind her. She turned around. "You should wait," she told him.

"Nope. We're partners and in this together."

"If you're sure."

He smirked at her. "As sure as I'll ever be. Let's go." He pointed toward the building's rear entrance.

Amanda tried the door handle, and it turned easily. "It's unlocked," she told him.

"I see that." Trent smiled at her.

Amanda silenced her phone, and Trent followed her lead. They then entered the building, taking slow steps ready to draw their weapons. It was dimly lit with just a few fluorescents buzzing overhead. She strained to listen beyond them and picked up the ticking and rumbling of an old register as they passed it. "If they are here for her body, the preparation room is likely in the basement. We just need to find the stairs."

"That's all," he mocked.

She felt the sting of his sarcasm too because the building was quite large. They passed a reception room, and then an office. The blind in the door's window was down, but there was a clicking noise coming from inside. "Do you hear that?"

Trent angled his head, pressed his forehead. "Yep."

"Slowly, on the count of three." The implication being they'd move into the room. She hand-signaled the countdown.

Trent opened the door and led the way inside with his gun raised, announcing, "Prince William County PD."

She ducked in after him, her gun at the ready. She scanned the room, following the clicking noise. It was getting louder, and there was mumbling. She rounded a desk and found the source of both sounds. A fifty-something man with a balding head and wide terrified eyes stared back at her. Strips of duct tape bound his wrists together, and one was plastered across his mouth. He had been tapping the desk with his nails.

Amanda held a finger to her lips as she moved closer to the man. Trent stood guard at the door.

"Murray Hickman?" she asked.

He nodded.

"You're safe now. This might hurt..." She yanked the tape off his face.

His eyes filled with tears, and he gave her a hushed thank-you as she worked to free his hands. "There's a... no, *two* women. One has a gun. She, ah, had the other one tie me up."

"Do you know where they went?" Amanda asked him.

"The prep room. It's in the basement."

"Where can we find the stairs?"

"Down the hall to the left, past three doors."

"Okay. Detective Stenson will take care of you."

Trent turned to look over his shoulder, shock evident on his face.

"He'll make sure you're fully out of harm's way." She was helping the man to his feet, and Trent nudged his elbow against her arm.

"You're coming with us," he told her.

"No, I'm not. I'm going to end this." Louder to Murray, she added, "As I said, Detective Stenson has you, sir. He'll get you outside to safety." She leaned into Trent's ear. "Make sure you call it in when you get out there."

"You're a stubborn ass sometimes, you know that? We can both go and wait on backup."

She shook her head. "I'm not going anywhere."

He breathed deeply, his chest visibly rising and falling, as he peered into her eyes. They were begging her to leave with him but also full of conflict. Like he'd stay with her given the choice.

"I'll be fine. Go."

And he did. As she watched Trent leave with Murray Hickman, a part of her wished she was with them. But when seconds mattered, she wasn't letting another one pass.

FORTY-SEVEN

Amanda's heart was beating a steady rhythm. Adrenaline had flooded her system and offered a familiar calming presence. She took each step cautiously. She hoped to avoid putting her weight on a creaky floorboard that would give away her position. Before she reached the bottom of the long staircase, she heard wailing and sobbing.

This is not going to be good... She'd anticipated high emotions, but this early demonstration made the situation more volatile.

She stepped onto the basement's concrete floor and was grateful for the soft soles in her boots. It should help her make a stealthy approach.

She followed the crying and found herself outside of a room. The air down here was cool and somewhat damp and carried the smell of embalming fluid, cleaners, and bleach.

"I'll do whatever you want, Cheryl!" Patty's piercing cry struck Amanda like a bullet. She was so close to her friend, but had to be careful of her next steps.

She crept closer to the open doorway, passing a ramp leading to a bay door. It was likely how they transported the bodies down here. It must have opened on the far side of the building, or she and Trent would have seen it from outside.

She reached the room and peeked inside. Her heart thumped at the sight before her, and she quickly drew back. She leaned against the wall to regain her bearings.

Michaela's body was on a steel slab that had been pulled out from a refrigeration drawer. Cheryl was hanging over her dead daughter, wailing, and she was holding on to the Beretta.

Patty was strapped to a gurney by strips of duct tape at the far end of the room.

Amanda needed to think through her next moves. If she blazed into the room, there was nothing to stop Cheryl from shooting Patty. Drawing Cheryl out to her was the only way. But how? There might be a chance if Amanda could think of something to make a noise and cause a distraction.

She looked around for something to toss, but saw nothing to use. She fished in her pocket and took out the key fob for her Honda. She could throw it to the concrete floor. But that would also blow the element of surprise. Cheryl was armed and could fire the gun. It took less than a second to pull a trigger.

"You can't bring her back! *I* can't bring her back. She should have just let me into her life." Cheryl wailed.

To hell with it...

If Amanda tossed her keys to the other side of the door that should lure Cheryl out and take her in the opposite direction. It would also place her back to Amanda and make her vulnerable. Then she could swoop in from behind and assume control of the situation.

She put her plan into action. As anticipated, the keyring clattered against the concrete.

"What was...?" Cheryl said, but Amanda heard no footsteps coming toward the door.

"Help!" Patty cried out, her instinct to survive winning over reason.

Amanda pinched her eyes shut for a second and took a steadying breath.

"Who's out there?" Cheryl's voice was riddled with panic and trembling with every word. "Is someone out there?"

Shoes slapped against the floor inside the room, but they weren't headed in the direction Amanda had wanted.

She had a decision to make. If she stepped into the doorway with her gun raised, it would escalate the situation rapidly. If she approached with a calm energy, the mood of reaching a compromise, Patty's survival would stand a better chance.

Amanda holstered her Glock and moved into the doorway, hands in the air.

"Who... *Who* are you?" Cheryl wiped at her wet eyes as if she half-thought Amanda was an apparition. "Go away!"

"I'm not here to cause any problems," Amanda stated calmly, moving forward as she spoke.

Cheryl mirrored her movements but at a quicker pace and stepped toward Patty on the gurney. Amanda refused to look at her friend. She'd been in a similar position in the past, having seen someone she'd cared about in a precarious situation. Her finger had frozen over the trigger.

"Don't come any closer, or I'll—" Cheryl leaned over her sister's upper body, holding the gun to Patty's head.

For Amanda to keep her focus, her calm, her center, she had to think of the person on the slab as a stranger who needed to be saved. "I'll stand right here. Just tell me what you want."

"What I want is for my daughter to come back. For all of this to have never happened. I didn't think it all the way through. I thought I could handle it. *I...*" She started sobbing so hard, she was hiccupping as her lungs tried to gulp in air.

"I am so sorry for the loss of your daughter." Amanda had to put the fact this woman was responsible for her death out of her mind.

"What would you know about it?"

"I lost my six-year-old girl, Lindsey, about nine years ago now." *And my son, Nathan, too...* She cleared her throat. "Losing a child is a pain that will never fully go away, but there's nothing you can do to bring Michaela back. And this—"

"Stop! I don't want to talk. I just want the pain to end." She gripped at her ear like she was hearing loud noises, but it was likely her conscience screaming at her. Guilt and grief were two very powerful emotions.

"That's your sister. You don't want to hurt her. It's not who you are." Amanda stabbed at her humanity hoping to make an impact.

"How would you know who I am?" she spat. "And how do you know she's my sister?"

Amanda extended a gesture of surrender and peace and said, "I'm her friend."

"No. I saw it! Right there!" She was pointing at Amanda's waist where her badge was clipped. "You're a cop. You're here to arrest me."

"Just let your sister go, Cheryl. No one else needs to get hurt."

Cheryl sniffled and mocked laughter. "Mick hurt *me*. She sent *me* away. Rejected *me*, but I'm her own flesh and blood. And now my sister won't help me."

All remorse seemed to have disappeared, smothered by this woman's greed. "You want money."

"I *need* money. I don't even have my own place."

She could ask what happened to the fifty grand she got in the fall, but now wasn't the time. "Just think about this, Cheryl. You're regretting killing Michaela. Do you really want the death of your sister on your conscience too?"

"What does it matter?" She raised her gun, pointed at Patty.

"Stop right there, or I will shoot you." Amanda had her gun drawn and leveled at the woman. At this short distance, she wouldn't miss.

"For that threat to work, you'd need to assume I want to live in the first pla—"

Amanda squeezed the trigger. The round hit Cheryl's left shoulder, the hand that held the gun, and the weapon fell to the floor.

"No!" Cheryl roared and lunged across the floor toward it. Amanda stomped on her hand, pinning her there. She cried out and writhed trying to get free to no avail.

"It's over," Amanda told her, releasing her boot from her hand and quickly kicking the gun farther away. She tucked her Glock back into her holster and bent to haul Cheryl to her feet.

Next thing she knew the woman had leaped up and turned to charge at her. She put her head right into Amanda's gut like a torpedo and slammed her backward. Amanda slapped against the wall. The wind was knocked out of her.

Cheryl spun around and grabbed a scalpel from a table and held it in Amanda's face. Amanda drew her gun again. The distance between them was only a few feet. But Cheryl must have anticipated Amanda's move, and she swiped out with the blade, nicking Amanda's right hand. It stung like acid, and instinct opened her palm. Her Glock clattered to the floor.

She and Cheryl stared at each other like two predators staring down their prey. *Who will make the first move?*

Amanda stood fast, holding her ground, but the slice to her hand was bleeding like mad. She didn't have time to tend to the injury for fear things could take a worse turn. Her focus had to be solely on Cheryl. "It's up to you. More police are on their way and will burst in at any moment. They won't hesitate to put a bullet in you."

Cheryl's chest was heaving as she continued to look Amanda in the eye. Then, ever so slowly, she lifted the scalpel to her own neck. Just before she had a chance to make the death incision, Amanda risked her life and rushed forward. She swatted the blade from the woman's hand, but her momentum took her and Cheryl to the floor, Amanda on top.

The woman wriggled beneath her, but Amanda held steady until Cheryl gave up her fight and started crying. Just then officers from the PWCPD moved in, including Trent.

Amanda took a deep breath and found her hands were trembling. She'd gotten lucky. Things could have gone a lot worse.

Amanda could tell she wasn't in Malone's good books from the second she'd seen his scowling face arrive on scene. The impending reprimand might even make it to her permanent record, but she couldn't have just stood by and waited. What if the cavalry hadn't arrived in time?

"You need to remember you're part of a team, Steele," Malone had mumbled, his face a bright red from his chin to the top of his forehead.

Patty had been treated on scene, and her physical injuries were cosmetic. The greater scars would be psychological. As for the damage to Amanda's hand, it required a few stitches, which she endured with a lot of hissing and silent swearing. But she'd be just fine. Cheryl had shown up at Patty's house and demanded half of Michaela's money, but Patty had told her there was no way in hell. Cheryl saw the funeral papers, and apparently her eyes had darkened and gone blank. She'd then threatened to kill Patty if she didn't take her to her daughter's body.

Cheryl would recover from the gunshot wound to her shoulder but would remain on round-the-clock monitoring for the foreseeable future. She was considered both a danger to herself and others.

Malone's words from last night were still repeating in Amanda's head as she headed toward Cheryl Glover's hospital room with Trent. She was grateful that she wasn't on her own.

"Thanks for everything," she told him.

"I'm not sure what you mean. I'm just doing my job."

"You're kidding right? You always go above and beyond. You have my back even when I go off the rails. That's the true definition of a good partner." She smiled at him, and he returned the expression.

"Are you sure you're all right?"

"Yeah, I'm fine."

"Talk to me."

"It's no big deal, but I do have a lot weighing on my mind. Logan and I decided to end things." *There, I said it...* But having it out there, in the light of day, wasn't that great. It just reminded her about the conversation she'd be having with Zoe once the week wrapped up. She might get off without saying more about Michaela though.

"I'm sorry. That's why you were upset the other morning?"

"Yeah, it just happened. But it's fine, you know. It just wasn't meant to be. We've worked at it for a couple of years. We tried. Twice technically."

"How did Zoe handle it?"

"She doesn't know yet. We decided to wait until the weekend to break it to Zoe, but she's going to be upset."

"Of course. Well, if you need anything, I'm here. Going above and beyond." He was smiling, but it faded. "Oh, I feel bad. The other day when you were upset, I was..."

"Excited about your relationship. I'm happy for you."

"Thanks, Amanda. Things with Kelsey are going great."

"I'd like to meet her sometime." She made the offering even though it hurt. She didn't begrudge him happiness, but she wondered what would be if he wasn't in a relationship. Would they give it a go? She shook the thought aside. She needed time to focus on herself and Zoe before she could get entangled in another romantic relationship.

"That would be nice." Trent smiled at her.

They entered Cheryl's room and found her cuffed to her hospital bed. She looked at Amanda and rolled her eyes.

"I regret what I did, but I'd probably do it again." Cheryl pushed out her chin. "She never gave me a chance to be a mother. I carried her for nine months and endured a day of labor, yet she just opens her heart to Darren."

Amanda wasn't swayed by the woman's defense. "Is that really why you killed your own daughter? Jealousy?"

"I gave her so much."

"Not from what I hear." Amanda didn't care if she tramped on the woman's feelings or ego.

"I gave her life," Cheryl hissed. "The greatest gift of all, or so they say."

"So because you gave her life, you saw fit to take it away?" Trent said, head angled.

"She turned her back on me, her own mother." Her eyes wet with tears but none fell. "Accepting me was all she had to do."

"Are you sure that's all? You weren't after any of her money?" Trent asked.

"So what if I was? She had some to spare."

"Your plan was to get close to her and then ask for a loan, that it?" Amanda was disgusted by the woman's selfishness.

"Again, so what?"

"But you didn't get that chance because she wouldn't let you get close," Amanda said.

"She was a spoiled brat."

"Michaela worked hard for all she had. It certainly wasn't because you made her life easy." Amanda's empathy was reserved for Patty and a young woman whose life was stolen. Even for Tara Coolidge, who had made bad decisions.

Cheryl scowled. "I gave her plenty of opportunities to change her mind."

"You saw her before the show?" Amanda asked.

"Uh-huh, and even gave her one last chance before I watched her drink her protein shake. She wanted nothing to do with me. So I stood there and watched her choke to death."

It was hard to stomach this woman's cold detachment even weighing in a mental illness. And given how her moods flip-flopped so quickly, she wasn't balanced.

Cheryl added, "Can you believe that I saw her early Saturday morning at Eagle Cemetery too?"

"At your mother's plot," Amanda said.

"That's right."

"You brought flowers tied with black ribbon," she pointed out. "The same kind you used to tie three roses for Michaela."

"Yes. *And* can you believe that she told me that I wasn't there for her all her life, so why should I let me in?"

"Why not just kill her then and there?" Trent asked.

"As I said I gave her many opportunities. At that time I was in shock and angry."

"But that rage continued to build until you decided to kill her," Amanda said.

"Uh-huh."

Her admission was offered lightly as if the consequence hadn't been murder. It was hard to reconcile the grieving mother at the funeral home with the woman in front of her.

"Mick had some nerve too. I gifted her this necklace with a beautiful pendant of a crescent moon with an emerald heart. I had to scrounge up pretty much every penny to afford it. Yet she tells me she brought it with her to give back to me. Did you find it? Can I have it back?"

"It's in evidence," Amanda said, "and once it's released, it will go to her beneficiary."

"But I bought it."

"You gifted it to Michaela. It's now part of her estate. Besides, you won't need money where you're going," Trent pointed out.

"Whatever. To think I bought that assuming it would help win her affection."

"It must have ticked you off when it didn't work," Amanda said.

"She didn't even reach out to thank me. She knew who sent it to her. Moons were our thing when she was really little, and emerald was her birthstone. Because she was such a spoiled brat, I set out to teach her a lesson."

"You sent her pot brownies," Amanda said, and Cheryl actually smiled.

"Yes, I did. It's hard to get brownies without nuts. I baked them myself and mailed them to her."

"Your daughter trusted you enough to eat them." A statement that would inject guilt into any reasonable person, but that didn't apply to Cheryl. She was teetering on psychopathic, if the pendulum didn't swing all the way there.

"My plan worked." Cheryl still had a resting smile on her face, which sickened Amanda. "But it didn't have to turn out the way it did. I originally wanted to reconnect and when that didn't happen, I wanted to knock her off her pedestal."

"But that didn't work either," Trent said. "So you killed her."

"It couldn't be helped, and it all sorted itself out like fate. Can you believe after telling me she wanted nothing to do with me, she still gave me a ticket to her show and told me, 'enjoy'?"

That revelation was nauseating. If Michaela hadn't given her a ticket, could she still be alive? Though it was just as likely that Cheryl would have found another way to get to her. "How did you even know Michaela's address to send the brownies?"

Cheryl smiled again. "I visited Tara at her house and appealed to her as a mother wanting to reconnect with her daughter and got Mick's address and phone number. As I think I've said already, having my daughter back in my life was my first intention."

"Are you sure it wasn't prompted because you heard that Darren Bolton was successful and you set out to prove something?" Amanda volleyed back and watched Cheryl's expression tighten. "I think you had a payday in your head from the start."

"As I said, she had enough to share. But the fact she accepted him with open arms yet turned me away...? Her own mother? She's lucky I gave her as many chances as I did to change her mind."

"Yeah, real lucky," Trent mumbled.

"So going on TV was also about coming across as some grieving mother to what? Gain sympathy?" Amanda didn't think there was anything this woman could say that would surprise her anymore.

Cheryl laughed. "I'm glad you liked the performance, but I did it to try to throw you off my back. I had a feeling you'd get to me, eventually. My prayer was you'd be fooled by the grieving mother act."

Master manipulator. That was just as Amanda had thought before.

"Prayer?" Trent spat. "You think God's going to help you get away with murder? You're more delusional than I already thought."

"Sticks and stones."

"Well, as you can tell you didn't fool us. You really messed up when you left your number with the reporter. It was the same one you used to blackmail Tara. Did you not think we'd be able to track that down?"

Cheryl's face soured.

Amanda went on. "Turns out the app you used to block your number stored your real info, so it just took a little warrant, and we had what we needed. But don't feel too bad. Most killers slip up, make stupid mistakes. Speaking of, I'm sure curious about a couple of other things. Why leave a card, and why throw out the one from the bouquet?" Since Cheryl's arrest, her prints were confirmed a match to those left on the florist card and Michaela's EpiPen.

"Did the lack of the card send you all over, wasting time? If so, mission accomplished."

Amanda wanted to knock the resting smirk off the woman's face, and it was rare she ever contemplated violence. She clenched her jaw. "Why leave a card in the first place?"

"I wanted Michaela to read it, maybe put some fear in her. I handed it to her right after her set at intermission. But she didn't see me as a threat. She actually read it and threw it at me. Big... No, *huge* mistake."

Amanda smirked. "Actually, leaving the note was a huge mistake on *your* part. You also handwrote one when you sent the necklace."

Cheryl's eyes narrowed. "Something I realized too late. It was another reason I thought going on TV would be a good idea. Clearly that backfired," she added in a mumble.

"Going back to the card in the dressing room," Amanda began. "She threw it at you, so you must have set it near her body before you left. Again, why leave it?"

"I wanted it to be seen as evidence. I assumed she'd have other people she'd pissed on. My hope was it would never link back to me of course. Though why should it? It wasn't like I was in her life as far as most knew. Darren wasn't going to say anything. That man has always been under my control, and Tara wasn't talking. I had her silence. All I'd have to do is expose her for hiding the fact that her client got high, and she'd be ruined."

To hear her talk so dismissively of Darren, it was hardly a surprise she used his name to rent the postal box, but Amanda would get to that. "For a time, your decision almost led to your son's arrest."

"It might have straightened him out, but he's not going to prison so..."

"Well, it seems you had it all figured out," Amanda said coolly.

"Thanks."

"We still caught you," Trent seethed, and Cheryl glowered. "One thing I'm left trying to understand though. How did Tara even know Michaela ingested the brownies? She's here in Woodbridge."

"I knew she was expected out to Colorado Springs to meet in person with a big sponsor. Don't remember the name."

"Active Spirit?" Amanda asked.

"That sounds right. She said she'd be seeing Michaela when she was there if I had a message for her."

"She was still under the impression you were a mother with sincere intentions."

"Tara was a fool. I couriered the brownies and set the delivery date to coincide with her arrival to Colorado Springs. What happened from there, Tara would have to tell you."

"Which isn't possible since you killed her too." That wasn't a question. They had the DNA results from the epithelium found under Tara's nails, and they had testimony from a neighbor who ID'd Cheryl as coming out of Tara's house Saturday night within the time-of-death window. This person had seen a man too, Darren Bolton, but he preceded Cheryl by thirty minutes. As for that fateful day in Colorado Springs, she thought back to the video on Tara's laptop. Michaela wasn't at a party. Rather it looked like she'd consumed the brownies in a private setting, possibly her home. She probably had some before Tara got there and was already high when her agent arrived. It was possible Michaela was already unhappy with Tara, who knew this, so she armed herself with photos and video to use if Michaela ever threatened to fire her. It was amazing that Jolene had never found out about this incident. Though it was understandable that Michaela kept silent. Her career would have been ruined.

Cheryl's nostrils were flaring. "That bitch accused me of killing my daughter, and she wasn't going to give me the one hundred and fifty K. She held a gun on me. We fought, and I hit her on the head. Self-defense."

Trent laughed. "Except it was murder in the course of a felony. In case you didn't know, blackmail is a felony offense."

Amanda watched with satisfaction as Cheryl's face morphed into an ugly mask. "And after she was down, you searched her house for the money. You must not have counted on her putting it in a safe."

"That bitch."

"What ever happened to the fifty K anyhow? And why triple the amount the next time?" Amanda asked.

"I thought I might be running out of time to make anything off this."

Amanda shouldn't be shocked by her lack of remorse for killing the agent. To Cheryl, Tara had simply been a ticket to an endless payday. When she stopped paying, her existence was meaningless. "Run us through what happened on Saturday."

"I arrived at the arena, early, before the show. I met Michaela in her dressing room. I brought her roses, the ones tied with black ribbon. But she told me that I couldn't buy her affections and stormed out of the room."

"And that's when you added the peanut oil to her drink?" Trent asked.

"Uh-huh, but all she had to do was change her mind and tell me she'd help me. She didn't. I gave her the chance. I did."

"But I'm guessing you took her EpiPen and phone when you tainted her shake. You didn't want her getting help or us finding your messages to her." The prepaid phone was on her person. The response from Universal Mobile came in that morning and supported their case against Cheryl. The SIM was activated at Idle Variety, a convenience store just around the corner from Deidre Robins's house.

"Sure did, but I still gave her another chance. After her set, around intermission, I slipped into her dressing room while she was talking to Tara. When Michaela came in, she told me to leave, or she'd scream. I put my hands up in surrender and acted as if I were going to leave. She drank some from her bottle and I handed her the card. She had just a few seconds to read it before she started to choke. Then she knew that she had made a big mistake. She threw the card at me and tried to get out of the room, but I stood there and blocked the door."

To hear Cheryl recount the murder of her daughter sent shivers down Amanda's arms. "And watched your daughter die."

"I'm not going to be guilt-tripped here. She brought this on herself. If she had just welcomed me into her life, I would have warned her not to drink from the bottle. She just needed to be a good girl."

"All because you were so crazy with jealousy about Darren's relationship with Michaela." Amanda was reeling at how this ran contrary to nature. Most mothers were wired to protect their young at all costs.

"Did you know that Tara was holding the pot brownies over Michaela's head?" The texts made it sound like it.

"I had a feeling when it didn't hit the news. In the least she was protecting her own pocketbook. Michaela would have made Tara a lot of money through sponsorships."

"I think you've just confirmed something else for me. The timing of the second request..." Amanda started. "You were already contemplating Michaela's murder when you asked for a hundred and fifty K. You wanted the money to flee the country if it came down to it."

"It wouldn't have hurt."

"Why didn't you then? You still had the fifty K?" Trent put in.

"Pft. Joking right. A couple of months ago I had it. I burned through it in quick time. I paid people I owed and partied."

It all went up in smoke... "Why request a cashier check to a post office box?"

"I didn't think they were traceable."

"This has more to do with the box. You opened it in Darren Bolton's name with the intention of setting him up as the blackmailer."

"Rather smart, eh? I figured you'd talk to him at some point."

Amanda enjoyed bringing this woman down at every possible turn. "Except he doesn't have the phone to go with the money requests and his banking wouldn't show the deposit. I had thought you cared about Darren but based on what you said a minute ago, it sounds like you took him for granted."

"Darren's my lapdog. He does anything I ask and would never turn on me."

Amanda smiled. "He's why we finally got you." *Damn, that felt good to say!*

"What do you know? He finally grew a backbone."

"Well, you'll have plenty of time to think about how a man you underestimated played a part in putting you away." Amanda turned to leave the room with Trent at her heels.

They got their killer, and if the system worked, there would be justice. It still felt bittersweet.

Her phone rang, and Malone showed on caller ID. When she answered, he wasted no time saying, "You and Trent are needed right away."

"Just tell me where."

A LETTER FROM CAROLYN

Dear reader,

I want to say a huge thank you for choosing to read *Her Deadly Rose*. If you enjoyed it and would like to hear about new releases in the Amanda Steele series, just sign up at the following link. Your email address will never be shared, and you can unsubscribe at any time.

www.bookouture.com/carolyn-arnold

Some books come together more easily than others. Thankfully I am blessed to be surrounded by supportive people.

To start, I'd like to thank my husband, George Arnold, who has been a rock by my side for nearly thirty years (how am I old enough?). He's always on hand to talk to and when I need to hear it, he's quick to say, "You've got this." If that support isn't enough, George goes beyond that. He researches things if I ask for it, whether that be finding the resources or revisiting previous books in the series to confirm things for me when I want to toss in Easter eggs for the loyal Amanda Steele readers. If I needed a coffee, chocolate, or a cheeseburger, he'd make it happen! Delivery straight to my desk! He also kept the household running without any complaints when I was hitting against a deadline. He's a true partner, and I love him!

Thank you to Carol Bennett, who shone as a true friend and cheerleader during the process of revisions. She was there with encouraging words and advice and helped me keep my head above water.

Thank you to my editor, Laura Deacon, at Bookouture, for her kindness, understanding, and flexibility when some deadlines might have had to be a teensy-weensy bit extended… (Ahem.) I also appreciate her valuable feedback.

And thanks to Claire Simmonds. She was my editor at Bookouture at the start of this book. Due to her encouragement, I reexamined that first draft closer, and I credit her observations for helping to get this book to where it is today.

But thanks to these people and my support system this book came together, and I'm so very proud of the final product! I hope you loved *Her Deadly Rose* too, and if you did, I would be incredibly grateful if you would write a brief, honest review.

You can also breathe with excitement because more Amanda Steele is on the way! But if you're an avid reader who devours books, you'll also be happy to know I offer several other bestselling crime fiction series for you to savor, as well as series in other genres.

One of my police procedural series features Detective Madison Knight, another kick-ass female detective like Amanda, though Madison might speak her mind a lot more… But she'll stop at nothing and risk it all to find justice for murder victims.

If you enjoy being in the Prince William County, Virginia, area and like dark serial killer novels, you must read my Brandon Fisher FBI series. While the home base puts it in Amanda's vicinity, it gets even closer to home than that. Brandon is dating Amanda's best friend. We could call this the expanded PWC Universe, or some other catchy name. (Let me think on it.)

Those of you familiar with the real Prince William County and the PWCPD will see that I've taken creative liberties and spun a fictional world of my making. My prerogative. I'm allowed to do that. It's just one perk of being an author!

Just before I sign off, though, I saved my largest gratitude until the end. Without you, my reader, I wouldn't be able to head to my desk every day and pound out words. So, a HUGE THANK YOU for your readership and support. And, please, don't underestimate the power and influence of word of mouth. Talk to your family and friends about my books, your local bookstores and librarians, your neighbors, the people at the checkout counter, your dentist, your... well, you get the point. Thank you!

And last but certainly not least, I would love to hear from you if you're inclined to drop me a note! You can reach me via email at Carolyn@CarolynArnold.net. You can also follow and interact with me on Facebook and X (formerly Twitter) at the links below. To investigate my full list of books, visit my website by following the link below.

Until next time, I wish you thrilling reads and twists you never saw coming!

Carolyn Arnold

www.carolynarnold.net

f facebook.com/AuthorCarolynArnold

X x.com/Carolyn_Arnold

g goodreads.com/carolyn_arnold

PUBLISHING TEAM

Turning a manuscript into a book requires the efforts of many people. The publishing team at Bookouture would like to acknowledge everyone who contributed to this publication.

Audio
Alba Proko
Sinead O'Connor
Melissa Tran

Commercial
Lauren Morrissette
Hannah Richmond
Imogen Allport

Cover design
Head Design Ltd

Data and analysis
Mark Alder
Mohamed Bussuri

Editorial
Laura Deacon
Sinead O'Connor

Made in United States
Orlando, FL
16 October 2024